.... Our deck wa
men before we drifte
be out of range of the Algerian riders. Only the fact that
I fell to the deck and played dead saved me from the
Algerian horse archers who were loosing their arrows
down on to our galley whilst riding their horses on the
quay. It would have been a different story if we had had
more of our archers on board. We would have
decimated them. But we did not; except for my two
companions and the few who had made it back to the
galley, all of our archers were either in the city or
trapped in the open on the cart path. ....

Book Ten of the saga of the Company of Archers

Sea Warriors

Preface

Taking a train full of currency or capturing a Spanish
treasure ship is nothing compared to the greatest theft
in history—when the captain of a company of English
archers and his men stole the entire treasury and

religious relics of the world's greatest and richest empire, and then escaped to Cornwall with chests and chests of gold coins and the priceless relics. This begins the story of what happened when he tried to turn the relics into coins for himself and his men.

Chapter One

We reach London with our French prizes.

We saw the French prizes from our expedition to Harfleur anchored everywhere as we rowed up the Thames on our way to where we usually moor in one of the berths along the long quay. The French transports we had taken were waiting to be towed further up the river so they could anchor closer to the quay and our dilapidated-appearing London post. It had been a derelict draper's shop near the quay before we bought it and began to fix it up to meet our needs—and perfect for us because it made us look poor and not worth hounding to pay taxes to the King or be asked to pay protection money by the local neighbourhood association run by the priests of the local parish church.

Not that we would pay the local association for their protection, mind you. If the priests were foolish enough to send the hard men in the tavern down the lane to us demanding coins, we would kill them and their leader knew it even if the priests did not.

King John was another matter. He was above it all, which was another way of saying he really did not have any idea of what was happening in his realm outside of Windsor and his hunting lands or might happen if he tried to interfere with us. Neither did we for that matter; so we treated him like a sleeping dog and tried not to wake him.

******

Spirits were sky high and the rowing drum beat steadily as we moved up the Thames under the grey sky with hordes of gulls wheeling and swooping overhead. We were cheered and waved at by prize crew after prize crew as we rowed past our French prizes where they waited at anchor for their tows to arrive.

Harold's galley was well known and the men all knew that the captain of the Company of Archers, that would be me, and one of my lieutenants, the major sergeant of all the galleys and transports in the Company's fleet, that would be Harold, were on board. So was my son George, newly promoted and proudly wearing the four stripes of a sergeant captain.

George was quite chipper for someone that had almost lost his life a few hours earlier. It was often like that for fighting men—there is nothing more exciting than having a sword stroke or arrow loosed at you to no effect, or, in George's case, all of the above and riding a falling mast into the water in the midst of a sea battle and being able to swim free.

"We will have no trouble recruiting sailor men and pilots after they hear about the prize money that will come out of this," Harold remarked cheerfully as we rowed past another cheering prize crew. "Though that has rarely been a problem."

"Hopefully, it will also help us recruit more strong young lads to apprentice with us as archers. And clerics to do our scribing and summing, although we are not be so desperate to find them now that more and more of Thomas's students are beginning to come of age. Priests are such trouble, especially those that are willing to make their marks on the Company's articles."

A moment later I realized what I had said when Harold smiled benignly. I hastily added, "My brother and my son and Thomas's students being exceptions, of course." *And me too.*

Truer words were never spoken; Thomas may be a priest, but he is a good archer and he bought his bishopric and his mitre and crosier fair and square with some of the coins we got from the refugees for carrying them to safety from the Saracens. He even paid both the King and the Pope to be sure his appointment would be good no matter what the outcome of their argument about who should name England's bishops and collect their bribes and tithes; yes, he did.

My son George and I and all the other apprentice-sergeants from Thomas's school are, of course, priests by virtue of having been learnt to read and gobble Latin and being prayed at by Thomas.

******

The excitement and anticipation of our prize crews was certainly no surprise; the men all knew they had soon each be receiving a goodly amount of prize money. And they were entitled to every coin of it—we had surprised the French at Harfleur and come away with much of the great armada of transport cogs and ships King Phillip had assembled to carry his army to England. It had been a splendid taking and my lieutenants and I wanted to make it a highly profitable one. That is why we had brought our prizes to London, so potential buyers would be able to inspect them and buy them.

Most of the prizes we passed as we rowed toward the quay were single-masted and double-masted cogs, but there were a few of the new, bigger and longer three-masted ships Harold and our port sergeants say are gaining favour with the sailor men because they can carry so much more cargo. The three-masters also, so it is said, make faster passages because they carry more sails. The problem, of course, is that they also require bigger crews.

******

It was only a few hours after sunrise but the scene on the quay was already gay and festive as we rowed up to it. The sky may have been murky and looking like rain, but the quay was crowded with people and our galleys were two and three deep at every berth along it.

We had no trouble mooring when we reached the quay because a berth had been kept open for us. Of course, it had been kept open; Yoram and my brother Thomas and a large force of our archers had ridden to London all the way from Cornwall so as to be here to meet us after we finished raiding Harfleur.

And I would wager Yoram and Thomas's arses are sore and blistered from riding so far so fast; they never were much for being riders, were they? Just like me.

We had a berth at the quay waiting for us because, as soon as Yoram and Thomas arrived, they had taken up all the other berths along the quay in addition to the two berths we bought years ago for our own use.

Yoram, of course, was my lieutenant in charge of the most important of all our trading posts, the fortified citadel we had built, and were still strengthening, on Cyprus near the Limassol city wall. He had come to England when I sent the recall notice to my sergeant captains to bring in their galleys and archers in for a big raid. I had not told Yoram or anyone else where we would be raiding, just that it would be a big one.

Most of the men had arrived thinking my lieutenants and I would be leading them against the Moorish shipping at Algiers. That was what I had wanted everyone to believe. In fact, I led them against the armada of French transports being assembled in Harfleur, the armada of transports Phillip of France had intended to use to carry a French army to invade England in support of the barons opposed to King John.

However sore his arse might be from having to sit on a horse for the first time before we sailed, I was greatly pleased that Yoram ridden all the way from Cornwall to participate—he was my first recruit after I became captain of the Company and, although I would never say it in front of the others, the best recruit that ever made his mark on our Company's articles.

We recruited him a few days after the eighteen of us, nineteen if you include George who was just a little tyke at the time, went over the wall at Lord Edmund's crusader castle in Bekka Valley. That was right after Thomas said a nice prayer and I gave poor Edmund a mercy from his horrible wound.

And why did we come to London with our French prizes instead of returning to our home base in Cornwall? Because London was then, as it still is to this very day, full of merchants and moneylenders and idle second sons looking for something to keep them busy and earn their bread, preferably without working too hard or having to join the Church and mumble prayers all the time.

All those people together in one place made London the best place this side of Lisbon to sell whatever of our French prizes we decided not to keep for the Company's own use. That was why we were towing them up the Thames and assembling them in front of the city.

Besides, if our French prizes did not fetch high enough prices here in London we could take them to Lisbon to sell or sail them out to the Holy Land to use in our own cargo-carrying and passenger-carrying operations.

Alternately, of course, we would use them as pirate-takers by concealing a large number of fighting men in their castles and cargo holds and releasing them after the pirates came aboard what they thought was a prize—and lose their galley to the Company when they themselves were cut down and their survivors thrown in the water to drown as the bible requires of pirates.

We have acquired many of the Company's galleys with our pirate catchers, we certainly have.

******

The rowing drum slowed as we approached the quay where we normally berth our galleys and cogs when they come to London. We could see that it was packed with people. Many of them were men from our recently arrived galleys that were tied up along the quay and from the dinghies of the prize captains that had rowed in to report where their prizes were anchored and arrange for towing. Our men were easy to pick out amongst the crowd because they were each wearing one of our simple, Egyptian linen tunics with the stripes of their rank sewed on across its front and back.

And it was not just our sailors and archers that were on the quay. It was packed with magicians and pedlars and what looked to be at least half the tavern and street tarts of London and their protectors.

It absolutely boggled my mind to think what might happen the next day on the quay and in the nearby taverns and lanes when we began paying every man at least two silver coins for his prize money and more to those of higher rank. Paying the men immediately was the plan Harold and I had discussed as we sailed and rowed here from Harfleur. Maybe we should reconsider it because of the size and nature of the crowd.

"Harold, look at all those people. Maybe we should wait to pay the men their prize money. What do you think?"

******

Yoram and Thomas were out of breath when they greeted us. One of the idlers on the quay had seen us approaching and ran to our nearby little shipping post to announce our arrival. They, in turn, had dashed to the quay in order to be waiting there when we arrived.

We greeted one another other with enthusiastic hugs and handshakes and back-slapping all around.

They were here because they had left for London as soon as we sailed for Harfleur. They had come overland from Cornwall on horseback with half of Raymond's squadron of horse-riding archers to keep them safe, almost sixty men.

There had been no trouble on their long ride from Cornwall to London and no one tried to collect a toll for their use of the road. Maybe, Yoram suggested later as we walked to the White Horse for a bowl of its juniper brew, it meant King John's new edict that had so upset the barons was being honoured—the one he had posted a few months earlier saying he and he alone as the King owned the all the roads and paths in the kingdom and no tolls were to be collected by anyone except with his permission.

I doubt it was the King's edict that made the barons along the road so law-abiding; there was not a baron or franklin in all of England that would think of threatening half a hundred tough-looking mounted men armed with longbows because they paid him no toll for crossing his lands.

My brother and Yoram had ridden to London and taken up the berthing spaces in the Company's London shipping post in the expectation that there would be prizes to inspect and sell. They had to ride to London with half a squadron of our Horse Archers as their guards because we had taken all of our available sailors and most of our galleys to France, every galley we had enough archers and sailors to fully crew.

Thomas and Yoram coming to London did not mean we left Cornwall and Devon unattended, of course. We did not dare. One of my most dependable lieutenants, Peter Sergeant, had stayed behind in command of Cornwall with Raymond at Launceston as his number two and commanding our mounted archers.

Raymond at that time was my recently promoted lieutenant in charge of all our Horse Archers and outriders. About half of our Horse Archers stayed behind with Raymond as a roving guard, the other half had been temporarily assigned to our galleys to fight as archers on our cutting-out expedition to take the ships and cogs the French were assembling in the harbour at Harfleur. The French were just starting to board their troops when we hit them and smashed the French armada by taking many of their transports as prizes.

If Cornwall had been attacked by the Earl of Devon or any of the other rebel barons whilst we were gone, Peter and his men would have retreated into the Company's three castles and waited for our counter-attack whilst Raymond and his Horse Archers roamed close around the invaders to pick off the attackers' stragglers and foragers.

Actually, Devon and the other barons opposing King John were lucky they did not try to take Cornwall whilst I was gone, for our response would have been overwhelming what with almost all of the Company of Archers' fighting men having been recalled to England for our big raid. Indeed, we would have used it as an excuse to get rid of Devon permanently.

My men certainly did not know until the last minute that I would be leading them against the French or that they might have to fight on land against the barons. They had been led to believe I would be taking them to Algiers, or perhaps Tangiers, to raid the Moors for prizes as we usually do on our way back and forth to Cyprus and the Holy Land ports.

Of course, they did not know, and neither did the King nor William Marshall who led his army; the French would have almost certainly have heard from their spies and supporters in King John's court that we were coming and been waiting for us.

In any event, Thomas and Yoram showed up on the quay and presented themselves red-faced and puffing just as our mooring lines were thrown to the many willing hands that reached out for them. It was a wonder they made it to us at all—they had to use their elbows to push themselves through the milling crowd of happy and cheering sergeants, sailors, archers, idlers, pedlars, pickpockets, and loose women of all ages and sizes and their protectors.

It was indeed a special and happy moment; one I never forgot. It seemed as if all of London was on the quay. It was packed with people calling out to one another and running about. Seagulls were swooping everywhere in search of food and adding to the noise. The place had a distinct smell of people and the sea mixed in with smell of the food the pedlars were hawking and the shite and piss of the people and dogs who had nowhere else to relieve themselves.

As we had learnt whilst coming up the Thames, our galleys and prizes from Harfleur had begun arriving yesterday morning. Our galleys were here at the quay because they were able to row all the way up the Thames.

The French cogs and ships we had taken as prizes were not near the quay, not yet at least, because most of our prize captains had had too few sailor men on board to claw their way up the crowded and busy river using their sails. So the prize captains did as they had been ordered and did not even try. Instead, they anchored further downstream near the mouth of the Thames and rowed up to the quay in their dinghies to report their arrival and ask for a galley to tow them.

Harold took charge of our galleys as soon as he set foot on the quay. Within minutes he began sending them out to tow our French prizes upriver to us. We still had absolutely no idea as to how many prizes we had taken, only that there were a lot of them. They were anchored everywhere and more were coming. We had surprised the armada of French transports being assembled to carry the French invasion army to England and came away with most of them.

"I expected prizes," said my priestly brother Thomas as he gave a hand to help pull me up from Harold's deck and then gave me quick hug before he reached down for George and Harold.

After an overly long pause whilst he was hauling up George he finally added, "But not so many. From the first of the galleys that arrived yesterday we heard that you caught the frog eaters by surprise and took a lot of prizes. It would appear you did better than anyone could have possibly hoped."

Then he gave me a stern look after he darted a quick glance to measure George.

"And what is this I have been hearing about George almost being lost?"

"It is a long story, Thomas, a long story. I will tell you all about it over a bowl of juniper brew at the White Horse. But one thing is for sure," I told him. "The best thing you ever did was make sure our George and the rest of your students were learnt to swim whilst wearing chain under their tunics."

******

We did not go straight to the White Horse for a joint and the bowl of the juniper brew I had been thinking about almost constantly ever since the fighting at Harfleur ended. We could not. First, we had to get control of the quay and organize our men and our prizes; then, we had to inspect our new shipping post so we could talk about it and "an unexpected development" whilst we drank and ate.

Harold's loud-talker shouted and his big booming voice soon had the galley sergeant captains pushing their way through the jovial crowd to join us. After much greetings and reports, often given excitedly by two or three of them at the same time, the galley sergeants went off to their galleys to search for our anchored prizes and tow them up the river so they could be seen and sold.

Towing our prizes up the river should have been organized earlier. I will have to speak to someone about forgetting to do that; probably me, damn it.

Thomas and George and I left Harold shouting orders to the sergeant captains of our galleys and walked to our nearby London post. My new sergeant apprentice, John, one of George's fellow students in Thomas's school for likely young lads, came with us. John was a bright lad of about sixteen summers and could jabber and scribe Latin with the best of them.

******

Our London post was in one of the city's derelict lanes near the quay. We went there to inspect the construction underway to strengthen the place and build its escape tunnel. Afterwards, we walked to our escape tunnel's destination. It was a small and rundown hovel on a narrow lane about eight hundred paces to the north of our post. It had a pig sty behind it with about two score of noisy and terrible-smelling pigs in it.

Earlier this year we had bought the place, pigs and pig shite and all. We had been digging an escape tunnel to reach it from our post ever since. It was our hope that the tunnel would come up under the low roof covering the pigs amongst their shite so no one would blunder into it.

More than likely, of course, it would come up somewhere nearby and we would have to move the pigs' roof to cover it.

Evan Miner, an archer from Wales, a thin man that had made his mark on the Company roll as Evan the miner, was the two-stripe chosen man in charge of the five archers digging the tunnel. Every one of them was an experienced Welsh tin miner temporarily assigned to our London post for the purpose of digging the escape tunnel. Evan and Robert Heath, our four-stripe post sergeant in London, accompanied us as we walked to the pigsty and the pig keeper's hovel. The pig keeper was a retired archer with a bad leg.

Robert's scrivener, a red-faced cleric from Kent named Rufus, should have been with us. Unfortunately, Robert told us ruefully, Rufus had disappeared several weeks ago.

Damn. Now we will have to find Robert another cleric to do his scribing and summing. Or perhaps one of Thomas's students is ready?

It was clear that the construction of our post's escape tunnel was well underway but that it was nowhere near complete. The tunnel's not being finished was important. Our London shipping post and its people and coins and cargos awaiting shipment would not be safe from the robbers and thieves that abound in the city of London until it was completed and its exit hidden. It meant that any coins we had get from the sale of our prizes, or from carrying cargos and passengers to and from London, would have to be kept under close guard on one of our galleys.

After we finished inspecting the pigsty where we hoped the tunnel would exit, Harold and Harold's apprentice sergeant, the lad that acted as his scrivener and did his sums, joined us and we walked to the White Horse public house for a bowl of juniper brew and an ox joint. I was lost in thought thinking about what Thomas and Yoram had told me on the quay when they explained why they had been at our post instead of being on the quay to greet us when we arrived—they had gone back to the post to meet with a messenger that had ridden in from Windsor.

The message the rider had brought was disconcerting to me and everyone else and prompted our immediate inspection of our new London post instead of going straight to the White Horse to celebrate—the King had heard about our victory and was coming to London tomorrow to see the French prizes for himself. William Marshal and others of King John's courtiers were coming with him.

******

The White Horse was crowded as the ten of us ducked our heads to get through the narrow door and make our way into the crowded and smoky room. The alewife recognized Thomas and raised her hand to signal him that there would be but a moment's wait. She quickly moved some drunken fishermen out of a corner table with the promise of a free bowl of juniper brew for every man if they would move to another table. They jumped at the chance and gave us big smiles.

There were a lot of nudges and pointing with their chins as some of the men recognized us when we walked in. No surprise in that; everyone except Thomas was wearing one of the Archer Company's simple but distinctive tunic gowns with the broad stripes signifying our ranks on our fronts and backs. Thomas was the only exception; he was wearing a simple priest's robe instead of the bishop's robe and mitre he was entitled to wear for the bishopric he had bought fair and square from both the King and the Pope. *He was also, of course, equally entitled to wear an archer's tunic with the six stripes of a lieutenant, for an archer and a lieutenant of the Company's captain he surely was.*

Harold whispered something to Robert Heath that caused him to promptly nod his head in agreement and get up and leave. Then Harold motioned the alewife over and whispered something in her ear as well.

"What was that all about?" I inquired of Harold. "I particularly invited Robert to join us. I want to hear how things are going here in London and what he is learnt."

"Robert is a good man, but I needed an errand run, and he is the best man to do it. He will be back soon. He can tell you about London's happenings and our prospects when he returns."

******

Ten minutes and one bowl of juniper brew later, Robert re-appeared leading almost a dozen archers carrying swords and galley shields. He settled into the empty space on the wooden bench next to George with a nod to Harold; the archers sat themselves on the benches along the two tables that the alewife's husband had pulled over to be a barrier between us and the rest of the smoke-filled room. The archers looked particularly determined.

I raised my eyebrows in a question and looked at Harold. He smiled back at me and explained.

"You have only got one good leg left and I am not taking any chances. Yoram told me there was fighting in the taverns last night between our men that were bragging about the prize money they were about to receive and some of the local lads that were jealous."

Then he smiled again and explained the determined looks on the archers' faces to me.

"I had Robert tell the archers that you intend to pass out their prize coins as early as tomorrow or the next day even if you had to personally borrow them from the moneylenders, and that it would not do to have you chopped down by a jealous local lad so you could not pay them."

Well, there goes my chance to change my mind about paying out the prize money.

Chapter Two

We borrow the prize money.

According to Yoram and Thomas, the King's messenger had commented that the King and his courtiers seemed quite excited and pleased by the news we had surprised the French army's transports at anchor in the Harfleur harbour and taken so many of them as prizes.

The courtiers' excitement and pleasure was certainly understandable. Our taking of the French armada almost certainly meant that there would be no French invasion this year, and, thus, there would be no additional scutage or extra taxes collected, as would be the case if the King had to pay for a war with Phillip of France and the rebel barons Phillip had been coming to support. Now only the rebel barons remained as an immediate threat to the King and the purses of the King's supporters and taxpayers.

The question for us, of course, was whether the King's coming to London was a danger to us because we attacked the French without his permission. Of course, we did not tell the King our plans. We could not. We were not totally daft; his court would have heard about it within minutes and the French spies would have known we were coming and been waiting for us.

What was also weighing on my mind as I sipped on my bowl of juniper ale was how the dissident barons, and particularly the Earl of Devon, would react to the French defeat. They were sure to be sorely unhappy and discomforted since they had offered the English throne to Phillip and pledged him their support if he would bring his army and help them overthrow John. Unfortunately, there was no telling how Devon and the rebellious barons would react to the news that Phillip's army would not be coming to join them when they rose against the King. Violently, would be my guess.

Indeed, it was probably a good thing Thomas and Yoram passed through Devonshire on their way to London whilst the barons and their men were still in Exeter waiting to greet the arrival of the French King and his army. Otherwise, they might have come up the old Roman road from Exeter Castle and attacked them as they passed by on their way to London.

Oh well, done is done and they can return to Cornwall on one of the Company's galleys, was my thought as I sniffed my bowl with appreciation and took another sip. Hopefully, the old archer and his wife we placed in an Exeter alehouse as spies would be able to tell us who was there with Devon and what their intentions might be now that the French would not be coming.

"Thomas, we have got to talk about the King's visit," I said to my priestly brother with a satisfied belch. "It complicates everything and it could be dangerous. The messenger may have said the King was happy about our victory, but with John you never know."

Then, after a pause, I added, "But I have an idea."

I let Robert and Evan listen so they could understand the role I wanted them to play for the King when he arrived.

******

The joint I gnawed on was tough and cold and the bowls of juniper brew burned my throat as they went down. All in all, it was a wonderful meal for a hungry and thirsty man. Afterwards, I walked with my lieutenants and our guards and apprentice sergeants back to our London post to get a goose feather and some parchments. I had decided to send a message to one of the city's moneylenders, the big one used by the King.

I intended to try to borrow enough coins to give every man two silver coins for his prize money and another two for every stripe he wears. And now that I knew the King was coming, I was going to try to do it immediately even before we attempted to sell the prizes we did not want to keep for our own use.

In fact, we had more than enough coins in our chests to pay the men that were with us on the raid without borrowing them, a hundred times more and perhaps even a thousand. But I wanted the word to get back to the King and his courtiers and tax farmers that we had to borrow the coins we needed to pay our men. As always, I wanted the King and everyone else to think we were poor and had no coins of our own to pay in taxes or scutages.

An hour or so later I sat on my sea chest in the forward deck castle of Harold's galley, the place where I live and sleep when I am on board it, and scribed a parchment to the merchant that had been named to me as the King's personal moneylender. I told him I would be coming to visit him in an hour or so and why.

As you might imagine, I actually hoped he would turn me down for the loan. Then the word of our poverty and the need to borrow in order to pay our men would get back to the King and his courtiers without us actually having to borrow the coins.

If the King's moneylender turned me down, as I hoped and expected, we would use our own coins from the captains' pouches on each of our galleys and pretend we had borrowed them from someone else.

******

The King's moneylender did not do as I hoped and turn me down. To the contrary, I immediately received a most cordial response saying he was sure he and the members of his guild could accommodate me and offering to come to me immediately or at any time of my choosing. He also said he would be equally honoured to have us visit his humble stall in the city market at our convenience to discuss whatever he and the other members of his moneylender's guild could do to assist us. He made his mark on his parchment as David Levi.

I did not know moneylenders had a guild; I wonder if the King taxes them. Surely, he does.

We promptly began to walk to the market with the moneylender's messenger scurrying on ahead to tell him we were on our way.

London's most important moneylender, David Levi, was standing in front of his stall waiting as I walked up to his shop with my lieutenants and guard of archers. George, of course, came with us. The market was crowded and we had drawn curious looks as we moved through it.

Good. The word would get about that we are so poor that we were forced to come grovelling, cap in hand, to a moneylender to borrow coins so we could pay our men.

The man we had come to see was tall and lean with intelligent eyes. He had a small black cap on the back of his head where the Church's priests and monks usually shave or pluck out their hairs to prove their humility and prevent itchy lice.

We bowed to each other as if we were courtiers and shook hands. He most courteously named himself as David Levi and seemed to know all about me and Cornwall and the Company of Archers that I had the honour of captaining.

He even knew that we sometimes operated under the name of the Order of Poor Landless Sailors and had shipping posts on Cyprus and elsewhere.

During the customary social and pleasantries period before getting down to business, my new friend mentioned that he had already heard about me and the Company of Archers from several merchants in Alexandria with whom he traded. Then he really surprised me by noting that one of our galleys had carried his brother and his family to safety from Constantinople when the crusaders attacked and sacked it instead of going to the Holy Land. David was a friendly sort and we were soon on a first-name basis.

Several of David's fellow moneylenders, all merchants with their own market stalls, were with him to greet us and so were two of his sons, Issac and Aaron. The terms for a loan of eight thousand silver coins surprised me by being quite reasonable, particularly since there would be no cost to us at all if we repaid them quickly. And that, of course, is exactly what I had every intention of quietly doing even before I returned to Cornwall.

In any event, I pledged my name and twenty of our prizes and borrowed eight thousand silver coins to pay out as prize money, more than enough so that every one of our men could receive two silver coins plus two more for each stripe he wore.

What was so interesting is that David seemed to understand why I was coming to him to borrow the coins to pay our men. He did not object at all when we conducted our business in the open area behind his stall so that all of the men with me could see and hear. It was almost as if he had read my mind and understood why I wanted my men and the market's merchants and the King's spies to listen.

The news that I had to pledge my name and prizes in order to borrow coins to pay my men their prize money would spread like a wildfire when my guards get back to our galleys and prizes. Hopefully, it would reach the King and his courtiers and tax collectors as well.

******

About an hour later, a heavily guarded horse cart carrying linen pouches filled with silver coins clattered up to David's stall as we toasted our new relationship with bowls of wine. The coins were in eighty linen sacks of exactly the same size. I could see that each of the sacks was exactly the same size as all the others and I instinctively knew the tally would be absolutely accurate.

I was not even going to bother to count the coins but David quietly insisted that I select at least one of the pouches and count them so everyone could see the coins as I counted them. I am sure he made the suggestion so my men and everyone else in the market could see that I had actually borrowed them.

It was a good idea and I should have thought of it myself. My men were already in a good mood from our successes, and it got even better as they saw the silver coins being counted whilst they were enjoying the cheeses and bowls of ale David's servants continued to press upon them. *David is definitely a man to know.*

"That is a man whose family we must get to know and befriend," I quietly told George afterwards as we walked together back to the quay. "Not to borrow more coins from him, mind you, but for information and other things that we might do together."

Thomas and Yoram nodded their heads in agreement.

I linked my arm with George's as we walked behind the horse cart and quietly explained why we had borrowed the coins to pay the men their prize money even though we did not need to do so. George listened intently and seemed to understand. Thomas walked on the other side of my son and chimed in or nodded from time to time to show his agreement. I spoke quietly so that no one else around us could hear.

As we approached the quay, I told George what I wanted him to do next.

"Tomorrow, after the King leaves, you would do well to send a message to David's sons and invite them to sup with you and John and Steven at whoever tavern or alehouse they would most enjoy. Take a file of guards to keep you safe and do your best to befriend them.

"You can talk about anything with Issac and Aaron except that we have coins and gold in Cornwall and on Cyprus. Tell them all about your family and schooling and adventures, but never ever even so much as hint or in any way suggest that we might have coins with us or even a small stock of coins and treasure in Cornwall or Cyprus. Even John and Steven did not need to know about such things.

"When asked by David Levi's sons or anyone else, you and your sons after you must always, absolutely always, now and forever, maintain that we never have any coins of our own because whenever we get them we must immediately share them with our men to keep them loyal.

"Making people think we are very poor but always dependable is important, George. You must always remember how important it is to make people think you and the Company are poor, but that you can always be counted on to be reliable and do the right thing.

"Moreover, you must make sure that the need to hide our wealth is passed on to your sons and their sons after them. In other words, George, you must always make sure that neither you nor your heirs after you nor anyone in the Company ever so much as hints or shows wealth to anyone at any time. That is the reason that you and your heirs in the years ahead must never, never do you hear, attend the King's court or dress in any finery of any kind. If you do, the King might come to think that you and the Company have coins and find an excuse to take them by force or in taxes."

It was a message George had heard many times before both from Thomas and from me; hopefully, he understands why we think is so important.

"Do you understand what I am telling you, George?"

"I believe so, father, yes I do."

******

We reached the quay with the cart full of coin pouches and loaded them into the forward castle of Harold's galley. Before we did, Harold moved his galley and lashed it on to two others already tied up along the quay. Robbers and thieves would have to come across those two galleys full of our fighting men to get to the coin pouches and carry away the men's prize money. Pigs would fly before that was likely to happen.

When we finished stowing the coin pouches, I used the shite nest in the galley's stern to put a turd in the harbour and led my intrepid band of archers back to the White Horse for another round of food and more of the juniper brew. The wind died down whilst we were inside and a light rain started. It had been a good day and we celebrated it by drinking too much and singing too loudly.

******

George, Thomas, and I spent the night in the forward castle of Harold's galley. We lit a candle lantern and talked for hours. Harold and my other lieutenants and apprentice sergeants slept in the castle in the stern.

Robert and Evan and the archers stationed in London spent the night somewhat safely tucked away in our post as they have been ever since we bought it. They and any coins we might keep in London would not be safe until the tunnel is completed and a false wall is built across the back of the shop to conceal the tunnel entrance and force anyone that wanted to use it to come down into the space behind the wall from the post captain's room above the shop.

The escape tunnel and false wall was Yoram's idea and a good one that we use at all our posts. The post sergeant sleeps with the post's coin chest in the room above the space where he meets merchants and potential passengers and the post's archers sleep at night. He and his family get to their room with a ladder that they pull up behind them every night. If he needs to escape, he lowers the ladder into the little room behind the wall and climbs down it and goes out the tunnel with his shipping post's coins and whatever other valuables he can carry.

Chapter Three

Prize money is paid and we gull the King.

The next morning, my lieutenants and I woke up as the dark of night ended, visited the shite nest, and ate bread and cheese with our men. Then I put on my mail shirt and George and Thomas and I walked through the morning fog to make a brief visit to our London post.

We were walking in the fog because I wanted to make sure everything was ready if the King decided to visit it, meaning primarily, of course, that the entrance to the escape tunnel had been properly concealed from the prying eyes of any of the men the King brings with him. Yoram and Harold and their apprentice sergeants began organising the distribution of the prize monies whilst we were off to visit the post.

The quay was already covered with people despite the early morning hour. Some of the pedlars and women had obviously spent the night and been providing their wares on credit in anticipation of the payout of prize monies to our men, and their willingness to quickly spend them.

******

We began handing out the prize coins to our men about three hours after daybreak. Harold had the coin sacks carried across the moored galleys between his galley and the quay and stacked on the quay. Whilst he was supervising the movement of the coins to the quay, he had everyone that was not wearing one of our tunics moved off the quay.

The pedlars, women, pimps, and pickpockets were not happy about being told to leave, but they had no choice and they did. Our men saw to it with great enthusiasm because they knew their prize coins would not be distributed until the onlookers were gone. As they moved them, dinghies continued to make trips back and forth to our anchored prizes to bring in their crews.

Soon there was a long line of happy and excited archers and sailors snaking up and down the quay— lieutenants and senior sergeants in the front, then sergeant captains, sergeants, chosen men, archers and sailors, and finally the apprentice archers, landsmen, and rowers without stripes. There must have been several thousand men in all, and it was a jolly bunch indeed.

Yoram sat on a chest and recorded each man's name, his galley or shore assignment, and the number of coins he was paid. Thomas and George and my other lieutenants and the young men that were their apprentice sergeants and scribes stood around them carrying swords and shields just in case. I bantered with each man as I handed his coin or coins, shook his hand, and thanked him for his service. There were no problems and lots of smiles.

Passing out the coins seemed to go on forever and many of those that were paid stayed to talk with old friends afterwards and watch the others receive their coins. Others hurried off to the women and taverns. Once I got a mighty roar of laughter and many bantering calls when I held up both hands with a big smile and hurried to the edge of the quay to lift my long tunic and piss in the harbour.

******

We had just finished paying the two-stripe chosen men and had started on the one-stripe archers and sailors when there was a great commotion at the north end of the quay and the crowd parted to admit the King and his guards. William Marshal and a number of courtiers were with him and they were on horseback; the King's household guards were walking behind him and looked a bit out of breath. They had heard we were here on the quay and had come here instead of to our London post.

The King was wearing a crown and looked quite regal and kingly. He was beaming and seemed quite pleased with his reception.

I made much of effusively bowing and kneeling as did my lieutenants around me. *Of course, I did; last night, Thomas, who has had much more experience dealing with the high and mighty, had reminded me that kings expect this sort of thing to remind everyone of their power.*

The men saw me do it and, in response to Yoram and Thomas's frantic motioning to them, got down on their knees and copied me as best they could. It was the first time most of them had ever seen the King or, for that matter, even knew we had one.

Except for being in attendance at the King's coronation, I myself had only seen King John one other time. That was in France when I had killed someone's arrogant second son right after getting the King's approval. Thomas, however, had met him several times during Thomas's visits to Windsor to bribe him and his courtiers for titles and lands and things like that. William

Marshal I knew from several meetings, and particularly from our meeting at Okehampton with the late and unlamented Brereton.

"Welcome, Your Majesty, your loyal subjects welcome you most warmly; Your Majesty has inspired them to a great victory over the French," I said as I knelt and swept my hand to indicate the men that were kneeling all around us.

Always lay the ox shite on with trowel when dealing with royalty and great nobles had been Thomas's advice when we discussed the King's visit. It seems to mean a lot to them. On the other hand, many of my men had come to the Company straight from the villages and did not even know they lived in England let alone that England had a King named John.

******

King John graciously lifted his hands to acknowledge the awkward men that were kneeling and bowing for the first time in their lives. Then, as he dismounted he waved his hand for me to rise and my men rose with me.

"I heard the joyous news and came to see for myself," said the King.

"It is true, Majesty, it is true indeed. These fine men were inspired by you. They have taken the French armada from Harfleur and are here receiving the prize monies they are rightly due."

I said it loudly so my men could hear and with more than a little pride in my voice as I waved my hand around to call the King's attention to the men.

"Pray then, carry on; I would see it for myself," said the King.

So I resumed paying the men their coins. After a while, I could sense the King was getting bored from not being the centre of attention so I had Thomas take my place and offered to take the King out in a galley to inspect the French transports we had taken as prizes. He declined most graciously and then surprised me by asking if it was true that I had borrowed coins from London's money lenders in order to pay my men. William Marshal and a couple of courtiers listened intently as I answered.

"Yes, Your Majesty. I regret to say that it is true. Unfortunately, borrowing coins to pay my men had to be done because Cornwall's lands are too poor to yield any revenues that might be used to pay them. I had no choice but to promptly pay the men to keep them available for your use, particularly since they have not yet been granted the same rights and freedoms as the men of the Cinque Ports." *I emphasised the word "yet."*

The King raised his eyes at my words so I explained further.

"Those of your loyal subjects that live and fight on the sea, as the archers of Cornwall do, expect to receive prize money and recognitions for their services in addition to their food and clothing; it was specified in the articles of the Company of Archers on that they make their marks. If I were to not pay them, they would undoubtedly leave and seek service elsewhere—and then they would not be available to fight for you against the next French armada.*"*

Actually, that was mostly true but not exactly. There was nothing in the articles of the Company that required an advance to be paid to each man for his share of the prize money before the prizes were sold.

The King nodded sagely, gave a good scratch to settle the lice in his crotch, and wandered over to the edge of the quay to look down at the galleys moored to it. He pondered them for a while. Then he looked again at the long line of men in line to be handed their prize coins and announced his departure.

"We are ready to leave now. You have our thanks, Earl William."

So "we" mounted his horse and trotted off the quay without looking back. Marshal and his retinue hurried along behind him.

******

"Well done," Thomas said to me with a smile as the last of the King's men double-timed off the quay in an effort to keep up with the King and his horsemen.

"I will draft a decree for John to sign extending the privileges of the Cinque Ports to Cornwall. I know just the man to get him to sign it. I heard a rumour that the services of the Keeper of John's Wardrobe are cheap to buy these days. It should not cost much because we have got such a fine argument and the King is in such a good mood."

Thomas thought for a moment, and then continued with a smile.

"I will put a 'whereas' in the parchment I draft to the effect that there are no revenues for the King to lose from Cornwall since the land outside the monasteries is not good enough to generate revenues—so extending the privileges of the Cinque Ports to Cornwall as a limb of, ... ahh, let us say Dover, that I heard is silting up, ... would cost the King nothing and get him access to more transports and ... ahh, let us say, ... thirty days use of a war galley each year whenever he needs one in the future."

It sounded like a good thing to do; little did we know it would almost lead to a disaster.

We agreed that when they return to London from visiting the Keeper, Thomas and George would take one of our galleys and sail for Rome to deliver the prayer coins needed to buy another year of the Pope's support. George was going with Thomas so he could visit Rome for the first time and learn how to pay the annual prayer coins that were the key to maintaining our good relationship with the Pope and the Church.

******

Whilst George and Thomas were off to Windsor to get the King's approval via the Keeper of the Wardrobe, Yoram and I, with the help of David and his sons, sold some of the French prizes for more than enough to *almost* fully repay the moneylenders. In fact, we had coins to add to our chests even though we immediately repaid every single penny except for one silver coin so that everyone could truthfully swear that we still had not been able to repay all the coins that we had borrowed.

At the suggestion of Harold and Yoram, I agreed to keep a number of the larger and better prizes for our own use. We will take some of them into the Company's service as pirate-takers and some as armed merchantmen with archer-heavy crews capable of fighting off pirates. The rest we will send east to sell in the Holy Land ports and along the way.

Properly armed merchantmen would be something new for the Mediterranean cargo trade. It was a good idea. We thought the merchants would like it because it would reduce their losses to pirates; our men would like it as well because it meant additional promotions since each merchantman's archers would need a sergeant and a chosen man. It also meant we would need to recruit more sailors and train more archers for duty at sea.

Harold really liked the idea of our operating merchantmen armed with a force of archers strong enough to fight off pirates. It would, he claimed, let us earn more coins for each cargo we carry and increase the number of prizes we take—because a single galley of pirates waving their swords without really knowing how to use them was much more likely to be taken by the archers on such a merchantman than the pirates on the galley would be to defeat our archers and take the merchantman.

At the very least, according to Harold, it would force the pirates to use multiple galleys to take one of our transports as a prize, and even then they might not be successful.

"It all depends on whether or not they have archers and how many boarding ladders the pirates use and how willing their thrusters are to die, not how many pirates and galleys."

"It is damn hard, you know, to climb up a grapple rope to the deck of a cargo transport when one of our archers is shooting arrows down at you or chopping down on you with one of our long-handled bladed pikes."

Harold immediately began thinking about how many archers each armed transport would need and how many arrows and bladed pikes and such each should carry. Strangely enough, he thought the bigger ships would need fewer archers since their decks are higher off the water above the decks of pirate galleys.

"They would have to climb further to get aboard, you see. And that is hard to do when someone is chopping down at you with a bladed pike or pushing arrows down at you. It is almost impossible if there is a defender for each boarding ladder—unless, of course, they have archers to clear the defenders away from the top of the ladders, as we well know."

The thought of more coins from carrying more cargos was enough to convince me and all of my lieutenants and senior sergeants. We decided to keep the bigger and newer prizes, meaning some of the three-masted ships and some of larger two-masted cogs. Only the smaller ones and those nearing the end of their useful lives would be sold. And that was what we set out to do with the aid of David Levi and his sons.

******

The days that followed whilst Thomas and George were away to Windsor were quite busy. Merchants, moneylenders, and idle gentry were constantly rowing out to inspect the French prizes we were willing to sell and climbing aboard those we were able to bring in and moor against the quay.

Yoram handled the negotiations to sell them and was quite good at it. It turned out that many of the prizes also had stores aboard them that had been intended for Phillip's army. We transferred those we wanted to the ships and cogs we decided to keep and sold the rest.

It was good to be alive, and we spent almost every evening in the White Horse sampling all of its fare except the women. *I had no wish for the French pox or the drips; I would never hear the end of it from Helen and her sisters—and I most sternly spoke to George and reminded him that the fear of the French pox and the drips was why I had agreed to his request that he marry the smith's daughters.*

"It looks as though I will have to report to the King's men that you could not sell your prizes for enough to totally repay us," David had said with a big smile one evening when Yoram and I joined him at his favourite tavern. "I am jealous." *Yes, now I am sure he knows we are trying to pretend to be poor so we will be left alone.*

Chapter Four

The King requests a favour and we leave London.

Thomas and George returned from Windsor four days later with, as we had hoped, the King's seal on the decree extending the privileges of the Cinque Ports to Cornwall. It cost twenty gold bezants. They also brought an unexpected task—King John had "asked" Thomas to carry a private parchment to the Pope when he and George sailed for Rome.

Thomas did not read King John's message himself, of course, but from the gossip he heard at court he was certain it asked the Pope to restore the king to the Church's good graces and withdraw the Pope's approval of the barons' refusal to submit to John as England's God-chosen king.

According to the courtiers, the King and the Pope had fallen out over the question of who should have the power to appoint England's bishops, the King or the Pope. They are lucrative appointments as we well know;

Thomas's crosier and mitre were quite pricey. I wonder what John promised the Pope this time.

"It was a good time for John to try to reconcile with the Pope," Thomas had explained to us. "The defeat of Phillip's armada has pulled the teeth from the barons' revolt, at least for this year, and the court thinks William Marshal has arranged a tentative peace with Devon and the other barons. If the Pope agrees to bless a meeting between the King and the barons, they would meet next year and try to work out their differences."

"Yes, you are right," I agreed. "But a peace between the King and the barons is bad for us. We need an excuse to kill Devon and take Exeter before Devon can get some of his friends together and try to take Cornwall. We would be in real trouble if he managed to get a big enough force together when most of our archers were in the east. Can you lose the king's message or change it so the King and the barons stay at each other's throats?"

"I dare not. Are you daft? It would be the end of us if John or the Pope found out, and they surely would. The King would almost certainly order our titles and lands forfeit and the Pope would agree. I do not know how you feel about being an earl, but I like being a bishop."

******

Our final week in London was a busy week. We spent our time finishing the repairs on our galleys that had been damaged fighting the French, selling a few more of our smaller and older prizes, recruiting sailors, and arranging cargos—and endlessly going over our lists of sailors and archers to put together crews for the galleys and the French transports we had decided to keep or take east to sell.

London was full of sailors and pilots because of all the shipping. They were easy to recruit because it was increasingly known in the ports that our Company provided opportunities for prize monies, fed our sailors decent food, and did not try to cheat them.

What we really needed, however, were useful longbow archers and dependable captains who could scribe and do sums, and they were few and far between. Accordingly, whilst we were in London we sent recruiting parties out to the villages to search for likely lads willing to come to Cornwall and make their marks as archer apprentices.

******

Finally, it was time for us to leave London. The transports and galleys sailing for Lisbon and Malta would not even attempt to stay all together as an armada. There was no need since our cogs and ships were sailing with archers on board to defend them. After they reached Ibiza, George and Thomas would move to another galley and sail for Rome whilst Yoram and Harold sailed on to Cyprus with most of our galleys and transports. Yoram was clearly anxious to get home to his wife and children and, truth to tell, so was I.

I was looking forward to returning to Cornwall and everyone going east was quite optimistic about returning to Cyprus and the Holy Land ports. They would all sail separately and try to pick up any prizes that they might run across. The rumour among the London merchants and on the London docks was that the Moorish pirates had become active again, so perhaps some of our galleys and pirate-taking cogs would run into some pirates or Moorish transports and get lucky.

I almost wished I was going with them instead of returning to Cornwall to spend the rest of the summer there. The French prizes and their prize monies have whetted everyone's appetite including mine.

******

I stood on the quay with John Farmer, my apprentice sergeant and scribe, and watched as Thomas and George sailed off for Rome in Harold's galley. Hopefully they would return in time so that Harold could carry me back to Cyprus in the fall. Martin Archer went with them to once again take up the command of our post in Rome. Martin and most of our men stationed at posts outside of Cornwall had come in when I recalled our galleys and archers for our attack on the French armada.

Now they were sailing off to return to their regular stations and posts in Cyprus, Constantinople, and along the Holy Land coast. Every able-bodied English sailor man and pilot we could recruit in London was going with them to help crew our unsold prizes. I would join them after I returned to Cornwall to spend a few months with my family and finish the summer season of construction and the training of our archer apprentices.

It had been a day of farewells when our armada and most of my lieutenants and archers sailed for Lisbon and the east. A surprisingly large number of people had come to the quay to see them off, including more than a few distraught girls and women. John Farmer and I would have gone down the Thames with them to sail for Cornwall but for the last-minute discovery of a rotten plank in the hull of Jeffrey's galley. The rotted plank was allowing far too much water to leak in and would probably worsen. It had to be repaired before we sailed.

The local boat-wrights initially assured us that they could fix it with a patch and we would not be delayed more than a few hours. So John and I stood on the quay amongst the crowd of well-wishers and lamenting women and watched as our galleys and transports cast off with bleating sheep and complaining chickens on their decks to begin to make their way down the Thames on the first leg of the long voyages each of them was about to undertake.

And they were indeed going on long voyages—my brother Thomas and my son George were sailing in Harold's galley to visit the Pope in Rome and deliver this year's prayer coins and the King's secret parchment. They would continue on to Rome after stopping for a few days in Lisbon and Ibiza to try to sell some of our prizes and set up trading posts in both of those important ports. *We had considered Palma instead of Ibiza but my bad experience there had soured me on the place. I still limp when the weather's bad from the sword that stuck me.*

Yoram and Harold and most of our galleys and almost all the transport prizes we decided to keep would call in at Ibiza for supplies and then sail all the way to our major post on Cyprus via Malta and Crete. From there, they would go on to ports along the coast of the Holy Land and Constantinople and put into our regular service of carrying cargos and passengers between ports and taking Moorish prizes.

No raids on Moorish ports were to be undertaken along the way by any of our galleys. I had made that clear to everyone early on and repeated it just before they sailed. Nothing of that sort was to occur until I came out to Cyprus in the autumn and could plan the raids on the Moorish ports and lead them myself.

On the other hand, it was always acceptable and greatly encouraged for our galleys and pirate-taking cogs to go after individual pirate galleys and Moorish transports. Taking prizes was, as you might imagine, constantly on everyone has mind because of the potential prize money. Raids on major Moorish ports, however, could be dangerous. They had to be carefully planned and executed.

Harold and Yoram and almost all the rest of our galleys and unsold prizes sailed for Cyprus at the same time as George and Thomas sailed for Rome. The first stop for all of them, as usual, would be Lisbon.

When they get there, Yoram and Thomas would tarry for a while and try to sell some of our prizes. They would also attempt to establish a permanent shipping post as we have been meaning to do for the past several years. Then Thomas and George would sail on to Rome via Malta whilst Yoram and most of our galleys and transports sailed to Malta and on to Cyprus and then the Holy Land ports.

John Heath, Robert's brother, had been given another stripe and was travelling with Thomas and George to become our four-stripe post sergeant in charge of our new Lisbon station. George's friend and fellow student, William the Ryder, was to be John's three-stripe apprentice sergeant and scribe.

Poor William Ryder; he had picked up the nickname of "the Ryder" because he kept falling off his horse when he was assigned to serve with Raymond and the Horse Archers as Raymond's apprentice and scribe.

******

Three days later, the repairs were finally completed and I sailed for Cornwall with one of Thomas's students, young John Farmer, as my apprentice and scribe. The quay was mostly empty when we left and many of the berths along it were empty. The distraught women and curious onlookers were long gone as the rowing drum started its beat and we began to move down the Thames. Only Robert Heath and David Levi and his sons were there to wave as our lines were cast off and the rowing drum began its monotonous beat.

Chapter Five

William is storm-wrecked near Hastings.

My voyage to Cornwall was star-crossed from the beginning. It had taken three days to repair the damage to the hull of Jeffrey's galley. We left on the tide as soon as the boat wrights pronounced it ready to sail. The sun was shining and the wind favourable when we finally cast off and got underway for Cornwall about an hour after sunrise. It stayed that way all day as we made our way down the Thames and for a few hours after we turned to run down the channel to Cornwall.

Late in the afternoon as the sun was almost finished passing overhead, the wind and weather suddenly began to rapidly worsen when we were off Dover. The wind changed direction and increased. And then it changed again and increased even more. It started blowing us towards shore and the seas got rougher and rougher amidst a driving rain.

We responded immediately. The sails were quickly lowered and everyone was sent to the oars including me. We lost sight of land, and the weather continued to worsen about the time our pilot and the sailors amongst us reckoned we were abeam of Folkston. That is when the repairs began to give way and we began taking on water far faster than we could possibly bail it out.

One minute, we were sailing with the sail up and the winds favourable; the next, the sky was black, the water dangerously rough, and the wind roaring. Then the patch gave way and we began to take on water and sink. It was as bad a storm as I had ever experienced and I was greatly weakened by being sea poxed. John was terrified and so were I and all the men seated on the rowing benches around us.

Jeffrey was the galley's sergeant captain and he had no choice when the patch gave way; he ran his galley aground and destroyed her on a rocky beach near Hastings. The wind was howling as a wave carried us up on the beach and I could feel the crunch through my sandals and knew instinctively that the hull was ruined beyond repair. Within an instant the galley started to slide back off the beach into the channel as the wave receded. That is when an even bigger wave pushed us further up on to the beach and slewed us sideways.

"Come on," I shouted as I grabbed John by his tunic and pulled him after me. All around us desperate and screaming men were leaving their rowing benches and running for the galley's railing to try to jump down on to the beach in a frenzied effort to escape. I jumped with them and so, I think, did John.

I landed with a splash in water well above my knees and stumbled forward just as another huge wave came in and moved the galley even closer to the beach and pushed me forward with it. Several men were crushed as the hull of the galley went over them and then we were all pulled back deeper into the water as the wave receded. More and more screaming and yelling men poured over the deck railing and jumped into the water all around me. I stumbled forward and desperately tried to run against the pull of the receding water to escape the next wave.

******

We pulled ourselves ashore with some of the stronger men helping those that were too exhausted or injured. A few minutes later, darkness closed in on thirty-seven wet and shivering men of a crew that had once numbered more than one hundred and fifty. John and Jeffrey were not among them.

It was the most terrible night of my entire life. It may have been summer but it did not feel like summer. It was dark and cold and windy with a driving rain that continued for hours. We had no shelter and nothing with that to start a fire, not that we could have lit one in the rain even if we had had the means.

"Sergeants, bring your men here to the captain; sergeants, rally here." I shouted in an effort to get some degree of control over our sad situation. Then I called out again in the pitch black dark and rain. "Everyone rally here for orders."

I sensed men moving towards me from their cries and the various noises I heard as they tried to move over the rocky beach.

"We have made it to safety, lads." I shouted into the rainy dark in an effort to encourage them. "We will have to buck up until dawn comes and we can walk to Hastings. It was close nearby even though we cannot see it for the dark. So it was jumping jacks for every man and run in place to stay warm; do not give up now. We are safe. It will be warm and we will be rescued in the morning."

******

All we could do all night in the darkness was stay awake, constantly jump up and down and run in place to keep our blood from thickening, and shiver and wait for the sun to finish circling the other side of the earth and bring dawn to us.

Dawn's early light finally came and found the thirty-seven of us still alive and shivering uncontrollably. Several of the men had lost their tunics and many had lost one or both of their sandals; I had lost the sandal on my right foot and one of my wrist knives. At first, my right foot hurt from wading ashore on the rocky beach and moving around to stay warm. Then it got so numb I was afraid that if I fell down I would not be able to get back up.

As soon as it was light enough in the morning to see we began wading into the cold surf to pull bodies ashore on to the fog-shrouded beach. What was left of the galley was grounded on its side just off the strand in water too deep to reach by wading. Clearly it was wrecked beyond repair and would never sail again.

Suddenly, there was a hail from what was left of the wreckage. Two men were alive. They had stayed aboard and somehow ridden out the storm.

"Do not try the water, Charlie. We will get help and save you," someone shouted from the beach to a mate whose voice he had recognized. "Do not give up."

I was busy taking a sandal off of one of the bodies and did not see who gave the order.

In the distance, as the light of dawn came up, we could see a castle on a hill overlooking the channel and rooftops below it. It had to be Hastings Castle and its village. Everyone instinctively began moving towards the shelter it promised without a word being spoken. Several of the men began to run. The rest of us walked as fast as we could.

Within seconds, the strand in front of the wreck was empty except for the dozen or so bodies at the edge of the water and a couple of men that were in very bad shape and could not move. One of them was moaning and holding his obviously broken leg; the other was sitting with his back against a large stone shaking his head.

"We will send someone back for you," I told them before I hurried off with the others. Reassuring them was all I could do; hope was all I had to offer.

The rain had stopped, but everyone was shivering uncontrollably in our wet clothes and the early morning chill as we walked as fast as possible across the rocky strand towards the village and rescue. Several of the running men were far ahead of us as we picked our way across the strand. It was summer in England but you would not know it on the beach near Hastings.

Then it dawned on me—thanks to God, the storm did not hit three days earlier and destroy our entire armada.

******

As we walked towards safety, we began to meet people coming the other way. First one man, and then another, and then a hurrying column of ragged men and women passed us going in other direction. None of them stopped to help us and most of them did not even slow down except to ask what our galley had been carrying.

They spoke the strange dialect of East Sussex, and we could barely understand their shouted questions as they went past us. The handful that paused to question us seemed disheartened when they heard it was a galley that had been stranded instead of a transport full of cargo.

The intentions of the men and women that came past us to salvage the wreck were immediately clear to all us; they were there for salvage, not for a rescue. There was nothing we could do but continue on to the hovels we could see ahead of us. I constantly shouted at the people streaming past us that I would pay twenty silver coins for each of our injured men on the beach and on the hull they brought in alive—and that I knew there were at least four of them.

******

Smoke was drifting up through the thatched roofs of several of the first group of daub and wattle hovels we reached. Our men had already broken into one of them by the time I got there. It was already full of shivering archers and sailors when I ducked my head and entered through its narrow door.

A young woman nursing a baby was the only other person in the bare room. She was crouching in a corner, and clearly overwhelmed and sobbing. So, for that matter, were several of the men. The men's emotion was different—one of relief and deliverance even though every one of us was wet and cold and still shivering, but at least we were out of the wind and the light rain that continued to fall.

I do believe that initially all thirty-seven of us squeezed into that little one-room daub and wattle hovel with its cooking fire smouldering on stones in one corner of the room. Even as wet as we were, our body heat seemed to warm the room even more as we crowded in. Within a few minutes some of the men had recovered and were leaving to break into the nearby hovels in search of food and dry clothing or bedding in that to wrap themselves.

We quickly understood that we had broken into the four or five hovels of a small fishing village on the outskirts of Hastings, people that were themselves always desperately poor and hungry. The village was virtually empty as all but one old man that was watching over some children and the young nursing mother were either away fishing or gone to salvage the wreck.

According to the old man, there was no sense going to the castle—it was no longer inhabited. It had been destroyed last month on King John's orders for fear of it being taken by the French. I was surprised and asked why.

The explanation I got from the nursing mother and then from the old man, to the extent I could understand their dialect, was that Hastings Castle belonged to one of the great French lords that was not at all loyal to England or King John. John had ordered it to be destroyed because he was afraid the lord's retainers would welcome the French when their invasion armada arrived. The castle's castellan and its soldiers had commandeered fishing boats and fled to France leaving their English servants behind to starve and the fishermen with no one to buy their catch.

******

Within the hour, the villagers that had rushed past us to get to the wreck began trickling back empty-handed to find their hovels occupied by our survivors. The tables had been turned; whilst they were gone, we had broken into their homes and looted them of food and bedding to wrap around ourselves in an effort to get warm.

Almost all of the would-be salvagers returned as soon as they saw the barren beach and the wreck aground in water too deep to reach by wading. Some ran back to launch their fishing boats as soon as they saw that the hull of the wreck was somewhat intact and could be reached by boat. As you might expect, they were very unhappy when they saw us in their hovels when they returned to pick up their oars so they could row their fishing boats out to the wreck.

I told the infuriated greybeard that stormed into the hovel where some of my men and I were huddled around the fire we had gotten going that I would pay twenty silver coins for each of our men he brought back alive and three silver coins for every galley sword, pike, and longbow he and the other fishermen could salvage. I promised a copper penny for every five arrows. His anger at finding strangers in his hovel turned to calculation, and he rushed off with a nod of his head.

It turned out to be an important offer because my telling him that we had coins to spend saved our lives.

******

The rain had finally stopped and most of the villagers had returned from the wreck to find their homes occupied. The first returnees did not bring in any of our survivors, so I sent a party of four volunteers off to the site of the wreck to retrieve our two injured men and see if the two men clinging to the wreck still needed to be rescued.

A few minutes after they left, a large party of armed men arrived on foot from the nearby town of Hastings. They did not act like rescuers and they were not poor fishermen; they were ship owners and sailors armed with swords and clubs. Worse, as it turned out, they knew who we were and they were not friendly.

It seems that one of the fishing boats that had reached the wreck, the first one on the scene, had rescued the two survivors on our galley and picked up a number of the galley's swords, longbows, and other weapons as salvage. They took our two men and their salvage to the Hastings city quay. Our rescued men had understandably identified themselves and told everyone who we were and what had happened. This caused us a great misfortune—not because we were wrecked on the strand and the people of Hastings were disappointed in the salvage, but because we were archers and sailors from a galley based in Cornwall.

Chapter Six

George and the troubles in Lisbon

On our third day out of London, a great storm blew us to the north and scattered our armada. We ran on and on before the wind in high seas. Not a one of our galleys or transports or anyone else's was in sight when the weather finally cleared. And when it did, Harold and our pilot had not the slightest idea as to where we might be located. There was only a great, empty, grey ocean stretching out to the horizon in every direction.

We fixed our position the best we could using the rising and setting sun and then sailed south and easterly knowing that sooner or later we would hit land. Two days later, there was a hail from the mast and in about an hour we could see the low, grey outline of a land mass to the south.

As we approached the unknown land, Harold's pilot, an old greybeard from London whose name was Samuel, said he thought it was almost certainly the southern tip of Ireland. He said he recognized an inlet where he had taken on water when sailing between Dublin and

Galway. I listened and learnt as Thomas and Harold consulted with Samuel and they talked at length about what to do and why to do it.

Should we head south for Cornwall to replenish our supplies or sail east to Lisbon? That was the question. In the end the winds made the decision for us—they were favourable for Lisbon.

******

We raised the galley's sail and rowed to keep the men busy and headed east. Six days later we raised the coast of Spain. Then we turned to our right and rowed along the Spanish coast until we reached Lisbon three days after that. It was a hot, summer day with hardly a cloud in the sky when we arrived.

Almost half of our galleys and French prizes were already in Lisbon's great harbour as we rowed through the harbour entrance. Several of them must have been quite battered in the storm because we could see repairs underway as we rowed past them. One of our galleys seemed to have been hit particularly hard by the storm; it was lashed to the quay and a crowd of men were on its deck trying to install a new mast.

Others of our galleys and cogs were moored to the quay taking on water and supplies. The place was bustling with stevedores and merchants despite the hot sun beating down. Many of the men were wearing little straw hats with wide brims to cool their hair.

Yoram's galley must have been one of those moored to the quay, for he walked up with a big smile on his face and his arms held wide in an enthusiastic greeting as our sailors prepared to throw their mooring lines to the men waiting to catch them.

"Hoy, Thomas; hoy, George. Welcome to Lisbon," he shouted as our galley bumped up against the quay. In the background I could hear a sergeant swearing at a luckless sailor that had not properly placed his big linen bag of rags and twigs to hold his galley's hull away from the quay.

******

"Come on up here and It is time to go have a bowl of wine and some olives and get out of the sun," Yoram said as we squinted up at him in the bright sunlight. "I have been out to visit our hospital and we have got a lot to talk about."

Yoram wanted to talk because we had been thinking about setting up our trading post in the hospital with John Heath as our post sergeant and young William Ryder as his scribe.

Our hospital was a small house with a walled courtyard near the harbour and in many ways ideal for us. It was one of the four hospitals we had set up for our archers that had been unable to continue on active service because they were elderly or disabled from wounds.

We had bought this one from one of Lisbon's merchants back when we left more than a dozen archers and a couple of sailors here to recover from poxes and the wounds they had received in the battle we fought with the Byzantines in front of Constantinople's walls. Now it only housed five of them.

The Company's other hospitals for our ill and elderly, as you might imagine, were located in Cornwall, Malta, and Cyprus. It was quite surprising how many of our retired and disabled archers and sailors preferred to live in warmer places than England.

Some of the men we originally left in the Lisbon hospital had died and others had recovered from their wounds and returned to Cornwall when my father recalled our men and galleys to fight the French. *And surprised us when he did—we had all thought we would be going on a big raid against the Moors in Tangiers or Algiers.*

Many of those that had recovered came out of the safety of an honourable retirement because they did not want to miss getting a share of the prize money from whatever raid was being planned. They had returned to active duty by joining our galleys bound for Cornwall to join the raid when they stopped in Lisbon to replenish their supplies.

Not all the men we left in Lisbon recovered and returned to active duty. Some of them had died, and five of our wounded men from Constantinople were still living in the hospital. They had remained in Lisbon when the recall came because they were too crippled or sick to continue as archers. They had been pensioned off with full pay and a bed of their own.

Making it known we would always take care of our sick and wounded men and those that lived long enough to be too old to fight or work as sailors greatly pleased our men. It was, according to my father and Uncle Thomas, a big reason so many archers and sailors were willing to make their marks on our Company's articles. They said it was a common fear of every man that he would be turned out and left to starve when he was no longer useful or needed, and that kings like John do it after every war. *It appears to be true; I had heard our men talking about it more than once.*

* * * * * *

What Yoram found at our hospital, he told us as we sat in the shade of a big tree behind one of Lisbon's taverns drinking a splendid wine, was that one of the five men that had remained in Lisbon had recently died when his leg turned black and rotted; the other four were still living there.

And just yesterday, two more men had been taken there to rest and recover because they were no longer fit—one whose arm had been broken by the log holding down his galley's sail when the wind suddenly shifted and another that had a great pain in his side and would most likely need a barber to bleed him.

When the hot sun began to go down and it was safe to walk without being made dizzy by the sun and falling down, Harold and Yoram and I went to see the place for ourselves. We were expected and warmly welcomed, but I could clearly see the worry on the faces of the men that greeted us and the women they had attracted as caretakers.

Our hospital was a one-room, stone building with a tiled roof, as is common in these parts, and a small walled garden. It was near the quay and had thick stone walls to keep it cool in the scorching hot summer days and the cold winds out in the winter. As was inevitably the case in all our hospitals and posts, our men were there with a number of women that had somehow moved in to care for them.

Using the house as a hospital for such men presented us with a problem. It obviously was not big enough to house both the invalids and John Heath and the sailors and guards he would need if we are to establish a permanent trading post in Lisbon.

"What do you think we should do?" my uncle asked me as we walked back to the quay in the dusk to spend the night on Harold's galley.

"We cannot turn them out," I said to my uncle and Harold as I used my tunic to wipe the sweat from my brow.

"It would not be right and it would dishearten our men. Being crippled and abandoned or getting too old scares our men more than being killed. There is nothing we can do except find a new place for either the men in the hospital or for our post."

"Good lad. You are absolutely right," said Harold.

With that, we began talking about how we should go about finding another place here in Lisbon for John Heath and his men—and we kept talking about it until Harold gave a little snore and Uncle Thomas blew out the candle lantern.

******

The next day Yoram took Harold and my Uncle Thomas to visit the merchants that had helped him sell five of our prizes and were provisioning our galleys and transports for the next leg of their voyages. Several of them spoke French and were able to translate for the others.

The merchants were enthusiastic about helping us establish a post to provide shipping services to Lisbon's merchants with armed transports and fast galleys. They described several places that might be empty and available.

One place in particular caught our attention. It was further away from the quay and the market and sounded as if it might be bigger than our hospital. According to the merchants, it had a much larger walled compound where we might be able to build another building if we needed more space. It had the additional virtue of not requiring many coins to buy it.

An older, French-speaking merchant walked next to me as we went to look at it early the next morning before it became unbearably hot. He was emphatic that merchants accompanying us, including him and his brother, wanted to help us locate in Lisbon.

"We want you here in the city because we like the idea of being able to ship our goods in armed transports," he said. He and his brother and the other merchants, he explained, had "lost too many cargos to the Moorish pirates by shipping them in the unarmed transports of the local ship owners."

Yoram had obviously told Lisbon's merchants about our plan for putting archers on our bigger prizes to defend them against pirates.

On the other hand, the merchant warned me, "The local shippers, even those that bought your prizes, would not want you here in Lisbon earning coins by carrying cargos that they would otherwise carry."

Do Harold and Uncle Thomas know this? I must remember to ask them.

"Be wary of the owners of Lisbon's shipping and remember what happened to the Venetians in Constantinople when they got too big," he quietly cautioned me under his breath.

"The local shippers know you English are interested in Lisbon and they are of two minds about it. They like the idea of having you here so they can buy your prizes, but they would not like losing some of their cargos to you even more. Besides that, some of them trade with the pirates."

It turned out that the owners of Lisbon's shipping would be the least of our problems, at least initially.

******

The first place the merchants showed us would have been perfect if it had been a little closer to the market and the quay. It was empty and just across a narrow lane from a church. There was a carriage-making yard on one side of it, a wood yard on the other, and its price was quite low.

We looked at several other places after we looked at the first one but they each had major drawbacks; one was much too small and expensive, and the other was poorly located up against a hill such that attackers and robbers could look down upon it.

After much discussion amongst ourselves, we bought the first place and took possession of it. John Heath and his men moved in immediately.

Our invalids in the hospital were mightily relieved and thankful when they heard about our purchase of the new post; so, to my surprise, were our able-bodied men as well. There were sighs of relief and morale and spirits seemed to lift everywhere when the decision was announced.

Uncle Thomas was right about the need to continue caring for the wounded men after a war or at the end of their useful service.

******

Two days later, we were about to follow the galleys and transports, that had already sailed for Ibiza as their next supply stop on their way east, when one of John Heath's men came running up the quay all out of breath and asked us to come quickly. There was a problem.

Uncle Thomas and I hurried to our new post with a couple of hastily summoned men from our galley's archers as our guards. One of whom, quite fortunately as it turned out, was wearing a sword and carrying a galley shield.

A red-faced and distressed John Heath was waiting for us when we arrived. He was clearly glad to see we were still in Lisbon.

"You need to talk to the priest," John said anxiously as he pointed to the church across the way. "Some local hard men just visited us and demanded a donation of fifteen silver coins for the church across the way. They said they came from the priest and we would have to pay that much each month or do without their protection and that of the Church."

"Do they now?" asked Uncle Thomas as he settled his mitre on his head. "Do they say what would happen if you do not pay?"

"Aye Lieutenant, err I mean Bishop, that they did. They said we would have the same fate as the previous two owners of this place if we did not pay; we would suffer and die as they did if we did not pay the necessary. I said I would talk to you immediately and get back to them this very day."

"Well then," said my uncle, "It is time for us to talk to the priest and sort this out."

******

We started towards the church with John Heath and our two guards. Then Uncle Thomas changed the direction he was walking. He turned around and we walked behind him in the hot sun as he went next door to visit the carriage works in the compound next to ours.

"Hello. Hello," cried Uncle Thomas jovially as he waved his crosier about as we followed him through the gate of compound next door.

I do not know how he can be so happy; I am hot and sweaty and uncomfortable.

A white-haired man wearing a leather apron and four or five workmen looked up in dismay as we walked through the gate. He was obviously the master carriage maker and he became quite distraught when he saw Thomas in his bishop's robe and mitre. He began waving his arms about and jabbering at us as his journeymen and apprentices looked at us with undisguised hostility.

We immediately had a problem, a big problem; none of the carriage-wrights could speak English or French and none of us could speak Portuguese. What the white-haired man could, and did do, was jabber away nonstop whilst tearing at his hair and over and over again shouting, "No mas dinero; no mas dinero," and pointing at the church across the way as he waved his hands around in a most pleading and defeated manner.

Uncle Thomas and I got the message. At least, I think we got it. Uncle Thomas waved his cross at the man, and then at his apprentices for good measure, and we left with the white-haired man still yelling at us. He was distraught and unhappy and being consoled by his apprentices and journeymen as we walked out of his yard.

After we left the carriage-wright's yard, Uncle Thomas sent John and our guards back to our post to get out of the heat. There was no one about as he and I marched in the sun's terrible heat across the dusty lane to the church and entered through its open door.

Chapter Seven

Meeting the priest and what happened next.

It was a rather common, everyday church such as one sees all over Christendom. That is to say it was about a dozen paces wide and about forty paces long with a dirt floor and a high ceiling with openings at the top of the side walls to let the light in and the hot air out. It was surprisingly cool because of its thick walls. There was an altar at one end and a confessional box on the left side. A small wooden table with short benches on both sides was in the far corner. A wooden cross was nailed up on the far wall.

What was unique about the church were the people in it—two slatternly women were sitting around a rough wooden table with a shirtless burly man that might have been a priest and a couple of rough-looking men who did not at all resemble clerics.

They looked up as we entered and the men stood up. The men with the priest did not look very friendly.

The looks they gave us were clearly intended to intimidate us.

"What do you want?" demanded the shirtless man in Portuguese as he took a sip of something from the wooden bowl he had in his hand and then stood up. We could not understand the words but their meaning was clear.

Uncle Thomas answered him in Latin.

"I am the Bishop of Cornwall and I have come to talk to you about your request for a monthly payment from the Pope's 'Order of Poor Landless Sailors,' the men that just moved in across the way."

"I do not care who you are or they are; they will pay if they know what is good for them. And what is it to you?" The man's response was in Latin; we had found the priest.

"I am the Pope's nuncio to his Order of Poor Landless Sailors and this," Uncle Thomas said nodding to me, "is Father George, one of their priests. We have come to ask you to reconsider."

The response of the shirtless priest was arrogant and surprising.

"Do not bother asking; we will not. Just pay us and go away until next month. We will protect you until then and each month thereafter if you pay. And did not bother telling me you will complain to the archbishop. My father's away to the north with the King and he would not pay any attention to you even if he was here."

He smirked as he told us about his relationship with the archbishop, and then moved closer to Uncle Thomas and gave him a little push in the chest with his finger to intimidate him as he said.

"You and your English merchants would pay us every month or you would not be able to stay in Lisbon."

"Ah well," said my uncle. "Perhaps it was God's Will that this priest and his men get what they deserve to be paid, is it not Father George?"

"God's Will?" I responded with a question in my voice.

"Yes, God's Will, George. God's Will is important. Have you forgotten its meaning?" Uncle Thomas gave me a hard look as he said it.

"What?" ... "Oh." ... "Oh, yes, now I remember. ... I am sorry," I said. ... "I forgot. It would not happen again."

"Are you ready to accept God's Will, Father George?" my uncle asked with an even harder look and a displeased edge to his voice. He looked at me intently. I nodded apologetically, and rightly so; I had missed his signal.

"Please be kind," I said to the two toughs in a pleading voice as I stepped towards them with both of my hands up next to my shoulders in supplication as if I was praying to the heavens. "It is important to accept God's Will."

The priest's two hard men sniggered at my abject behaviour even though they could not understand the words. They stopped sniggering, and the looks on their faces turned to dismay as my wrist knives came out, and then stunned disbelief as they flashed towards them.

They did not even have time to cry out or get their hands up before I got one of the men fully in his throat with the knife in my right hand. I felt the tip of my knife hit bone and gave it another hard push and a twist. At the same time, the other man, the one I had almost missed and merely nicked on the side of his neck, flinched backwards and instinctively twisted and turned away from my knife. He stumbled against the table and knocked it over. It overturned with a great crash.

I never did see how Uncle Thomas took the bare-chested priest. I was too busy stepping forward to get to the other hard man. He had instinctively turned away and stumbled into the table in response to my thrust and his sliced neck. He did not have time to react before I crowded up against him, put my arm around his neck, and cut his throat from behind with a great ripping pull.

The younger of the women just stood there with her mouth open in amazement and her hands held up to cover it. Then she started screaming. The other woman made a run for the door as Uncle Thomas was bending down to pick up his mitre that had fallen off in the brawl. She did not make it. Uncle Thomas was on her like a cat on a mouse and knocked her to the ground. That is when she started screaming and he punched her in the mouth. His mitre fell off again. It never did fit properly.

The younger woman stopped screaming as I pushed my second man to the floor. She just stood there with her eyes wide in surprise and her mouth open in dismay as she watched him clutch at his throat amidst a rapidly widening pool of blood. She had no teeth in front; the priest or one of his men must have knocked them out.

******

Both of the women were sobbing and trembling with fear by the time Uncle Thomas got to the front door and put the wooden bar in place so no one could enter. The younger woman looked at the little priest's door in the rear of the church. I could tell she was considering trying to make for it in any effort to escape. I shook my head at her and said, "Do not even think about it." She could not understand me, of course, but she got the message and did not move.

We waited whilst the priest and his hard men finished their dying in the great pools of blood that began forming around them. The first man I had gotten in the neck bone did not begin his leg trembles so, after a minute or two, Uncle Thomas used a leg that had broken off the table to hit him in the head to give him a mercy.

"Now then, Young George. We must tidy things up here and disappear the priest and his friends in case the archbishop really is the priest's father. Here is what I want you to do."

******

That evening, after it got totally dark, a horse cart pulled by a dozen heavily armed archers from one of our galleys still in port pulled up to the door of the church and I unbarred it. The archers carried the bodies out of the church and threw them in the cart. It went quickly because we had already wrapped them in some rough linen bedding we found in the Priest's hovel next door and the pools of blood had soaked into the church's dirt floor. There had been people walking in the lane, but they disappeared as if by magic when our men arrived at the church pulling the horse cart.

The women were thrown into the wagon on top of the bodies with their hands tied and their feet hobbled. They did not know it but they were about to be taken to the quay and loaded upon a galley that would immediately row out of the harbour bound for Malta and Cyprus. The dead priest and his hard men would go overboard to feed the fish when we were far enough away from Lisbon; the women would travel as passengers and help the cook.

A parchment describing the situation was hastily scribed for John Heath to send to Yoram. It would be up to Yoram to decide the disposition of the women.

If the past is any guide, they would probably be spoken for or married by the time they reach Cyprus, unless, of course, they were poxed, and even then they may find someone if they did not smell too bad.

However it ends, they would never return to Lisbon or be heard from again. Yoram would make sure of that.

Chapter Eight

William is held for Ransom.

We were marched into the village of Hastings and up the hill to the castle. It had not been completely destroyed. Only its battlements and roofs had been cast down; its dungeons were intact.

It quickly became clear from the treatment and beatings we received in the days that followed that those of us that survived the stranding of Jeffrey's galley had not been rescued; we had been captured.

The men that had captured us were the portsmen of the Cinque Ports, the men who were "King's barons of the Cinque Ports"—as all free men in those ports were titled on the premise that their military service at sea for the King was equivalent to the military service on land required of England's landed barons, including me even though I had not much in the way of land and neither serfs nor knights fees.

As such, the "portsmen" who owned ships and cogs were entitled to attend the King's parliaments with the landed barons. Up until recently, the portsmen had been steady for the King in his dispute with the northern barons. Adding Cornwall's ports to those where goods could be landed tax-free changed everything because it threatened their trade. It was the last piece of straw that broke the horse's back; now they were ready to change sides and support the dissident barons against the King.

Our guards soon made clear even more reasons why the portsmen of Hastings were unhappy—because making Cornwall a limb of Dover threatened the Cinque Ports' monopoly in the provision of boats and sailors for the King in time of war. It also suggested that Dover might replace Hastings as the chief port. The Hastings men were mostly unhappy, however, because the archers of Cornwall had received the King's pleasure and the prize monies from taking the French armada and they had not even been asked to participate.

In essence, the men of Hastings were thoroughly pissed because they thought the King had sent us against the French armada to get the French prizes instead of sending them and their fellow portsmen as they thought the King was obliged to do. Their best answer to the

King's snub, some claimed, was to join the rebellious barons and eliminate us so it would not happen again.

The fact that the King had not sent us and the portsmen of the Cinque Ports had neither the fighting men nor the galleys needed to take the French armada did not deter their anger. It soon became clear that the men of Hastings were particularly unhappy with the King because their future was uncertain due to the recent destruction of Hastings Castle.

"Dover Castle did not get torn down, did it?"

******

Conditions in the dungeon were terrible, and we were all hobbled with leg irons. The sailor with the broken arm was alive when they put a line around him and lowered him down into the dungeon. But he had died the next day and was already beginning to rot. Also dead was one of the archers. He had been beaten to death by one of the portsmen because he had protested my being kicked.

Our guards were all hastily recruited fishing boat crewmen and unhappy in their duties and our treatment at the hands of the portsmen. They lowered buckets of water to us when the portsmen were not around. If they had not lowered the water down to us, we would have surely died. As it was we were starving to death amidst our piss and shite.

According to what we were able to gather from what our guards shouted down to us when the Hastings portsmen were not around, the portsmen that held us were undecided as to what to do with us. Some of them wanted to kill us; the others wanted to hold us for ransom.

My offer on the beach of twenty silver coins for every man they rescued was mentioned by the guards more than once. We got the impression my offer of silver coins was known to all the Hastings men and held great appeal. I was asked almost every day by both the guards and portsmen if they could actually get a ransom of silver coins for each of my men and many more for me.

"Of course, you can get them," I had gasped to one of the portsmen that had climbed down a wooden ladder to see us and kicked me in the ribs for no reason before he asked me.

"We took many prizes. They have already been sold and the coins are waiting for you to carry us to Cornwall and get them."

I will kill you the first chance I get, you poxy bastard.

******

There was a great disturbance with much shouting and uproar in the guard room above us on the sixth or seventh day of our captivity. We could hear screams and shouts and the distinctive thuds of clubs hitting shields and the men that were holding them. Our spirits rose even though we did not know who was fighting or why.

A few minutes later, a candle lantern lit the room above us and in its flickering light we could see men standing around the hole above and looking down at us.

"Are any of you Cornishmen from the stranded galley?" a voice shouted down as we gathered below the opening and looked up.

"Yes. Yes," we all shouted at once.

"Is the captain of the archers there?"

"I am here. I am here," I shouted as the excited men around me chimed in to voice their agreement.

A minute or so later a wooden ladder was lowered into the dungeon and we were told to climb out. Some of the younger and stronger men immediately went up the ladder towards the light. Others were too weak to make the climb. I waited for fear that once I came up to the light the ladder would be withdrawn and my men trapped. Also, truth be told, I was afraid I was not strong enough to make it.

"You will have to help us up or drop a line and haul us up," I shouted. "Some of us are too weak to climb by ourselves."

There was a lot of talk and movement up above me and, all of sudden, to my horror, the light disappeared. All around me in the darkness the remaining men moaned and cried out in despair. Then, miraculously it seemed, the light returned and someone leaned over the edge of the hole and held it so as to light the dungeon.

The man that came down the ladder was obviously an able-bodied sailor man. I could tell by the way he moved and acted.

In the flickering light of the candle lantern, we watched as he quickly tied the line around under a man's arms to so those above could pull him as he attempted to climb the ladder. When he finished, the sailor went up close behind him to hold him against the ladder and help him place his feet on the cross boards.

With the sailor's help and the men pulling from above, the process was repeated and the remaining survivors slowly climbed the ladder one at a time. After all but three of my men had climbed the ladder, a second flickering light appeared and a second very large man carried another candle lantern down the ladder into the foul hole that had been our home for almost a week.

Our new rescuer set the lantern on the floor. Then he stood back amidst the flickering light whilst he tied one line under his arms to steady himself and then tied another as a safety line under the shoulders of the man he intended to carry up the ladder. We could tell he was an experienced sailor man by speed at that he rigged the lines and tied the knots.

Three times he slung one of my last three men over his shoulder and climbed the ladder with him. I went last with him climbing beneath me to steady me and help my feet find the cross boards.

We left behind the flickering candle lantern, a great pile of shite, and two dead men. One of the dead men was Rufus, an archer from York that had gone through our apprentice program in Cornwall and been beaten to death in a Hastings dungeon for trying to save me. The other was the sailor with a broken arm whose name I never knew.

******

The light of the sun blinded my eyes when someone took my arm and guided me out of the guard room over the dungeon and into the roofless room next to it. I had to cover them with my hands for several moments. When I could see again, I found myself in a dimly lit, large hall filled with several dozen armed men and sailors staring at me with great curiosity.

My similarly bedraggled and foul-smelling men were off to one side wolfing down pieces of bread and queuing to suckle water from a couple of water skins. They gave a little cheer and smiling nods when they saw me. I was desperate for food and water and moved towards them as fast as I could stagger. A burly, three-stripe archer sergeant named Tom Black pulled a water skin out of the mouth of the archer sucking on it and pushed it towards me.

A well-dressed man in the robes of a rich cleric came up to me as I wolfed down some bread and cheese and then took another drink of water.

"Hello," he said as he held out his hand. "I am William of Wrotham. I rode here with my men to help arrange your ransom as soon as I heard."

He said it as if I would know who he was. I must have looked at him blankly for he hastened to explain.

"You know me even though we never met—I used to be the King's sheriff in Cornwall and Devon. That was before you and your archers arrived. Then I was one of the wardens of the Cinque Ports. Now I am in charge of all of the shipping in the kingdom. Indeed, I led some of them to Poitou a few years back to fight the French."

Then I knew who he was. He was the priest who loaded some of the King's men on to the Cinque Port cogs and sent them off to fight the French in Poitou's harbour. Well, he was going to have fewer transports and galleys to command in the near future after I finished destroying Hastings's.

"So we are to be ransomed, are we? And for how much and where? *And how much is your cut and that of the King?*

"The Hastings captains want thirty-five silver coins for each of your men and one thousand for you. A rather modest amount, would not you say, in view of all the prizes you just took? Particularly as you will be well-fed and watered until the coins arrive."

Chapter Nine

A ransom is demanded

Our treatment immediately improved although we continued to be closely guarded and held in the dark. We were marched to the Hastings quay and loaded into the hold of a small cog with inadequate and infrequently delivered amounts of food and water.

That very afternoon, I was brought on deck and given a pen and parchment to scribe a message to Peter describing our fate. In my message I directed him to borrow the required coins from David Levi, the London money lender, and exchange them for us on the London dock where our galleys were usually berthed. William Wrotham approved of what I had written and so did the Hastings portsmen. I was immediately returned to the hold.

The possibility of being ransomed raised our spirits whilst we waited for several weeks in the galley's cold and damp hold. Whilst we waited in the darkness, we talked about how we might take the cog and sail it to Cornwall.

Our plans were well underway when I was again brought up on deck. William Wrotham was there with several of the Hastings portsmen including the man that had kicked me in the ribs and then beaten to death the archer who had protested.

They were all smiles and good will—the required coins were ready to be paid and the Hastings men were ready to collect them. The cog would be sailing to London as soon as the wind turned favourable. The coins would be paid in London and that is where we would be freed.

We were to be freed one at a time on the agreed London quay as the ransom coins were received. I smiled with relief and nodded my agreement. *What else could I do?*

******

To my surprise, I was briefly given the freedom of the deck as the Hastings cog finished clawing its way up the Thames. I think it was because two of the five Hastings portsmen, the men who owned the Hastings transports, had never seen me and they were all curious to find out more about me. All five of the Hastings portsmen were on board to share the ransom and they were all in a good mood. They were willing to talk and quite forthcoming about their cogs and galleys and the advantages Cornwall would enjoy as a limb of Dover.

They smiled with satisfaction when I lamented about having to borrow the ransom to pay them. I, in turn, listened intently as they humoured me by responding to my questions about their cogs and other transports and where they sailed. One of the bastards even told me about the house he intended to build with his share of my ransom.

All but one of my men remained confined in the hold whilst the Hastings cog clawed its way up the Thames with the tide. The exception was one of my experienced sailors. He was allowed to come up from the cog's hold to help pilot the cog to the particular quay where the ransom coins waited, the one we usually used in London as I had specified in my parchment. He and I looked at each other and never said a word or made a gesture as we passed one of our galleys and it fell in behind us.

******

Peter and Raymond and a large group of heavily armed archers were waiting on the quay when the Hastings cog approached the quay. Their bows were strung but not nocked. We lifted our arms in silent greeting to each other but no words were spoken.

If William Wrotham had not been standing next to me in his priest's robes I think I might have fallen to the deck of the cog so Peter's archers could sweep its deck and take it. I did not do so because Wrotham would probably have been killed and I did not know his relationship with the King, or how the King would respond if he did not get whatever share of the ransom the Hastings men may have promised him. Also, truth be told, I did not act because I was afraid some of us would be hit when the arrows started flying, and me and my men killed, if our effort failed.

Peter and the archers waiting on the quay were clearly angry at the foul and pitiful state of the ransomed survivors they saw coming off the Hastings cog. Curses and cries of rage and horror greeted each of my men as he came out of the cog's hold in his foul rags and tried to walk across the deck to the quay.

Even so, the exchange of the ransom coins for the survivors went quite smoothly. The men being ransomed came out of the hold one at a time, inevitably holding their hands over their eyes to protect them from the sudden light and needing help from the Hastings men to walk. They staggered over the deck to the quay each time a handful of coins was handed to one of the portsmen. Several had to be carried.

Getting the survivors on to the quay was easily done as the tide was such that the deck of the cog was almost level with the quay and welcoming hands reached out to help them. Each was quickly surrounded and assisted by some of the waiting and increasingly angry archers.

Finally, it was my turn. The portsmen's eyes widened in appreciation and they crowded forward as the counting of the coins began for my ransom. No one stopped me when I stepped on to the quay as the count went past nine hundred.

"It was God's Will," I muttered under my breath as I stepped over the railing and briefly into Peter's embrace—and at the same time lifted Peter's knife from his belt and slid it into mine.

"Bishop William," I said to Wrotham as I turned and stepped towards him and the portsmen on the cog's deck that were watching with keen eyes as the final coins were being counted in the sack one of them held. "How do you think God would receive a man that beat an archer of my company to death for no reason but his own pleasure?"

Wrotham did not have time to answer before I pulled Peter's knife out of my belt and leaned over the deck railing to grab the tunic of the portsman that had kicked my ribs and beaten poor Rufus to death with his club.

He did not even have time to take his eyes off the ransom coins or scream before I pulled him towards me and stuck the knife into his belly up to its hilt and ripped it upward with all the strength I could muster. As I did and the portsman's eyes bugged out in disbelief and he began screaming, I shouted an order to Peter's stunned men as they were beginning to reach towards their quivers for arrows.

"Do not loose; let them leave in peace."

Then to the stunned Hastings men I shouted my terms over the screams and panicked cries of the dying portsman.

"Now here is my ransom demand for you lot from Hastings. You have thirty days to deliver every single one of those silver ransom coins to the King as a gift from his loyal Company of Archers, and two thousand more to the archers' post here in London for our trouble.

"If King John and the Company of Archers do not get them within thirty days, we will sail to Hastings and hang you all, burn your hovels and the entire village to the ground, and take all of Hastings's cogs and galleys as prizes and turn them over to loyal Englishmen that support the king."

Then I spit in the face of the still-screaming man and let go of his tunic so he could fall to the cog's deck amidst his stunned fellows. My only regret was that I could not piss on him as well.

"Cast off its mooring lines and push it away," I ordered with a nod of my head towards the Hastings cog and the open-mouthed men on its deck—and then watched with satisfaction as the archers on the quay hurried to obey.

Chapter Ten

William returns to Cornwall.

Peter and Raymond recovered quickly as the lines were thrown off and the Hastings cog began to very slowly drift away from the quay. They immediately understood what had just happened and where this was going to lead. Raymond even sneered and gave the cog a disdainful push with his foot to help move it out into the Thames.

The archers and the survivors that had climbed off the Hastings galley ahead of me stood for a moment with their mouths gaping open in surprise—then they began cheering and shouting insults and threats at the cog as the slowly moving current of the Thames caught the cog and it very slowly began drifting away from the quay.

"These men need food and drink, and so do I," I told a smiling Peter. "Please take us to the White Horse and see that every man gets all he wants."

"Good idea. I have already sent a man running to the market to buy tunics for the men that need them—

which would be just about every man from the look of you."

****

Some of the men that came out of the cog's hold were in such bad shape that they needed help to walk even the short distance to the White Horse. Fortunately, Peter and Raymond had bought a strong force of Raymond's Horse Archers to London. As a result, every one of our new freed men was instantly surrounded and assisted by concerned and solicitous helpers as we moved down the quay with everyone talking at once.

I must have stumbled or staggered because I suddenly realized Peter was holding me up by one elbow and Raymond the other. I felt relieved and tired, terribly tired.

"Help them sit; Help them sit," Raymond shouted over the babble of voices as we made our way into the White Horse for the food and drink we so desperately craved.

The White Horse quickly became so packed with our men that every survivor was assigned one man to help him and everybody else was sent outside with their weapons to "stand guard." Even then, the stench from the men and the clothes of the survivors was extreme. There was little wonder in that—we had had no choice but to lie among the piss and shite in the pitch-black dungeon for almost a month. Then we had been moved to the cargo hold of the cog from which we had just emerged.

Things became quite emotional as the food and drink began to be delivered to us by the alewife and the tavern servants. At the same time, our fellow archers stripped us naked right there in the tavern and helped us to put on the new tunics that a hurriedly despatched detail of archers had rushed to us from a nearby market.

Several of the still-dazed survivors were soon openly weeping at their deliverance. For some reason, I felt like weeping myself when I realized I had been in here happily celebrating our great triumph over the French less than a month ago.

My hands shook as I lifted a cold joint of chicken and bit into it; it felt like I had last been in the White Horse long ago in the far distant past.

******

Our stay in London lasted three days. Most of the ransomed survivors, all but me actually, were bedded down and cared for at our London shipping post. Robert Heath and his men and their families temporarily moved to join Raymond's archers in the stalls of the nearby stables to provide the survivors with space to sleep.

I did not stay in our post with the rest of the survivors. Peter and Raymond were concerned about how King John would react to my killing of the Hastings portsman. As a result, I joined my two lieutenants in the little forward castle of the only galley we had in London at the time. They had it anchored off the quay so they could cut the anchor line and move away instantly if trouble arrived in the form of the King's sheriff and his men.

We still had not heard anything from the King three days later. That is when all the survivors were much stronger from lots of good food and drink and we left London together for a leisurely overland trip to Cornwall. Over a hundred of Raymond's horse archers escorted us. The survivors and I had an easy time of it as we slept and ate whilst travelling in comfort in the horse carts Peter had hired from the stable.

Most of us recovered rapidly and were soon joining the daily archery contests. Only one of the survivors, an archer named Miles, did not make it to Cornwall. He developed great chills and died in his sleep before we could find a barber to properly bleed him. One of the men carved a cross from a tree limb and I said some nice prayers in Latin over his body as we buried him in a cow pasture near Salisbury.

"Is it safe to travel on the old Roman road to Cornwall?" I had asked before we left London. "What happened to Devon and the barons that were waiting in Exeter for Phillip?"

"Not to worry," had been Peter's answer. Then he explained.

"We got word from the spies we planted in Exeter. The barons scattered and many went north as soon as word came that you had taken Phillip's armada. The Earl of Devon has not been seen since. Rumour has it that he has fled to France for fear the king would take his head."

"Do we know if he took his knights and soldiers with him?" I had asked. "If he did, it might be time for us to take Exeter Castle and eliminate the Earl once and for all."

After I thought about the possibility for a few moments, I added, "Thomas and George should be back soon. We could use Thomas's contacts at court to see if the King would allow us to get rid of the Earl and keep Exeter after we do."

"Aye," Peter had agreed. "But we will have to be careful. It would do us no good to rid ourselves of a lord the King hates only to have the King replace him with an equally dangerous lord the King favours." *Peter is very smart; he is a good man.*

"Exactly so. Has there been any word of Thomas and George?"

******

There were no rains so the old Roman road was fast and we made good time, even though we travelled leisurely and stopped for bowls of ale at almost every public house along the way. We sighted Okehampton nine days after we left London. By then, we survivors had all been rested and fattened up such that I had begun riding at times with the horse archers instead of staying in the wagons with the other survivors.

We were altogether a happy band of men and we were going home.

Our welcome when we reached Okehampton Castle near the border between Devon and Cornwall, our Horse

Archers' base of operations, was not at all what I expected. I had anticipated seeing Isabel and perhaps staying and enjoying a few days with her whilst I continued to recover my strength.

I had heard Isabel still had not remarried and her husband, Lord Courtenay, he who had "sold" Okehampton to me just before he married Isabel and went off crusading, was still missing and had not yet been reported as dead in the Holy Land. He apparently never met the son he sired before he sailed.

It was not to be. I had not even dismounted after clattering over Okehampton's drawbridge when who should come rushing across the bailey to greet me but Helen.

Helen had heard from one of Raymond's gallopers that I had been successfully ransomed and was on my way to Cornwall in bad condition. She had immediately started for London to care for me and had gotten as far as Okehampton.

Peter and Raymond had already told me it was all they could do to keep her from coming to London with them; only their insistence that she would burden them if they had to fight to rescue me had kept her away.

Isabel and Wanda, Raymond's wife from the land beyond the sea, smiled as they watched our reunion whilst the castle servants rushed to bring bowls of ale to the sergeants among the arriving men and hold their horses' reins.

Isabel's smile seemed to be both bemused and resigned as she and Wanda came forward to give me a searching look and a welcoming hug and a kiss on my cheek. But then Raymond and the local men began clattering into the bailey over the drawbridge and the two women forgot all about us as they went to greet them.

Helen never let go of me. She ignored the bustle of everyone around us and immediately began searching me all over with her hands.

"No wounds," I told her as she did. "Just bad treatment." After a pause, I added, "and for that one man has already paid with his life and others soon will."

I did not tell Helen or anyone else what I had already decided to do—I was going to take the heads of the other four Hastings portsmen even if we were paid the two thousand silver coins that would save the village's boats and hovels. On the other hand, I was uncertain as to what should happen to William Wrotham. It would

depend on what the Hastings men we take tell me about
his involvement. It was possible he deserves my thanks.
If he does, he will get it; if not, he will die most horrible.

Helen was most affectionate. She immediately led me into the great hall and sat me on the bench whilst she ran to the kitchen to fetch bread and cheese and another bowl of ale. Then she sat next to me and held my arm and put her head on my shoulder whilst I ate.

"We were so worried. I prayed for you constantly and made many promises to God. So did Anne and Tori. All the children are well but Anne's little Alicia. She has a cough that will not go away. We are afraid for her."

After a while Raymond and Peter came in and joined us.

Later that evening, Helen washed me all over with a rag dipped in warm water, picked off the lice she could find, and used a blade to cut back my hair and beard. And all the time and afterwards she was more affectionate than usual.

******

We reached Restormel three days later and there was much joy and merriment at our return. The next day gallopers carrying a parchment from our London post brought a message from David Levi, the King's moneylender.

"The Hastings men have sent the ransom coins to the King and borrowed two thousand more to meet your demands. I have the two thousand waiting for you or whomever you send. Please do not kill them until I am repaid." *He had read my mind.*

Chapter Eleven

George and Thomas sail for Rome.

Uncle Thomas and I left two armed trading cogs in Lisbon and sailed for Ibiza the next morning on Harold's galley. The cogs would seek cargos to carry to ports in the pirate-infested Mediterranean as they sailed to Cyprus.

Sergeant Heath and fifty-two archer volunteers and the cogs' sailors stayed behind to operate the post and crew the armed cogs when they finished loading their cargos. The two women from the Lisbon church and the three dead men were already on a galley bound for Cyprus via Ibiza and Malta. It had cast off and rowed out of the harbour as soon they were carried on board. The men would be put over the side and the women carried to the next port and abandoned.

The weather was good and Harold's rowers were strong and they were well fed and watered. Uncle Thomas and I participated in the daily archery required on all our galleys and played chess. We also helped row to keep our arms and shoulders strong, and speculated endlessly with each other and the men as to what the Moors were doing and how the archers in the galleys and pirate-takers that left Lisbon before us might have done in terms of taking Moorish prizes.

We passed Gibraltar and reached Ibiza without seeing any Moors. Everyone agreed that it was not surprising that we did not see any Moors to take as prizes since so many of our own galleys had passed this way just a few days earlier.

In Ibiza, Uncle Thomas and I switched to the eighty-oar galley of James Tinker so Harold could take his galley on to Cyprus and resume command of all of the Company's fleet in the Mediterranean.

Sergeant Captain Tinker and his galley had been among the first of the Company galleys to leave Lisbon and had arrived in Ibiza several days earlier. His galley was already provisioned and ready to sail as soon as we arrived.

We supped well and drank too much wine until late in the evening of our arrival, and then did not get up the next morning in time to watch Lisbon disappear behind us as Captain Tinker's galley rowed out of the harbour the next morning. We would go through the ocean strait between Corsica and Sardinia and on to Rome.

******

The winds were good after we left Ibiza so Captain Tinker decided to try to sail all the way to Rome without making another port call. It was a popular decision and the men in Tinker's crew that had been to Rome previously told many tales about the great city and its delights to those that had not. This was my first visit to the great city, and I listened closely even when it was obvious that much of what we were being told could not possibly be true.

All in all, it was an altogether pleasant voyage. Every day we would have an archery contest that lasted for hours since every archer, including me and Uncle Thomas, was required to rapid-push fifty arrows every day at a linen target pinned on one of the hamstrung cattle or sheep we were carrying for food. That is how we killed it if it had not already died.

Each day's winner got a copper coin from Captain Tinker's galley pouch and anyone whose arrow missed and flew into the sea was mightily embarrassed—and required to spend the rest of the day helping the cook bake his never-ending stream of flatbreads and bailing water out of the bottom of the hull all that night. One day I almost won a coin.

The archers spent their days alternating between rowing, fletching their arrows, and practicing all the things the men on our galleys must do every day. All the while they yarned about everything imaginable; the sailors tended to the galley and engaged in mock battles with each other and the archers using galley shields and practice swords. There was moors dancing on the main deck and test matches between the dancing teams every day that, for some reason I never could understand, the sailors inevitably won.

Once there was a cry from the lookout on the mast that brought everyone on deck.

"Hoy, the deck. There is a big whale fish off our port side."

"There it is," Uncle Thomas said as he pointed. "Look at the size of that thing."

It was the biggest fish I had ever seen and it was swimming right next to us. It was almost as long as our galley and it was just swimming along near the surface. There was a much smaller big fish swimming right next to it. They must have been frolicking, for every so often they blew water into the air.

We watched for quite some time but then they suddenly disappeared with a flap of their tails to wave us a farewell. Uncle Thomas said they are mentioned in the Bible as swallowing fishermen and sailors that misbehave.

******

The sun had almost finished passing overhead on its endless circling of the earth when we finally reached the mouth of the Tiber River eleven days after leaving Ibiza. Our pilot said he and Captain Tinker would need to see clearly in order for us to safely thread our way through all the shipping in the mouth of the Tiber and in the river. So we laid offshore until the next morning when sun began coming up over the horizon on its daily trip around the earth.

Candle lanterns flickered all around us all that night; we were not the only ones waiting for the next arrival of the sun to head up the river.

At first light, we joined a great mass of shipping attempting to move up and down the placid brown river. The Tiber was bustling with everything from fishermen in small dinghies to barges and cogs and great three-masted ships under tow.

Our pilot's problem, of course, was compounded because many other vessels of all sizes and kinds were anchored in the river or moored along the shore or to one of the river's many wharves. The only saving grace that I could see was that generally all the traffic coming down river to the sea moved on one side of the river; the traffic going up the river to the city on the other side. There were a lot of exceptions and many near collisions.

Captain Tinker took no chances. He manned his galley's rowing benches, posted lookouts in the bow and on the mast, and had sailors with poles and pikes ready to push us away from anything with that his galley might otherwise collide. Until it got too hot, Uncle Thomas and I spent most of the morning standing with the sergeant and his pilot on the roof of the forward castle where the three of us slept at night and played chess when it was too cold or wet on deck. I was fascinated. Even the Thames had not been this crowded and busy.

One thing that immediately struck me was that the people here seemed quite excitable, probably, according to Uncle Thomas, because Italy was closer to the sun and the heat had thinned their blood. There were countless shouts and gestures and shaken fists as we worked our way up the river until we reached Rome's great walls. The walls around the city were even taller and more impressive than those I had seen in Lisbon and so were the great castles and houses along the river.

Uncle Thomas came out from the shade where he had been hiding from the sun and began naming what I was seeing when we came around a bend in the river and the city walls and buildings came into view. It was a big city for sure, certainly the biggest I had ever seen. It was no wonder that Jesus decided to move his Church here and the Pope lives here.

******* *Thomas*

Our galley moored at the narrow, wooden wharf running along the bank of the river where we always try to tie up when we are in Rome. It was a good place to berth in the summer because it was so close to the city wall that the wall itself shaded us later in the day. There also was a riverside tavern and shade trees between the wharf and the wall. I had been here before and always enjoyed it.

We had arrived on a hot summer day and numerous pedlars and petty merchants came out from the shade of the trees along the river and descended on us as soon as we began tying up. Many of them were selling wooden crosses and prayer beads; others were selling bowls of wine from the skins they were carrying and offering the services of all types of women. My nephew and the crew were wide-eyed with excitement at seeing the city and all the people and activity. It had been a good trip from Ibiza, but a long one. We were all happy to be here.

George and I immediately climbed off the galley and walked to the nearest riverfront tavern for a glass of cooling wine and a plate of nuts and olives. *I had been here before and knew where to go.* We sat on benches in the shade provided by the trees in front of tavern stall and watched the constantly growing activity around the galley.

It was not until we began our second bowl that I realized that in the excitement of arriving we had gotten off the galley without putting on our mail shirts. I sent George running back to the galley to get them. "And bring a couple of galley swords and shields as well," I shouted after him. He raised his hand in acknowledgement as he trotted over to the galley. *He is a good lad.*

It was pleasant sitting there under the trees with my nephew and a bowl of wine. No one seemed to notice or care when we stripped off our lightweight Egyptian tunics, put on our mail shirts, and then donned our thin tunics again. It was much too hot to wear my much heavier bishop's robe.

We watched benevolently when, after a while, Captain Tinker passed out the traditional arrival coins to his crew. Many of them promptly came over to the tavern and, of course, the pedlars and pimps followed them. Several of their women lingered in the shade of the wall fanning themselves and making gestures to attract the men. Our men and the women were soon sitting all around us chatting enthusiastically.

******

My nephew and I were cooling off in the shade and well into our third bowl of wine and happily munching on some fresh bread and olives when we had a surprising visitor—Cardinal Bertoli wearing the cassock of a simple priest and escorted by a couple of sword-carrying men. The Church must have spies along the river, for he showed up little more than an hour after our mooring and came straight to tavern.

Well, of course, the Church has spies about. These are dangerous times in Rome what with yet another effort by its citizens to seize control of the city from the Church and its priests. Last year when I was here to pay the Pope, there had been riots and fighting in the streets. I wonder what was happening this year. Some say it was the summer heat that causes a man's blood to get so hot that he wants to fight and riot. Others say it is behaviour of the city's priests and the night watch.

For a second, I did not recognize the man in the priest's cassock that stood in front of us with a big smile on his face.

"Antonio. Antonio. Eminence, is that you?" I said in Latin as I leapt to my feet and embraced him.

"Welcome, Thomas. Welcome to Rome. Yes, it is me. I am returned to Rome."

The Cardinal was a fine fellow and we had shared many experiences together including being captured and imprisoned by the Venetians. He and I greeted each other as long lost brothers with hugs and cheek kisses. I introduced George as "Father George, my nephew and assistant."

We waved at one of the tavern's servants to bring us more drinks and moved to sit on the ground so we could talk privately in Latin under a tree on the side of the riverbank. George came with us and so did the

Cardinal's guards. Antonio was full of information and spoke freely as soon as his guards moved out of earshot.

Antonio said he had come as soon as he heard we arrived because he wanted to warn us that the Pope was not happy about Phillip of France losing his armada. He became quite serious when he leaned forward and quietly told us we might be in danger despite bringing the Pope his share of this year's prayer coins from the refugees and other passengers our galleys and transports had carried.

It was all about the Church, Antonio explained, and the fact that two German princes were claiming to be the Emperor of the Holy Roman Empire. One of them backed by King John claimed that Italy was part of the empire and should be ruled by the Emperor; the other backed by King Phillip said Italy was not part of the empire and agreed it should be ruled by the Pope.

"Of course, the Pope backed Phillip and the barons against John," Antonio sniffed. "What else could he do if he wants the Church to rule both Rome and Italy as Jesus intended?"

Another reason, my friend said primly, was that Phillip and the dissident barons were agreeable to the Pope appointing England's bishops; whereas King John wanted to continue the practice of appointing them himself.

Ah, that explained it. The appointment of bishops was always a lucrative source of revenues for he that appoints them. I certainly knew that.

"It was because of John's refusal to let the Pope appoint the bishops that caused the Pope to excommunicate him a few years earlier and support his overthrow by the barons and Phillip. But now that is not likely to happen, at least not this year, due to Phillip's defeat at Harfleur by your brother."

Then the rotund little cleric took a sip of wine and added, "And, of course, John made it worse by meddling in the Church's affairs by supporting the election of the wrong German prince for Emperor—one that claimed he was the King of Italy even though it rightly belongs to the Church."

******

I was concerned, deeply concerned, by what my friend had told me and tried to make the best of it.

"Antonio, my friend, I am coming to the Pope with much more than just his share of the prayer coins from the refugees and pilgrims; I am carrying a parchment for the Pope from King John. I think King John is offering concessions in order to be reconciled with the Pope and restored to the Church. But, of course, I do not know if that is true or what might be in the King's parchment."

"Bringing an offer from King John would help your cause considerably; yes, it would, most certainly it would," exclaimed my portly friend as he looked at me intently.

"But the Holy Father is more interested in the relics that disappeared from Constantinople when the crusaders took it, particularly Saint John's gold-coated right hand and the silver-coated head of Saint Paul because they mean so much to the Orthodox. He is heard rumours that the English archers might know where they are. There are those that could very well have you tortured to find out if the rumours are true." *Tortured? Oh my God!*

"Well, torture is not necessary for me to tell the Pope everything I know. Surely, you know that. I was not there, of course, but it is true that our galleys were paid to carry the Emperor in Constantinople and some of his courtiers and priests to safety. And it is also true that the Emperor and his men may have taken the most valuable relics with them when they fled.

"But, as I am sure you know by now, our men were not allowed to go ashore when the cargos were unloaded at isolated spots along the Greek coast. They do not know where the crates might have been taken after that."

I was telling a lie, of course. I knew exactly where the relics were located and who has them—we have them and they are in Cornwall.

After a pause, I added.

"We are loyal to the Pope so, of course, we would be willing to help find the missing relics for him. *What else could I say, eh?*

"But why is the Pope so interested in having the relics from Constantinople? I thought Rome already had enough bits and pieces of Saint John and Saint Paul to attract the faithful and their coins."

Antonio's explanation was most interesting and not at all what I expected. I said as much and, after taking a break to piss against a tree and think things over, I suggested a plan that might benefit us all. Antonio liked it immensely, and agreed to speak to the Holy Father and do his part.

Chapter Twelve

We meet with the Pope.

George and I went to the Pope's residence in Rome early the next morning before the sun got high enough overhead to absolutely cook us. I was wearing my heavy embroidered bishop's robe and carrying my crosier and mitre; George was wearing the plain brown robe of a simple priest.

We engaged a horse cart with a roof of woven palm branches to carry us because of the heat. We had left early in an effort to avoid the heat, but it was already too warm to walk; it would have been unbearable wearing my robe despite the strange coolness provided by the mail shirts George and I both wore under our robes. What we were not wearing were our wrist knives—because I knew we would be carefully searched before we met with the Pope. We brought a guard of ten heavily armed archers from the galley instead.

Captain Tinker had selected steady men that had never been here before to accompany us so they would have a chance to see some of Rome beyond the riverfront taverns and whorehouses. They clattered along behind us in a horse-drawn wain and gawked and pointed at the magnificent buildings and the plazas with their ornate fountains and larger-than-life statues.

I did some pointing myself and explained to George what we were passing.

"It is a pity that the fountains are no longer working for they are truly a wonder," I told him. "They were not working last year either."

******

Our arrival at the big, carved, wooden gate leading into the square in front of the Pope's residence was expected. From here, we would have to walk and our guards and carts would have to wait.

"Greetings, Eminence," the officer of the guards said. "We were told to expect you. Father Pietro would take you to the Holy Father."

Father Pietro turned out to be an unctuous and sallow-faced youth that took himself and his role quite seriously. He kissed my ring, nodded dismissively to

George, and led us over the cobblestones to the big stone building where the Pope lived.

We did not go directly in to see the Pope, of course. First, we went through a door into a room where several priests and three papal guards were waiting. They searched us rather thoroughly with our hands held high. As usual, they did not reach up to search our wrists and totally ignored the linen pouch of coins I was carrying in my hand and did not put down.

Similarly, as usual, I did not bring their failure to search our wrists to anyone has attention. George seemed quite intrigued by the process even though I had several times described it to him. He had never been searched before.

Immediately afterwards Father Pietro led us to another room with wooden benches along its walls, told us water and fruit would be arriving momentarily and that we should use the corner of the room if we needed to piss or shite. Then he took his leave with a graceful bow that suggested he would have a long and profitable career in the Church. He would, Father Pietro said as he went out the door, make sure our men also received water and fruit whilst they waited for our return.

We waited for quite some time. Then Cardinal Bertoli hurried in without saying a word, gave me a great and approving nod of agreement, and motioned for us to follow him.

I hope I can remember the story I made up.

******

"Yes, that is it exactly, Holy Father. No one could have said it better. With God's help and your prayers the English archers may be able to find the missing relics because we carried the Orthodox priests and the crates with their relics to safety in three different galleys when Constantinople fell.

"They may be able to find where the Orthodox priests hid them because we know from the sergeant captains of our galleys where they landed the priests and how long it took them to bury the relics and return to each galley. That is important because it helps the archers know where they need to search.

"The problem, of course, is that those lands are hostile to the True Church. There would likely be heavy fighting when the archers come ashore and begin searching. Our archers are always willing to fight for valuable prizes and the relics would be great prizes. But here is the thing, Holy Father—if the archers fail to find the relics they would be content with their wounds and lost friends just as they are when they fail to take a Moorish prize; but if they find the relics they would expect to share in the prize money as provided in the Company articles on that they made their marks. What should we do?"

The Pope solemnly considered the problem and came up with the solution I had suggested to Bertoli—if we found the relics, we would sell them to the highest bidder to get the money necessary to pay the men—on the condition that whomever won them would then offer them as a gift to the Church.

The prince making such a grand gift, of course, would receive a similarly grand gift in exchange—he would avoid a stay in purgatory and be given great recognitions during his time on earth—such as, for example, being the only prince the Holy Father would accept as the Holy Roman Emperor or the King of England.

"Why, that is a wonderful idea, inspired by God for sure," I exclaimed as I crossed myself. "There is undoubtedly a good Christian prince somewhere that would pay so much that there would even be excess coins for the church."

George never said a word, but he was wide-eyed at the exchange; he knew we already had the relics safely at Restormel. He did not know the half of it.

******

"Do not say a word until we can talk privately," I said as George and I were led back to our waiting carts and escorts.

It was already very warm and groups of pilgrims were forming up everywhere in the square to be led inside to pray. The smell from their unwashed bodies and the piss and shite in the square from the pilgrims and pedlars that had visited the Pope since the last good rain, which had obviously been some days ago, was overwhelming.

As we walked back to the horse carts and our men, I once again wondered if never washing or wiping the shite off your arse and clothes was really necessary to emulate Jesus who, being a God, of course, never had to do such things. I have never believed it myself; on the other hand, that is what the Templars believe and they have become rich in lands and have so many coins that they are well known as money lenders.

We found our guards lounging up against the wall of a building to catch the shade. They were talking and pointing as they watched the groups of pilgrims in the square and the pedlars and pickpockets they attracted.

A young priest was standing with our men. He had, as we had been promised, provided them with several jugs of good water and bowls to drink from. We could also see that he had also brought them some fruit; there were apple cores on the ground and several of the men were still eating apples as we arrived. *And, for some reason, I wondered if the apple cores were collected and given to the poor, or just left for Rome's many rats. I did not ask.*

George obeyed my orders and did not say a word until we reached our men and the waiting carts and began clattering away over the cobblestones on our way back to Captain Tinker's galley.

"Uncle, I do not understand. We have some relics in the coin room at Restormel. Are those the ones you were talking about?"

"Of course, we have them, George, of course we do. We probably have all of them. But we do not want anyone to know that, do we? If the Pope had known we had them, he might have held us hostage to get them or sent an army to take them."

I continued to explain after a pause when our cart lurched over a particularly large rock in the street.

"This way, we will get coins for the relics and the Pope will end up with the relics *and* some of the coins. It is a win-win situation for everyone, eh?" *Unless my plan works.*

"But why does the Pope want more pieces of Saint John and Saint Paul if the Church already has some here in Rome?"

"Who knows? Maybe he wants to put their bodies back together for some religious reason even though I cannot think of one. But he is a cagey one, Pope Innocent is, so he is sure to have a good reason for wanting them; we will have to ask Cardinal Bertoli when we see him later today."

After a pause I once again reminded George that it was a secret that we have the Orthodox relics from Constantinople at Restormel.

"You must always remember to never tell anyone that we already have the relics, not even our own men;

although, some of them undoubtedly know. It is a deep family secret and must remain so."

******

Cardinal Bertoli settled on to the wooden bench that evening with a sigh of relief. A moment later, he waved his hand to signal one of the tavern girls to bring him a bowl of wine and to take a bowl to each of the three papal guards that had escorted him to meet with us.

I raised my hand and pointed at George and myself for another round. Then we all leaned forward to talk. What Bertoli said was quite encouraging.

"I told the Pope that your company was so poor that your brother had to borrow money to pay his archers and sailors for the French prizes. That is why he agreed to give such valuable indulgences to whomever buys the relics from you and gives them to the Church. That is, of course, if you can find them."

Then he gave me a sly look and added, "Or at least something that looks like them." *Looks like them? Is he suggesting what I think he is suggesting?*

George was listening carefully as I took a big gulp of wine from the wooden bowl I had been given by the tavern girl, and asked Antonio the question that had been perplexing us.

"I would, of course, be sending parchments to my brother and his lieutenants telling them to organize the search for the missing relics from Constantinople and get it underway as soon as possible. But we do not understand why the Pope is willing to do so much to get them. Can you tell us?"

"To increase his power, of course. The misguided followers of the church in Constantinople set great store in the miracles that have occurred when prayers were offered to the relics. The Pope believes it likely some or all of the Constantinople believers would return to the True Church if they believe we have the relics in Rome.

"And they would believe the relics are in Rome if one or more great princes thinks he has bought the relics from you and donates them to the Church. He will proudly announce it and the Pope would confirm it." *Thinks? Did he just say "thinks?" Hmm.*

We spent the rest of the evening drinking wine and discussing both who might buy the relics "if the archers are able to find them" and the significantly more important question of how the coins that result from selling the relics would be divided.

"Pope Innocent himself," Antonio proclaimed as he asked for a large share, "would be willing to send a secret parchment to each of the Princes that might be potential buyers informing them of the great opportunity to help the Church and themselves by buying the relics from those who are searching for them.

"Indeed, with the right encouragement the Holy Father might even be willing to suggest that the men of the Company of Archers are the *only* ones who are likely to find them and explain why?

"The parchments the Pope sends out would be written so as to encourage the potential buyers to contact you and let you know that they are willing to help you pay your men if they are able to find them."

Antonio said he could be absolutely sure that was what the parchments would say because he himself had been ordered to scribe them for the Pope despite the great expenses he would have to bear if he were to handle everything.

As you might imagine, because each of the Pope's parchments would have to be worded to generate the maximum amount of coins, we spent quite a bit of time discussing what the Pope' parchments should and should not say to each prince, and even more time talking about how the resulting coins would be divided.

"His Holiness would be satisfied with the relics and my needs are modest," Antonio told us. "Does only one coin for every ten you receive sound fair for me and three in ten for His Holiness?"

One in ten and three in ten sounded eminently fair. George beamed his approval as Antonio and I spit on our palms and shook on it.

We also discussed that princes should be informed of the Pope's generous offer of "no purgatory" and "other more worldly benefits" for donating the relics. It was clear that Otto and Frederick, the two German princes that both claim to have been elected by their fellow princes to the throne of the Holy Roman Empire, were at the top of the list of those to receive a parchment from the Pope—they were our best hope for a large amount of coins because the Emperor needed to receive his crown from the hands of Pope in order to be recognized by the other princes as their Emperor.

King Phillip of France and King John were also good prospects to buy the relics because they both wanted the throne of England. So was a Swedish prince I had never heard of who had asked the Pope to proclaim that he owned Finland. *I thought of a couple of additional people to contact but I did not mention them.*

We stayed and talked at the riverfront tavern for so long and drank so much wine that Antonio's guards had to hire a cart and carry him home. George and I were so tipsy that we staggered over to spend the night on Captain Tinker's galley, the one that had carried us to Rome and at was moored only a few steps away against the riverbank wharf. We went there instead of going back into the city to spend the night with Martin Archer and his men at our shipping post in Rome.

Our non-arrival worried Martin, the senior sergeant captaining our post in Rome, so much so that when we did not show up he turned out his men and sent them searching for us. The next morning, we heard that his archers showed up at the galley in the middle of the night and would not leave until someone fetched a candle lantern and held it up so they could see us sleeping. *Martin always was such a worrywart.*

Chapter Thirteen

Thomas and George sail for Cornwall.

A big storm blew in during the night so we did not leave the next day. It was just as well; after all of last night's wine, I was in no shape to handle even the gentlest of seas. It was an easy decision to put off our sailing until the weather cleared and, instead, take George on a tour of the city.

We hired a horse cart with a sun roof of palm fronds to armour us against the rain and off we went. A second, similarly roofed horse cart filled with a guard of archers followed us. It was quite enjoyable and made more so because a fellow recommended by the tavern keeper rode in the cart with us to tell us what we were seeing. There was no sense courting trouble so neither George nor I wore our clerical robes, just our mail shirts with an armoured plate in front and our lightweight Egyptian robes with our rank stripes.

Our guide's stories were entertaining but far-fetched. We spent an enjoyable day listening to them and seeing the sights, particularly after the rain stopped in the early afternoon. The streets and markets were packed with people but no one bothered us or paid us any attention. Pilgrims and merchants from distant lands were common in Rome. My headache from the previous night's drinking stopped after George and I and our guide stopped for some olives and we had another bowl of wine

George and I returned from our sight-seeing in the city to find Cardinal Bertoli and a handful of papal guards waiting for us. This time Antonio was wearing a simple, lightweight peasant's gown in order to stay cool in the summer heat and safer in the streets by drawing less attention.

"I heard you had stayed over because of the weather so I brought you these to read," he said.

With that, Antonio handed me copies of the secret parchments that would be going out to various princes with the Pope's great seal affixed to them. He also gave me the original of the parchment we had decided *not* send to King John of England because he had no coins. Then we walked to the nearby tavern to read the parchments, celebrate working together once again, and talk about the world and the Pope and the various princes that might be gulled out of their coins *if* we found the relics.

******

We rowed down the Tiber and out into the Mediterranean the next morning with our deck crowded with a great mass of squawking and fluttering chickens whose legs had been tied together in bundles of ten and a couple of bawling steers whose hamstrings had been cut.

It was a fine day. We were bound for Cornwall and happy about it. George and I spent most of the morning of our first day at sea taking turns being sea poxed and once again reading the Pope's secret parchments and talking about them.

There were subtle differences in each of the parchments and none of them mentioned English archers, just that the relics of Constantinople were missing and the Church was willing to make great concessions to get them, especially the gold-covered right hand of Saint John that had baptised Jesus and the silver-covered head of Saint Paul. The parchment for the King of England was quite interesting even though the Pope had decided not to send it.

The Pope's requirements for King John of England avoiding a stay in purgatory, those we had decided not to send, were by far more demanding than those that were actually sent to the other princes. John's avoidance of purgatory and the end of his excommunication would have required not only that he provide the relics but also required an agreement with his barons as to their rights, a peace treaty with Phillip of France, his acceptance of whomever the Pope crowned as the new Holy Roman Emperor, and his acceptance of the Pope's right to name England's bishops.

Pope Innocent's concerns about King John made sense, particularly the part about the Holy Roman Empire. What Antonio had told me about John's meddling in the German princes' election of a new Emperor had surprised me since neither England nor France were part of the empire.

According to Antonio, John had several years earlier sent messages to the German princes in support of the election of a German prince named Otto who had agreed to leave Italy to the Pope—but then Otto changed his mind immediately after he was elected and demanded that the Pope also crown him King of Italy at his coronation. The Pope had refused to do either and was still furious with King John for supporting Otto.

"Otto acted too quickly," Antonio had sniffed with a great deal of pleasure.

"He should have waited until the Pope crowned him as the Emperor of the Germans before he started claiming Italy. As a result of the Pope's refusal to crown Otto, another group of German princes elected another prince named Frederick to be Emperor despite efforts of Otto and his supporters to keep the second election from occurring."

Antonio had hardly been able to contain his pleasure when he had told us about it.

"Now there are two German princes claiming to have been elected as the Emperor and neither has been crowned. They are sure to bid against each other and pay too much for the relics if you find them."

Neither the Pope nor Antonio, nor I for that matter, could understand why John tried to influence that German prince was elected Emperor. He must have been promised something. But what?

"Even the Pope could not understand why John scribed to the princes supporting Otto," Antonio admitted.

All in all, the Pope's requirements were so great that King John did not sound like a good candidate to buy the relics and donate them to the church. Moreover, I knew John would not have enough coins with that to buy them unless he levied a new and very large tax, a tax that would almost certainly drive more of his barons to rebel.

What John did sound like was a good candidate to send William Marshal and an army to seize the relics and offer them to the Pope. When we were ready to sell them, we would have to take them under very heavy guard to someplace where it would be safe to exchange them for the coins.

"Antonio," I had said when we were discussing potential buyers, "I am concerned about wasting the Holy Father's time by having you offer King John a way to escape a well-deserved stay in purgatory.

"The more I think of it, the more I am sure that King John does not have enough coins to cover the expenses that would have to be born to recover the relics and no way to get them without causing such a great unrest that it would prevent us from searching for the relics.

"Worse, because John does not have enough coins to cover the expenses of finding the relics, and no way to get them, he might send an army to seize the relics from us if we are able to find them. Then there would be no coins to pay our men for recovering them." *Or send you your one coin in ten for your trouble and expenses.*

Antonio had immediately understood why the Pope should not encourage John to seek the relics so he could donate them to the church. He assured George and me that the Pope would not mention the relics to King John. Giving us his draft parchment was Antonio's way of assuring us that he meant what he had said when we discussed whether John should be offered a chance to bid on the relics.

"The Pope is a good man and very busy. He certainly would not want to waste his time nor do anything to prevent you and me and your dear archers from receiving the coins needed to cover our relic-related expenses, such as by offering the King of England an incentive to avoid purgatory by taking them from you without payment."

******

We had rowed through the strait between Corsica and Sardinia with our sails up and were about two days out of Ibiza when opportunity struck. There was a hail from the lookout's nest on the mast alerting us that three sails were in sight on the horizon off to our starboard side. Sergeant Captain Tinker raced up the mast to see for himself and soon began shouting orders down to his sailing sergeant. A few minutes later a three-masted ship of a strange design could be seen from the deck. It had three masts with big triangular sails and was accompanied by what appeared to be a couple Moorish war galleys.

"It is a big Moorish transport with three masts and strange sails, and it is being escorted by war galleys so it must have a valuable cargo," Captain Tinker had said as he came down the mast and he and his loud-talker and sailing sergeant joined us on the roof of the stern castle.

Captain Tinker's words spread like wildfire through our galley's crew. Spirits and the level of activity rose everywhere. They increased even more as our rudder men turned our galley towards the Moors and Captain Tinker ordered the arrow bales brought to the deck for the archers and every rower to have a sword and shield and his rowing bench.

"Arrow parties to bring the bales on deck and open them; swords and shields to every man."

Our lookouts were not the only ones with good eyes. The two Moorish galleys had seen us before we had seen them. They had turned and begun rowing toward us even before Captain Tinker had raced down the deck to join us on the castle roof and begin to give his orders. With a little luck, we told each other, the Moorish galleys may consider us a potential prize until it was too late for one or both of them to get away.

"Fetch our mail shirts and bows," I ordered George, "and a bale of arrows for the castle roof." All around us sergeants were swearing great oaths and excited men were racing about to gather supplies and prepare their weapons. I could see archers climbing on to the roof of the stern galley and others climbing with their bows to the lookout's nest on the mast. Even our usually silent bales of chickens and our two remaining sheep were making noises and flopping about.

Our galley's deck looked chaotic as the men ran this way and that to man their positions and get ready for a fight, but it was not; retrieving their weapons and getting ready to fight was something every galley's crew practiced doing at least once every day.

Only the cook was waiting for someone to tell him what to do. He would not be told to throw his hot coals over the side until the battle was about to begin; he might need them to cook the bread and meat strips needed to sustain the rowers in the event of a long chase. He had already placed a short sword and galley shield where he could instantly pick them up.

When George came back I told him to put on his mail shirt and then go get a couple of galley swords and shields for us in case we need them. *It never hurts to be ready with a sword and shield, does it?* Then I took off my tunic and put on my mail shirt.

******

"String your bows; string your bows," cried the sergeants as the two Moorish galleys rapidly closed with us. Most of the archers had done so already but someone might have forgotten in all the excitement.

The strange three-masted sailing ship the Moorish galleys were protecting was not taking any chances. It adjusted its three triangular sails and turned away to flee before the wind. The two galleys, however, came straight at us. From the look of them, they intended to come upon us from both sides, perhaps breaking off our oars so we could not escape.

"Bows free," roared Tinker. "Archers push when you have targets." His loud-talker and archer sergeants immediately repeated Tinker's command at the top of their voices. Seconds later our arrows began to fly.

"Get ready to instantly ship your oars," roared Tinker as the Moors closed with us. "Ready grappling irons and throw as soon as you can hook her," he said. His loud-talker repeated the order a moment later.

Suddenly, one of the Moorish galleys lost its nerve and turned away as a storm of arrows descended on it and its lookout fell off the mast with an arrow in his chest. The other Moor kept coming.

"In oars; in oars," shouted Tinker just before we closed with the on-rushing Moor. He was standing next to me with an arrow nocked and ready to push. Every man including the sergeant captain fights on our galleys, including passengers such as me and George.

Tinker's orders reached our men just in time. Their oars came in fast and I did not think we lost a single one. The Moor was not so lucky. There was a crash and the distinctive sound and screams that occur when oars are sheared off and snapped back against their rowers. Our veterans had heard it before.

Our galley's deck was packed with men and so was the Moor's. Out of the corner of my eye, as I pushed an arrow into a Moor standing on his galley's castle roof, I could see sailors on both galleys begin to throw their grappling irons. We were so close I could clearly see the shock and surprise on the faces of the men on the Moor's deck as they realized we were so many and armed with longbows—and we were throwing grapples to keep *them* from getting away.

The sword-waving men on the Moorish galley were cut down by our archers like a Damascus blade going through cheese as our grapple throwers strained to get their galley tight up against ours. A few seconds later, there was the familiar sound of two hulls banging together and we all staggered slightly from the initial collision. By then, there was almost no one left standing on the Moor's deck. They were either down on the deck with arrows in them or had dived below to hide among the slaves on their lower rowing deck.

As our boarders jumped on to our victim's deck, the other Moorish galley started to turn back to join the battle, but then its captain thought better of it and turned away to follow the three-master.

"Prize crew number one board the prize; prize crew number one board the prize," screamed an excited and enthusiastic Tinker and his loud-talker. "Hurry, lads; do not let the bastards get away.

Chapter Fourteen

We take another prize.

We pushed off from our new prize so quickly that we left almost a dozen men of the boarding party on board in addition to our prize crew. I thought it might have been a mistake since it would leave us short of men when we went after the fleeing Moors, but I did not say anything to Captain Tinker. Besides, he will certainly have done the right thing if we catch another one of them as a prize with the men that remain.

There had been casualties—two dead archers and three wounded, one seriously. Thankfully, George and I were not among them. The Moors must have had a few archers in their crew. We will undoubtedly learn more when we rendezvous with our prize in Ibiza.

Captain Tinker ran up the mast to join the archers in the lookout's nest as soon as we pushed off from our prize, but not before he ordered the sail raised and everyone to the oars including me and George. We were going to try to take another prize.

Within a few moments, the oars on the lower bank were fully manned and pulling hard with two men on every oar; on the upper bank, there were two men on every oar but only about half of the oars were manned because of our casualties and the prize crew and the boarding party still on our new prize. The rowing drum began to beat faster and faster as we began to pick up speed.

Our galley ignored the second Moorish galley, the one that veered away to the south. We rowed instead straight for the big sailing ship as it slipped over the horizon to the east and ran before the wind. The other Moorish galley soon went over the southern horizon. We never saw it again.

*****

It was already dark when we finally pulled up next to the big and very strange-looking Moorish ship with its three masts and its big and little triangle sails. The sky was partly cloudy and in the moonlight we could barely see it looming in the night off to our starboard. That is where we stayed all night long—one or two galley lengths behind it. We were afraid to come any closer to board it until we could see it better. Speculation as to what kind of ship it was and what it might be carrying continued all night long.

We got our first good look at the big Moorish three-master in the morning as the sun began to move overhead to start its never-ending move around the earth.

"It is a big dhow," our white-haired pilot assured us. "They come from far to the east where there are dragons and the women are rigged differently. I saw one once when we was blown far to the east during old King Henry's day."

The dhow kept going and we kept following closely. Captain Tinker put our best archers up in the lookout's nest and they quickly cleared off both of the Moor's lookouts and that part of her deck that could be seen from the mast. Clearing part of the Moor's deck, however, was not enough to stop the Moors on the dhow from continuing to try to flee and causing us to have to chase after them.

That was the state of affairs when one of our sailors came up with an idea. He climbed up past the lookout's nest to the very top of the mast with a roll of galley rope slung over his shoulder. When he got to the very top, he fixed a line to tie an archer up there above the lookouts.

Captain Tinker said the sailor's name was Alan. We watched as he helped one of the archers climb up from the nest and get into the harness he had tied. Then Alan handed the archer his bow and a quiver of arrows and gave him an encouraging pat on his leg. It sounded easy but was altogether quite difficult because the top of the mast was constantly swaying and jerking back and forth as our galley bumped over the waves and responded to wind gusts.

Finally, the archer settled in and began to push out his arrows. It was difficult because of the swaying and jerking mast, but he did it even though his waist and shoulders were up above the top of the mast.

"He is the best archer I have got," commented Tinker out of the side of his mouth as we stood looking up at the archer high above us. "Wins all the tournaments is what he does."

As Alan the sailor came down the mast I looked over at Captain Tinker and mouthed "It was a good idea; another stripe for sure, maybe two." Tinker nodded back.

George said nothing but he nodded in silent approval with Tinker. *Good. It was important the lad understand that good men must be recognized, and the sooner the better.*

Other sailors began carrying quivers of arrows up to the lookout's nest and on up the mast to the lone archer above them. Another archer climbed the mast to join those already in the lookout's nest.

Our galley's sailors had been continuing to throw grapples to lash us tighter to the Moor whilst Alan was working at the top of the mast. Every grapple we had was hooked on the big Moor, including several new ones Captain Tinker's crew put together in record time using our anchors. We were soon lashed tightly up against the big Moor and being pulled along by it sails.

We were just placing one of our galley's two wooden ladders against the side of the dhow when the Moors began something new, despite the steady stream of well-aimed arrows coming down on them from the archer at the top of our mast—they began tipping heavy chests and wooden boxes over the side of their deck railing to fall down upon us.

The first chest caught us totally by surprise, even though our men up on the mast had seen it coming and tried to warn us as they launched arrows at the men carrying it. We had not understood what they were saying until the first chest came crashing down and squashed one of the sailors trying to hold the ladder in place—so an ambitious volunteer could climb it to reach the big dhow is deck.

Dropping the chests stopped our boarding efforts for what seemed like hours. Every time a ladder was raised someone on the deck above us would brave our archer's arrows and drop something down on the men below or both. Finally, the archer at the top of the mast shouted that the deck was clear—the dhow had either run out of men willing to brave the archer's arrows or things to drop on us.

Both of the ladders were hurriedly set up and a long line of anxious archers climbed them and poured on to the deck of our new prize. The Moors quickly surrendered and were secured in the cargo hold. Things moved quickly after that and the dhow soon joined our prize galley and sailed for Cyprus via Malta with a prize captain and some sailors and archers on board to work its sails and protect it.

It would be up to Harold and Yoram to decide whether to sell the prizes or take them into our service. Either way, our men would get their prize coins. The men who are crewing the prizes would get their coins when they reach Cyprus; those who continued on with us would get theirs at the next port we reach.

If the good weather holds, our next port would probably be Ibiza now that we have stopped calling in at Palma ever since William was attacked in Palma's market.

******

George and Captain Tinker and I spent a good deal of time discussing our prizes and how we took them as we accompanied our prizes to Ibiza. We agreed that it was a damn good thing the dhow did not have any infantry shields on board to protect its crew from our brave archer. Infantry shields being the large shields soldiers fighting on land can hold above their heads to ward off arrows.

I asked George to remind me to send a parchment to Harold telling him how difficult it had been to take the dhow.

"If I know Harold and your father," I told George, "I suspect each of our transports, even those with a force of archers on board to protect them, will soon have some of the bigger shields on board and big rocks or

chests to throw down on galleys trying to take them."
Hmm. Could the ballast rocks be used?

"Surely, there must be pirates in the waters where big boats like the dhow come from," said George. "I wonder how the pirates take them?" It was a very good question.

Chapter Fifteen

Thomas and George Learn of William's travails.

George and I made a port call at the Moorish port of Ibiza and enjoyed three days of rest in a sleeping room that a local merchant, one of the merchants that provide our galleys and cogs with foodstuffs, had quickly arranged for us in a taverna near the quay.

It was a beautiful place with a garden with large shade trees where we could sit and talk. The food and wine was excellent and we enjoyed meeting the local people who sat at its tables and ate and drank late in the evenings when the temperature cooled.

Each day we ignored the heat and walked through the city gate to visit the market and talk to the multi-lingual local merchants. Many of whom I already knew from the tavern and my many previous visits. They all said they liked the idea of armed cogs and ships. George was very excited about the response. I was a bit more cynical.

"Of course, the merchants told us they liked the idea of using armed cogs and ships to carry their cargos and passengers. We are good customers because we make so many port calls in Ibiza. They probably would have been equally enthusiastic if we had inquired about their interest in using unarmed cogs and ships."

Our sailors and archers, as you might imagine, were pleased with our calling in at Ibiza to replenish our water and supplies. They took advantage of our visit and their prize monies to gorge themselves on wine, good food, and women. All in all, Ibiza was a sailor's delight and the price of supplies was quite reasonable after a bit of bargaining.

In general, the merchants in Ibiza's market were pleased at our custom and did not try to take advantage of us. They knew that if they did we would take our coins to the other ports in this part of the Mediterranean. It helped, of course, that the merchants were inevitably easy to deal with as they spoke many languages including French.

They all knew our galleys and cogs going back and forth between England and the Holy Land used to make port calls to take on supplies in Palma—and that we stopped calling in at Palma after William was attacked and terribly wounded.

******

Whilst we were in Ibiza, George and I worked together to draft a "just in case" parchment to send to William on the next galley or cog of ours that resupplied in Ibiza on its way to Cornwall. We would do the same when we reach Lisbon. We also sent a parchment off to Cyprus to Harold and William telling them about our three-masted prize and how we took it with the help of an archer strapped to the top of the mast.

In the "just in case" parchment, I commented on the peacefulness of the local situation despite it having a Moorish ruler, reported once again on our prizes, and added some additional thoughts about our sale of the relics. I wanted William to know as much as possible in case we ran into bad weather or pirates and did not make it to Cornwall.

George and I also decided we needed to begin the process of getting the ambitious and purgatory-fearing princes to buy the priceless relics that went missing from Constantinople "if our searches uncover any of them." Accordingly, we began drafting parchments for William to sign and send to the Christian princes after they had received the Pope's generous offer of avoiding purgatory and personal advancement for themselves. Drafting the parchments and arguing about how they should be worded helped us pass the time.

******

It was with mixed emotions when we cast off our mooring lines and began to sail for Lisbon and on to Cornwall on our fourth morning in Ibiza. It had been a most enjoyable port call even though some of the men came down with the dripping pox from dipping their dingles in the slaves that were the local public women. To everyone has astonishment, not one man deserted; probably, of course, because the island was small and Islamic.

Everything changed a few days later when we reached the Lisbon quay. John Heath, our post sergeant in Lisbon, had jumped on to our galley's deck even before we finished mooring to tell us about William's shipwreck and capture. All John knew was that William's galley had been wrecked in a storm whilst it was on its way to Cornwall and that William and the other survivors were being held for ransom in Hastings.

He knew about the travails of my brother and his men because Peter Sergeant, the lieutenant in command of our forces in Cornwall, had immediately begun preparing for a war of rescue. Peter had, quite rightly, sent out an emergency recall notice ordering all of our galleys and archers back to Cornwall.

The news and the recall notice turned what was left of our leisurely passage into one of great urgency.

Gone was any thought of spending a few days resting and enjoying the city's pleasures. Our men barely had enough time to run to one of the many taverns along the waterfront for a bowl of the surprisingly good local wine before our galley finished being resupplied. We immediately rowed out of the harbour with the sail up and every oar double-manned and pulling hard.

Leaving Lisbon so quickly did not seem to bother the men at all. To the contrary, it pleased them; rescuing their fellow archers always took precedence over everything so far as the men of the Company were concerned, and rightly so—promising never to abandon a fellow archer was, after all, in the articles of the Company on that every one of us had made his mark.

Besides, the men told each other, fighting to free their fellow archers and sailors from the Hastings portsmen might mean more prize money since each of the portsmen owned at least one galley or cog. Only one man ran despite Lisbon's obvious charms. We often lost more.

We had gotten the news about the shipwreck and ransom from John Heath as soon as we tied up at the Lisbon quay. Almost immediately heavily loaded horse carts and porters descended on us and began to hurriedly load water and supplies. John had arranged them.

There were also a number of strong, young Portuguese fishermen standing by at our local post to join us. They were volunteers willing to come to England with us as additional rowers. John had recruited them so that there could always be two men on each of our galley's oars and there would always be fresh arms available to spell the rowers when they needed to rest or eat or use the shite nest.

According to John, he had had many volunteers as soon as he put out the word among the local fishermen. The Portuguese, he told us, seem to always have trouble finding things to keep their young men busy and the fish catches from the waters off Lisbon had been down this year. In any event, recruiting additional rowers for our galleys returning to England and arranging for their rapid provisioning were splendid ideas and put John squarely into my good books.

John also brought us three galley slaves that were Englishmen and one that claimed to be either a Scot or a

Welshman depending on who he was telling. He had bought their freedom as our post-sergeants were always to do when they find British or French slaves—if they cannot safely free them by force or persuasion. *Killing their owners and overseers to free them is allowed, but only if there is no other way and can be done quietly so no one knows who did it.*

According to John, three of our galleys had already come through Lisbon on their way back to Cornwall, "with their crews rowing hard and spoiling for a fight."

It was all he could do, John told us, to keep the handful of archers assigned to guarding our Lisbon post from deserting to join them. *Though we all immediately assured each other within the hearing of some of the crew that an archer leaving his post in order to fight to free his fellow archers might be accused of poor judgment, but never desertion.*

******

We rowed night and day and made a very fast passage from Lisbon directly to Cornwall. Indeed, the entire voyage had gone rather quickly despite our overly long stay in Ibiza. It had only taken us four weeks from the time we cast off the mooring lines on the Tiber until we entered the mouth of the River Fowey.

George and I were anxious and worried and pacing about on the deck as our galley moved up the Fowey towards Restormel and the riverside camp where the apprentice archers were learnt to push arrows from a longbow and walk together to the beat of a rowing drum.

"Hoy there, what is the news of the captain?" I shouted as we rowed up to the little floating wharf lashed to the side of the river in front of our training camp. "Do you know where he is?"

"He is up to the castle with his women taking care of him and the men who came back. They are all doing right nicely is the word."

"Was he hurt?" George asked as he vaulted over the deck railing and began running up the footpath along the river. He was away and running before I even had a chance to climb on to the floating wharf that was now bobbing up and down from George jumping on it.

"Not much," the man called after him. "The bastards just starved and beat him and the other lads. Beat some of them to death, so they did. But he learnt them good and then some."

I breathed a sigh of relief when I heard the news and began trudging up the path to follow George to the castle, all whilst mumbling thank you prayers under my breath and wondering what had really happened.

Well, I will know soon enough.

******

The evening began as one big family reunion with all of William's children running around and trying to get our attention. We started supping early, long before it got dark. After we finished eating all the wives and children retired to their rooms so we could talk private-like, including Peter's new wife and George's very pregnant Beth and her sister who were now somewhat recovered from when they were clinging to him and weeping for joy at his arrival when I first reached the castle.

Raymond and his men had started back to Okehampton yesterday after delivering William and the survivors. Raymond had not known that George and I would be arriving or I am sure he would have stayed. As a result, only four archers were present for what turned out to be one of the most important councils we ever held—William, George, Peter, and me.

We had much to talk about and many things to consider. The future of the Company of Archers seemed a bit uncertain and we needed to decide what to do next. It would have been helpful if Yoram and the Company's other lieutenants and senior sergeants had been there to give us their opinions and help us decide, but they were not.

After the women retired to feed their infants, William led off by walking us through everything that had happened to him after George and I left London to sail to Rome. The details were quite upsetting and reminded me of how Yoram and his men suffered when they were captured by the King of Cyprus. George was visibly upset and angry at his father's treatment and that of the men that had been stranded with him.

"Do you think the King knew the Hastings men were holding you and approved?" he asked his father.

"Well, William Wrotham showed up and told me about the ransom. So the King must have known. But then again, maybe he sent Wrotham to free us. It was hard to know? I did not have a chance to talk to him."

"That bastard," George said to his father with a great deal of indignation in his voice. "Letting you and the men suffer like that; maybe we should help the barons top the King after all."

"Steady, lad, steady; we are playing the long game here," I said. *I should not have to tell him this.* "And I should not need to remind you of that."

George looked a little chagrined at being chastised to try to ease him a bit.

"The Earl of Devon's our main threat and he is John's enemy for sure. We need to get rid of the Earl of Devon first and we damn well need to do it in such a way that we end up with Exeter and the Earl's holdings. We can settle things with the King and Wrotham afterwards—*if* they deserve it."

"Your Uncle Thomas is right, George," Peter said. "It sounds bad about the King, yes, it does; but we did not know enough about the role of the King and William Wrotham to be sure, do we? We need to get our hands on one of the Hastings men and find out what really happened."

Then Peter took a sip from his bowl of ale and added something important that had us all nodding in agreement.

"Besides, we may not yet be strong enough to take on the King and all the barons and knights that might step forward to help him—but we are getting there and we would be sooner or later—particularly if we kill the Earl of Devon and put a good fear on the men of the Cinque Ports by eliminating the portsmen of Hastings and their boats."

We all growled our agreement. The time had come, I thought, to tell William and Peter about the Pope's interest in acquiring the relics.

"There is something else, something very important, that might change everything," I told them. George nodded in agreement as I said it.

"The Pope has come up with something big, and it does not include King John."

With that, George and I told William and Peter about the Holy Father's plan for acquiring the Orthodox relics, including two of John the Baptist's gold-covered right hands and Saint Paul's silver-covered head, that went missing from Constantinople when the crusaders sacked the city—the relics we had removed from the Patriarch's residence and carried to Cornwall. William and Peter were as astonished as George and I had been when we first heard about the Pope's plan and how much we and Cardinal Bertoli and the Pope might profit from it.

"Is it possible?" exclaimed William when we finished telling them about it.

"Yes, it is," I told William, "particularly since we already have both of John the Baptist's missing hands and the rest of the Orthodox relics right here in Cornwall and no one knows we have them.

"All anyone knows, except us, is what the Pope has told them—that the relics are believed to be hidden by the Orthodox priests at several places in Greece and are actively being sought by good Christians with the help of many prayers."

Then I took another sip of wine, wiped my beard that one of my lads had trimmed for me, and told them my plan.

"I have been thinking about it; perhaps there is a way we can do things a little differently and get more coins for them than we would fetch if we adopted the Pope's plan."

Then I told them my idea and we talked and laughed and planned late into the night.

Chapter Sixteen
Thomas's plan takes shape.

My ribs stopped being sore and I recovered my
strength as I settled back into the routine of life in
Restormel. Life with my family was immensely enjoyable
and I soon joined Peter in the training of our archer
apprentices.

Similarly, Thomas returned to his students, and
George went off to Fowey Village with his pregnant
wife's sister to help put the learning on our archer
apprentices as to how to capture galleys and cogs at sea.
Thomas put on his bishop's robe and said the words in
the little church in Restormel Village that made it right
and proper for George and Becky to know each other.
Beth seemed quite pleased and Becky promised to
return to help when the baby was ready.

******

My lieutenants and I spent the weeks after Thomas's
and George's return from Rome talking and arguing

about how and when we should follow up on the Pope's parchments to the princes. The Pope had offered the princes various earthly benefits and an opportunity to avoid purgatory in exchange for the Orthodox relics we carried out of Constantinople and now have in Restormel. That offer gave the relics a huge value and neither the Pope nor the princes nor anyone else knew we had them.

"So how can we safely convert the relics into coins, lots of coins?"

That was the question we quietly and privately asked each other whenever we met. *Safely*, of course, was the key word. So far as we know, no one outside of a few senior men in the Company knew we already had them safely tucked away in Cornwall—but many of our men were with William when we carried them out of Constantinople, and many others saw the crates when they were unloaded in Cornwall and carried into Restormel.

"You are right," I told Thomas a few days later when the four of us were together. "Word that we have got them is likely to get out sooner or later despite the Pope saying the relics are in Greece. Only God knows what would happen then."

"Aye," said George, who had come up from Fowey Village with Becky to check on Beth. "You are right about that, Father. We could be in danger. Four galleys came in besides Captain Tinker's before the recall was cancelled and more may have already left Lisbon and still be on their way here. Do you think we should hold their men here to beef up our defences just in case?"

Ahh. Good on my son; he is thinking like a captain should. Yes, he is.

We all agreed that temporarily keeping more of the archers in Cornwall was a good idea. We also continued to agree that one thing was certain—it was too dangerous and too soon for anyone associated with the Company of Archers to carry a parchment to France's King Phillip asking if he would be interested in covering the expenses of the searchers "if we found the relics" in exchange for owning them.

Helping to "cover the expenses if they were found," of course, was another way of saying the princes would have to pay us enough to get us to part with them—and, unfortunately, it also told them we might sooner or later have the relics available to be stolen from us.

Despite the risk of motivating potential robbers and thieves, we were keen on asking the German princes the

Swedish and French kings if they were ready to "help cover the expenses if they are found" in exchange for some or all of the relics the Pope wanted.

"We will have to always deny we have them and only claim to be searching for them at great expense to ourselves. Our story for the princes has to be the same as we told Cardinal Bertoli and the Pope. So next spring we will announce that William and his men 'found' some of the relics in Greece. That is when we will offer them to the princes that have expressed an interest in buying them."

******* Thomas

As autumn approached and my brother, William, prepared to leave for his annual trip to spend the winter in the Holy Land and "find" the missing relics, Peter Sergeant was sent in a galley to carry parchments to the German and Swedish princes that the Pope had identified as potential buyers. One of my students was hurriedly promoted to be a sergeant apprentice and sent with him. He would be Peter's scribe and Latin interpreter if one was needed.

We spent long hours talking about when we should contact the princes and who should do it; and whether or not we should contact the French king and his heir,

Prince Louis. Ideally, of course, it would have been me to carry the inquiry since I could go as a bishop representing the Pope.

William, however, had been shaken by his experience and near-death in Hastings whilst George and I were in Rome. He had decided that either he or I should always be in Cornwall to make decisions. I could not talk him out of it. Peter will deliver some of the parchments instead of me.

Peter's task was to deliver two parchments to each of the two German princes vying to be anointed as the Holy Roman Emperor and to the Swedish king who wanted the Pope to approve his takeover of someplace called Finland. Someone else would have to contact the French and the Venetian Doge. But who?

The first parchment was a 'confidential' message from the Pope to each of the princes and the French and Venetians. Thomas and George had gotten it from Cardinal Bertoli when they were in Rome. It was a follow-up to the Pope's original message to each of the princes.

It merely informed each prince that it was the Company of English Archers, also known as the Papal

Order of Poor Landless Sailors, that were organising a major expedition to search for the missing relics.

The second parchment for each prince was from me writing as the Bishop of Cornwall. I told the princes I was writing at the Pope's request to let them know I had just blessed some of the men and galleys that would be sailing for the coast of Greece to search for the missing relics. I noted that the relics were worth a king's ransom and inquired as to each prince's interest in acquiring them "in the event they are found."

"If you are interested in acquiring the relics," I scribed. "Please inform the man that delivers this message. I will let you know if the relics are found."

******

"Deliver both parchments and then wait for one week before you sail on," my brother told Peter. "In case they have questions."

Peter was excited about going and very anxious; he had never met a prince before. The thought that he might not act appropriately worried him.

I told him the best thing to do if he met a real prince was kneel down and touch his head to the floor twice and then stay down until the prince motioned for him to rise. *They like that sort of thing, you know.*

"Everyone else you should treat as you would if you were just meeting one of your fellow lieutenants and senior sergeants for the first time."

"What should I say if they ask questions about the relics?"

"The prince and his courtiers would undoubtedly have many questions. Tell them you are only a messenger from the Bishop of Cornwall and do not know much about the relics. The only thing you absolutely cannot tell anyone, or even hint, is that we might already have the relics in Cornwall and the search is a sham to cover up the fact that we already have them."

Peter still seemed quite uncertain so, with William and George listening carefully, I told Peter exactly what to say and made him repeat it back to me several times so I could be sure he had it learnt correctly.

"I was not there, Your Highness, and I am just the messenger. But what I heard from one of my fellow captains who were was that when Constantinople was falling to the crusaders, several of our galleys carried Orthodox priests and crates containing religious relics to various places along the Greek coastline. At each stop, the Orthodox priests left for a period of time with the crates they were carrying and returned without them.

"The captains of the galleys know where the priests landed the crates. They also know how long it took the priests to walk from where the galleys put them ashore to where they hid the crates and then returned to the galleys. As a result, our Company has a rough and general idea as to where the relics might be hidden.

"Our problem, of course, is that our galley captains do not know how much time the priests spent hiding the relics instead of walking back and forth. So all our captains really know is the general area where the relics might be hidden. Each will be intensively searched by an army of English archers and sailors until we find them, even if we have to fight our way ashore to do it."

****** *Captain William*

In the days that followed Peter's departure, we talked almost constantly about how the relics might be sold so as to fetch the most coins for us.

"I have been thinking," I told George and my three lieutenants one evening whilst we were supping together, as we did almost every day.

"When I go east in the fall to raid the Moorish coast and winter in the Holy Land, I could additionally send somewhat the same inquiry to the new Doge in Venice and the princes of two biggest of the new crusader states that arose from the ashes of the Byzantine Empire. They are all three ambitious to get ahead and are likely to need the Pope's blessing. And there may be others.

"In addition, without Thomas mentioning it to Cardinal Bertoli and the Pope, I could even secretly send a parchment mentioning the possibility of recovering the relics to the Patriarch of the Orthodox Church, wherever he might be now that he is fled Constantinople. I suspect he would be willing to pay a lot for them.

"Thomas," I nodded over to my brother who was busy pulling apart a greasy chicken and periodically throwing little pieces of it to the cats that were prowling around under the long table, "is of the opinion I should ask the Pope's permission before I send inquiries to the Doge and the princes of the crusader states.

"He thinks it would be too dangerous to contact them unless I get the Pope's permission and can additionally offer them an escape from purgatory and other papal benefits. He is also worried that thieves and robbers would be drawn to us if more and more people find out we might be selling the missing relics.

"What do you think?" I asked George and the others.

****** *Captain William*

How to safely reach out to the King of France continued to worry us. We were sure he hated us so much for destroying his fleet that he would kill any of us that approached him. The same was almost certainly true of the Doge of Venice.

Finally, about a week after Peter sailed for Germany and Sweden, the Abbot of the Bodmin Monastery was contacted and he agreed to carry the two parchments to France. He was keen to help the Pope, the Abbot said, and agreed to accept a "donation" of one hundred gold bezants for his personal use and deliver the two parchments to King Phillip. Two of his monks will carry copies of the parchments to Venice's Doge for another hundred.

The Abbot later confided to Thomas that he intended to use the coins to buy a position in Rome; God, he told Thomas most sincerely, "must have wanted him to do this for God determines everything and he was making the Abbot weary of Cornwall's weather."

In any event, we used the Bodmin Abbot to deliver copies of the parchments to King Phillip and his son, Prince Louis, because we thought it would be too dangerous for any of our men to carry a secret inquiry to them—because the French were still no doubt seething over their recent naval defeat at Harfleur.

The problem was that the French might think it another ruse and not believe us. Using a senior official of the Church, we hoped, would reinforce the idea that the Church was determined to obtain the relics and, in so-doing, enhance their value in the eyes of King Phillip and his heir.

Our best guess was that it would take the Bodmin Abbot three or four weeks to deliver our inquiry to the French King and return. One of Thomas's older students was promoted to sergeant, ordained as a priest, and sent with the Abbot to act as his assistant and our spy.

It was a good appointment; the Abbot delivered the parchments and the lad came back and, strangely enough, recommended to Thomas that we should burn down the Bodmin Monastery as a den of the devil. He would not tell us why.

Chapter Seventeen

William sails for the Holy Land.

Two weeks after Peter left to deliver the parchment announcements of our search, one of our galleys sailed for Rome carrying a message from Thomas to Cardinal Bertoli. It explained our proposed addition to the original plan and included the names of additional potential buyers of the relics and the parchments Bertoli could send to each of them "on behalf of the Holy Father."

In his private message to Bertoli Thomas explained that had drafted the additional parchments in the hope that they too would be send out with the Pope's signature and seal. Thomas went on to explain that they involved several changes in the "Pope's splendid original plan" in order to help additional generous princes avoid purgatory. It was possible because there may be more of the priceless relics than we initially thought.

Thomas read to us what was on the parchment he proposed to send to Cardinal Bertoli to encourage him to send out messages to additional princes.

"It appears the priceless missing relics have been hidden in a number of different places by the various Orthodox priests that carried them away from Constantinople and also that there might be more of them than we first thought. This, of course, will greatly increase the expense of recovering them to such an extent that it is likely they all cannot be found before the archers are forced to stop looking in order to earn their daily bread elsewhere.

"Accordingly, the Company of Archers has a problem that may become a big problem that might reduce the amount of coins that are available to be distributed— offering all of the relics to one prince who values them the most would require the archers to wait for their coins until all the relics are recovered. "That might take years and we would never know when all of them had been found."

"The problem is that whilst the archers are waiting for *all* the relics to be recovered, a good and generous prince that might have happily provided the coins needed to cover the cost of finding *all* the relics and donating them *all* to the Church might be taken by the pox or unlucky in battle and thus unfairly doomed to purgatory—leaving the Company of Archers without his coins and the Pope without the relics.

"There is a solution for such an unchristian fate for a good prince that would have acquired and donated all the relics but did not live long enough—let him quickly buy and donate to the Church some of the relics before we find the rest of them. Then the good man would avoid purgatory and the Church would, at least, get some of the relics. Other princes can then be offered the relics that are subsequently recovered.

"Moreover, if the Pope is willing to allow a few *additional* carefully selected princes avoid purgatory, we could offer some of the additional relics we recover to the new crusader princes when we find them. That would help more princes avoid purgatory and, of course, there would be more coins coming in to keep the relic searches going and cover the additional expenses of both you and the Holy Father.

"The major relics such as John the Baptist's gold-coated hand and Saint Paul's silver-coated head would, of course, be reserved for the most important princes and only one major relic, such as the silver-coated head or gold-coated hand, would be offered to the two German princes so they would have to bid against each other to get the Pope's blessing with whatever coins God has seen fit to endow them. That way the choice would be made by God.

"Letting the Germans bid against each other for Saint Paul's head when we find it is the most Christian way to proceed. It ensures 'God's Will' would decide the outcome by providing more coins to the winner. Similarly, if the Pope approves, we will offer Saint John's gold-covered hand to both Phillip of France and the Swede and let them bid for it and perhaps even to the Patriarch and the Doge of Venice." *What I did tell anyone was that I also had another idea.*

"In each case, the loser might, if the Holy Father agrees, subsequently be offered some of the subsequently recovered relics and the same benefits for donating them except those benefits that God has already given to someone else."

"We have reason to be optimistic," I said to William as we watched one of our galleys depart to begin its voyage to Rome carrying the parchments to Cardinal Bertoli for the Pope to approve.

"I know Antonio Bertoli. He will read between the lines and do his best to convince the Holy Father to put his seal on the parchments and send them out—he will like the idea of getting a share of the additional coins and so will the Holy Father."

******* *Captain William*

Six days later, it was my turn to sail on my annual trip to spend Cornwall's cold months in the relative warmth of Cyprus and the Holy Land. I sailed on Harold's galley. He had hurried all the way back to Cornwall in response to Peter's recall and arrived two days ago to find out, as he put it, "what the hell happened."

All the rest of the galleys that arrived before word of the recall's cancellation reached them, all six of them, were to stay in Cornwall so their archers could be used to increase our guard force. Thomas and George would stay in Cornwall to make sure it was properly defended. George wanted to come with me, but I would not allow it; I promised him he could come with me next year.

We let some of the men on the six galleys exchange places with men in Harold's galley so they could return to their wives and families. There were not all that many who requested an exchange—archers and sailor men do not usually put down roots and want to stay.

This time Anne went with me. Her baby died last year and she had been in poor spirits ever since. Both Helen and Tori insisted I take her and asked me to let her visit her mother. They said it would help her regain her good thoughts.

Anne was very pleased when I invited her to accompany me and enthusiastically agreed. We will travel in the little forward castle where the galley's sergeant captain usually sleeps. Harold would move to the bigger castle in the stern of the galley and share it with his sergeants and my new apprentice sergeant, Andrew. Andrew was a priest's son from Acre and made his mark on our articles as Andrew Priest.

Andrew was one of Thomas's students that had been several years behind George in Thomas's school. Thomas had made Andrew up to sergeant apprentice and said the words that made him a priest when he selected him to take the place of my previous apprentice, the lad who had been lost when we were wrecked on the Hastings strand.

******

It was quite a scene as Anne and I stood on the floating wharf and climbed aboard Harold's galley. Harold was going out with a full crew of fighting men so there would be two men on every oar if we needed to row our way out of trouble or needed extra men for a prize crew. Accordingly, his galley was stuffed full of supplies with numerous ten-chicken bundles of hens tied together by their legs all flapping and cackling, a pile of a dozen or so sheep with nobbled legs struggling and bleating, and four similarly situated old oxen fit only for roasting strips and the stew pot.

My brother Thomas and son George were there to wave us off as the mooring lines were cast off and we began drifting down the river to the channel. So were Anne's sisters and all of our children and a number of sergeants and senior sergeants. It was a cheerful group even if some of the cheer was forced, and rightly so. We were, after all, heading out into the Atlantic Sea to make a run for Lisbon and the Holy Land. No one knew what weather and dangers might be ahead of us or whether they would ever see us again.

******

The first leg of our voyage was to Lisbon. The weather and winds were favourable and we made such a good passage we did not even have to time to slaughter all the chickens and sheep we were carrying. After I recovered from an initial two days of being sea poxed, Harold and I spent a lot of time talking as I brought him up to date and filled him in with the details about the relics he had not learnt during his brief visit to Cornwall. We saw a few sails, and ignored them as they were unlikely to be Moors in this part of the Atlantic Sea.

Harold was one of my key lieutenants, the man in charge of all our galleys and cogs and sailors. He knew we had the relics safely inside Restormel Castle. Of course he knew; they had been carried to Cornwall on his galley. He also understood, from our talks at Restormel during his short visit, why the most important thing I would be doing during the next six months would be pretending to lead the search to "find" the missing relics so we could sell them without being blamed for stealing them.

My voyage to Lisbon was a pleasure. Anne took particularly good care of me by doing many nice wifely things to please me—she trimmed my beard and hair, squished the lice she found between her fingernails, washed me down with a rag and a bucket of warm water, gave me nice massages to make me feel good, and promptly emptied the chamber pot.

It was so nice lazing about with Anne that I was almost sorry when the lookout on the mast cried out that he saw land and we turned south to run along the coast until we reached Lisbon.

Chapter Eighteen

An unexpected tragedy.

Lisbon was initially a joy for everyone. We stayed an entire week and Anne went shopping in the market every day. Every man was given a copper coin each day as an advance on his annual pay. Some took them all; others left all or part of their coins on the galley's books.

One of the first things we did was give our post sergeant, John Heath, greetings from his brother Robert who was our post sergeant in London, and get a report from John. It was encouraging in many ways. He and his men had heard nothing about the priest that had disappeared when Thomas and George had been here and no one had inquired.

The only thing of note, he told us, was that one of his men had run, his scribe.

"That was a great surprise to me as he was the last person I would have expected to run. Had it soft, he did."

That very day, Harold and I and Anne visited our hospital to inquire into the health of our wounded and retired men to see if they needed anything. Whilst we were visiting, we casually asked if they or the women they had attracted had heard anything of interest or concern about the archers or our trading post. They had not.

They did not know Thomas and George had disappeared the priest and his men into the sea, and we did not tell them.

John Heath arranged for Anne and me to have our own sleeping room in one of the local taverns. He said Thomas and George always enjoy staying there when they come through on their way back and forth from Rome. Harold and my apprentice sergeant would stay on the galley.

"They did not have a chance to enjoy staying there on their last return voyage, of course, because they rushed home when they heard about you being held for ransom."

Our room was quiet and clean and with a chamber pot emptied every morning by one of the taverna's slaves. After the slave emptied the pot she brought us bread and cheese to eat whilst Anne and I sat outside in the shade of a huge tree of a type I had never seen before. A little while later a guard of archers would arrive and we would walk to the city's great market.

It was a fine room and quite safe. Its only door was into the tavern but there was a small window with a wooden shutter that could be barred from the inside to prevent thieves from entering in the night.

******

Everything was fine until the afternoon of our sixth day in Lisbon. Harold and his apprentice sergeant came to visit me after Anne and me and our four guards and Andrew Priest, my new apprentice sergeant, returned from the market.

We were all sitting outside in the taverna's garden talking when we saw a group of men with clubs and swords walking down the lane towards the entrance to the taverna. Anne had gone inside to put away some sewing linen we had just bought into a painted chest with pictures of angels and saints all over it. She had bought the chest on the very first day we arrived.

Somehow the arrival of so many armed men at the tavern did not feel right. Suddenly I knew.

"Hurry," I said as I stood up and started around to the other side of the tavern where our room was located. I was running with my sword drawn by the time I reached the tavern and started around it to reach the window into our room. The others caught my urgency and were pounding along behind me. The archers were stringing their longbows as they ran.

Anne was squatting over the chamber pot as we arrived at the little window. She gave a little scream and looked surprised when she saw me looking in, then she looked quite perplexed and uncertain.

"Hurry, come to the window. Now. You can water your arse later. Hurry." ... "Now, goddamnit Anne; now."

Anne finally understood and came to the window just as there was a knock on the door to the room—and an instant later, it opened and men poured into the room with a lot of shouting. I grabbed Anne's arm and tried to pull her through the window. Someone in the room grabbed her and pulled her out of my hands. She screamed as they pulled her away from the window.

"They have got her. Quick; around to the front," I shouted as Harold swore great oaths and we all began running. He had been standing next to me and seen her pulled from my grasp. The rest of the men did not know what was up, but they had heard the noise and had seen the looks of alarm on our faces and us pulling our swords. They grasped their weapons most firmly and hurried after us.

******

I led the way as we raced around the stone-and-mud walls of the taverna to the narrow entrance door in its front. We got there just as the first man ducked his head to get clear of the low entrance and came out.

"We have got them trapped," I said grimly as I swung my short galley sword down in a great chop on the head of the first man who started through the door.

There was a solid "chunking" sound similar to that when a woodcutter's axe bites into a tree, and I literally pulled him clear of the doorway with my sword stuck deep in his skull. He never said a word as he threw has hands out wildly and went down with my sword stuck in his skull. About then I became aware that there was a great commotion and much shouting and the sounds of fighting from inside the tavern.

I was still trying to get my sword free when Harold took the man that came out right behind him with a great thrusting stab into his side. It went in almost to the hilt. Harold's man was a swarthy bearded man and he screamed and jumped forward and tried to twist away in a desperate effort to get off Harold's blade.

The third man through the door got clear of us and started running. He got about twenty fast, running steps when there was the familiar thud of an arrow hitting home followed almost instantly by a second. Both arrows took him full in the back and drove him screaming to his knees with his hands out in front to hold his face off the ground. There was noise on the other side of the door but no one else came out.

"How many do you think are in there?" Harold asked over the screams and shouting, even though we all more or less already knew because we had seen them walking up to the tavern—eight or nine for sure. We were in good shape; there were eight of us and we had them trapped inside with Anne and the taverna's owner and servants.

"There is a door out to the kitchen on the other side of the taverna," I shouted at two of the archers that were standing behind me and anxiously trying to look over my shoulder to see inside the door.

"Get over there and cover it. Stand back so they come out and then take them with your arrows. Give a shout if they try. Let the tavern servants and all the women go free."

After a few moments, I turned to Harold and said, "Go around to the side door with the lads. We need to take at least one of the bastards alive if we can. Hurry."

Who are these men and why are they here?

Then I heard Anne scream. It was a piercing cry of agony over the shouting and loud talk coming from inside the tavern, and it ended abruptly.

"Give me your shield," I said as I looked over my shoulder at the nearest of the guards that had remained with me.

The guard handed it to me without saying a word. I took a firm grasp on it with my left hand and moved towards the door with my short galley sword in my right. I do not remember the guard's name; I wish I could.

Chapter Nineteen

The tavern battle and its aftermath.

I charged through the door and pushed my shield into the face of one of the men standing just inside it with a knife in his hand, whilst, at the same time, I stabbed, and missed, at another man that had jumped back and turned to run. The archers who had not gone to the kitchen door with Harold came charging in on my heels.

The men on the other side of the entrance had seen what had happened to the three who had tried to run for it; they wanted no part of us. They were used to waving their weapons and intimidating people, not standing up to heavily armed men who were coming after them and spoiling for a fight. There were three of them and they ran.

They tried to escape through the benches and tables in the public room. One of them darted down the corridor towards the sleeping rooms where I had last seen Anne, the other two towards the opening in the other corner leading to the outside kitchen.

Three frightened men and a woman were huddled in a corner of the public room, the taverna master and his servants. I followed the man who ran into the sleeping room corridor—and instantly saw Anne on the corridor floor. She was lying in a great pool of blood; her eyes were open and unseeing.

There is no other way to describe what happened next, except to say, I went mad. The man I was chasing ran down the corridor and through the open door to our sleeping room.

I went in after him and he did not have a chance. I fell upon him as a hungry cat would fall upon a fat mouse. I was still weeping and screaming and slashing away at what was left of him when Harold came in and pulled me away.

******

I struggled briefly to get away, but Harold got both of his arms around me and held me up against the wall until I finished sobbing and hiccupping and gasping for breath.

"We have taken two live ones that are able to talk, and I sent Archie running to the galley for reinforcements," Harold said as he partially released me.

"Anne is in one of the rooms. We will take care of her."

All I could do was nod. I was too exhausted to say a word.

Harold held me by the arm and led me through the public room with its overturned tables and benches and out into the bright sunlight. I was literally drenched in the blood of the man I had cut to pieces.

Some of our men were in the public room. They stood silently among the wreckage and stared with sympathy as Harold put his arm around my shoulders and led me out. A few of them solemnly nodded as I passed.

Somewhere along the line, I must have given Harold my sword for I saw him hand it to one of the men as we passed among them. I do not know what happened to the shield I had borrowed.

Our men filled the tavern courtyard. They were all heavily armed and more were arriving at a run. The talking and murmuring stopped as Harold led me out and I held my hand up to protect against the bright light. I was drenched in blood.

The bodies of the men Harold and I had killed lay where they had fallen. It was warm and flies were already starting to buzz about them.

"Where are the prisoners?" I asked Harold.

******

Four of Anne's murderers had been taken alive. One of them had an arrow through his gut and was clearly not going to survive. He was lying on his side in the dirt near the tavern wall and holding on to the feathers on the end of the arrow shaft. He was groaning and crying out in agony.

Another of her murderers was sitting against the tavern wall with a painful arrow in his shoulder. He would probably live, in the unlikely event we let him, and if the arrow was pulled out and his shoulder did not turn black and begin to smell. Two others had minor slices and were sitting with their hands clasped on top of their heads.

"Take them all to the galley and bring the captain's wife," Harold ordered over his shoulder as he began walking me back to the quay. "No mercies until we question them."

Harold was surprisingly gentle and held me by the elbow all the way to the quay. Most of the people in the lane took one look at me and the faces of the heavily armed men surrounding me and quickly disappeared. Others just stood silently as we passed. I was weeping and did not realize it until we reached the galley and I started to lift my leg to swing it over the deck railing to climb on board.

"We will find out who did it, Captain, you do not need to worry about that," Harold said as he sat me down on a sea trunk in the forward castle and someone handed me a bowl of wine.

Harold walked into the forward castle an hour or so later to report. By then, someone had wiped the blood off my face and arms with a wet rag and an elderly sergeant with white hair had helped me into a new tunic one of his men had brought from the galley's clothes chest.

"One of the prisoners has died from his wounds and we have sent for John Heath's interpreter so we can question the other three. The men we caught only speak the local dialect of Spanish."

"Anne. Where is Anne?" I asked.

"We wrapped her in some bedding and brought her on board," Harold replied sorrowfully as he reached out to put a hand on my shoulder.

"She was an innocent," I said. "We have to bury her nice and proper with all the words."

"Of course, we will. I will have John Heath arrange it." ... "Um. There is been a development. Three men of the city guard are here on the quay. They were asking about the fighting at the taverna and about the rumour in the city that we have taken some prisoners. John Heath and his interpreter are with them on the quay.

"All we have told them so far is that we have no idea what happened or why. I have come see if you want to talk to them."

There were three sword-carrying men wearing similar clothes standing on the quay with John Heath and an older man that was obviously his interpreter, obviously the city guards. A large number of heavily armed archers were on the quay around them.

Everyone turned and stared with great curiosity as I approached. Little wonder in that; my face and hair and hands were still totally covered in dried blood.

Our conversation was what one would expect under the circumstances. They bowed and were most respectful and gentle. They wanted to know what had happened at the taverna and why.

Through John's interpreter, I told them some of what I knew and asked them why someone would want to murder my wife. Then I acknowledged we had caught some of the murderers and rather grimly told the city's guardsmen I intended to keep them and question them. I promised them we would share our prisoners' answers with them when we got them.

The guardsmen murmured their agreement, bowed most respectfully, and walked away. They were clearly intimidated by seeing so many armed and angry men and happy to leave. Then we visited the prisoners and questioned them separately.

It soon became clear that the wounded man and the younger of two unwounded men knew virtually nothing. The older unwounded man and one of the dead men had recruited them to come along and help rough up some English sailors. They both swore it was one of the dead men that had killed Anne.

The older man's name was Julio and, unfortunately for him, both Harold and I recognized him as one of the men who had pulled Anne out of my arms as I tried to pull her through the window to safety.

Julio initially refused to tell us who had sent him and why. He quickly changed his mind when Harold went for one of his eyes and slashed him across his face a couple of times with his knife as he turned away. He began chirping like a bird. *It burns most terrible to have your face slashed; I ought to know.*

Once Julio began talking he would not stop. He told us he worked for one of the local bishops. Blood dripped through Julio's fingers as he held his slashed face and told us he and the other men had been ordered to kill an Englishman, preferably an archer or sailor, by a bishop whose name was Pedro Resende.

Killing an Englishman, Bishop Resende had told Julio, was to be a lesson to the English about the folly of interfering with the clergy of the church in Lisbon. He and his men were not really fighting men, Julio told us, just members of a church-sponsored neighbourhood "protection society."

According to Julio, others of the Bishop's men had seized and tortured John Heath's missing scrivener and found out that it was two Englishmen—*Thomas and George for sure*—that had interfered with their collections from merchants in the parish where our post was located. They also found out that the missing men had been carried away in an English galley.

Anne's death, it soon became clear, had nothing at all to do with the priest Thomas had killed and everything to do with the archers interfering with the ability of the parish priests to get additional coins for their parishes by extorting them from the local merchants and artisans in exchange for "protecting" them from thieves and robbers.

Selling protection, Julio said, was a common practice of the church to provide coins and employment to men who would otherwise have to earn their bread as thieves and robbers. Anne's death, he said, was nothing personal, just business.

They had come after me, Julio explained with a sob, because they had heard there was an Englishman and his wife staying at the tavern. They thought I would be the most vulnerable Englishman they could find since I would be alone with my wife. Killing Anne was an afterthought when they did not find me.

Julio gave us a detailed description of the Bishop and where to find him. He kept talking until I could stand the sight of him no longer. That was when I plunged my knife in his belly and ripped it upward and he started howling and screaming.

Then, for some reason, I felt badly about killing him and decided to let our other two captured men live with what many would consider an even worse revenge—we would take them with us and sell them to the Moors to be galley slaves. Who knows, maybe we will run into them again and they would be freed with all the other slaves as we always do when we take a prize galley off the Moors.

"Robert," I said to our port sergeant as Julio was tipped still screaming over the deck railing into the harbour whilst still trying to hold his guts in, "Please take your interpreter and find a cemetery where we can bury Anne. And be sure to hire a local priest to say the words so they will let her bide there. Then go to the tavern owner. He is another innocent victim in all this. Please go to him with some coins and make things right."

I immediately set about finding a parchment on that I could scribe a message to Bishop Resende.

Chapter Twenty

We sail to Cyprus and the Holy Land.

Harold and many of his archers and sailors assembled with me the next morning at a cemetery next to a church somewhere in Lisbon. A Portuguese priest chanted some prayers, said a few words, and then waved a pot with smoke coming out of it over my dear Anne as a couple of church slaves covered her up. It was most unsatisfying.

Our heavily armed archers were clearly angry as they marched from the cemetery back to the galley to the beat of a rowing drum. They had threatening looks on their faces and were glaring at the people on the streets as we marched past them. It was almost as if they hoped someone would say or do something to start a fight. I was too depressed to think about it at the time, but a chance to strike out at someone, anyone, probably would have helped my sour mood.

Harold and I walked behind the marching archers with John Heath and our sergeant apprentices. Our sailors had been ordered to stay on the galley to defend it in case of trouble and prepare it to row out of the harbour as soon as we returned. No one said a word as we passed through the streets with people scattering out of the way in front of us. Several times people did not move out of the way fast enough and had swords swung at them by the two burly archers walking ahead of our marching column.

I thought about the parchment I had sent to Bishop Resende as I walked and became angry with myself for being much too lenient. *Maybe I should forget the promise I made and just kill the bastard whilst I am here and be done with it; I wish Thomas was here to help me decide, him being a bishop and all.*

The parchment I sent to the bishop had been wrapped around the bloody knife I had used to gut his man. It appointed him as the man personally responsible for the safety of all Englishmen in Lisbon, and told him exactly what would happen the next time an Englishman died or disappeared or anyone attempted to collect protection coins in the parishes where our hospital and post were located.

More specifically, I said his stomach would be sliced from one end to the other. Then, after a long and painful wait, we would get tired of listening to him babble and he would be tossed alive and screaming into the harbour with his guts falling out just as had been done with his men that killed my wife.

In the back of my mind, I hoped Bishop Resende would not believe me, although I expected he would. It did not matter.

My mind was made up. If he did not believe me, I would kill him immediately; if he did, I would wait a year or two until our shipping post and hospital were firmly established in the minds of the local toughs and churchmen as untouchable. Then I would kill him most painful.

******

Harold raised his sail and we rowed out of Lisbon's great harbour as soon as we returned to the galley. Our destination, if the weather held good, was Ibiza to replenish our water and supplies.

The weather held good, as was usually the case during the sailing season, and we easily reached Ibiza with water and supplies to spare. I was still greatly undone when I stepped ashore but much improved after days of rowing and taking part in the archery tournaments and village dancing on the main deck.

Yes, I had often taken a seat on the benches and rowed. For some reason, making myself tired by rowing seemed to help drive away my dark thoughts and helped me sleep at night. The men went out of their way to treat me most kindly. They washed my tunic and even emptied my chamber pot until I once again began using the shite nest in the stern.

******

Ibiza was a port on a Moorish island whose heathen prince was so poor, the merchants said, that he tolerated Christian and Jewish merchants and land owners so he could tax them. The city itself even had a couple of churches from some long ago Christian invasion.

The Prince's main concern, according to Ibiza's merchants, was an invasion by either the Prince's more powerful Moorish cousin on the other side of the sea or Christians coming from Spain. He was worried about everyone and did not want to alienate anyone. The result was a peaceful city with Jewish and Christian merchants on a beautiful island.

We knew this about Ibiza because we had begun replenishing our galleys and cogs in Ibiza after our unfortunate experience on Palma when several of our men were killed and I myself was severely wounded.

Our stay in Ibiza lasted longer than usual. I was the cause of the delay because I insisted on exploring the possibility of establishing a permanent post here. In the end, nothing came of it.

"It was one thing to stop here to take on water and supplies and drink some of the local wine," Harold finally told me. "But there are not any refugees to carry enough cargo being shipped in and out to justify basing a transport galley or cog here. Moreover, the Moslem King probably would stop us from taking Islamic prizes if we based pirate-takers here.

"Besides that, our men and property would be at great risk when the next Christian or Moorish invasion occurs, as the merchants think it surely would."

I reluctantly agreed, and we sailed for Malta where we already had a well-established post. Brindisi was the Christian prince holding Malta on behalf of the King of Sicily. He was somehow different from most princes, perhaps because he was not born to it. In any event, we had become friends. He liked the idea of taking Islamic prizes and, indeed, used to do it himself until he got himself nobled and Malta for helping Sicily's King take

Sicily's throne when his predecessor died without an heir.

Our post near the Grand Harbour of the Island of Malta was important because it functioned as a way station for our cogs and galleys coming and going between Europe and both Athens and Constantinople to the north and the Holy Land and Egypt to the east.

Even more important, at least to me and our prize-oriented men, Malta was a splendid base from which to intercept Moorish pirates heading into the Christian waters of the Eastern Mediterranean and to send our prizes when we take them in the waters off Algiers and Tunis in the Western Mediterranean.

Besides that, the Grand Harbour was a fine liberty port for our men even if the women did smell uncommonly foul. We routinely stationed some of our pirate-taking galleys and cogs there.

******

We had barely entered the Grand Harbour and moored at the quay when Brindisi himself appeared on his huge grey horse, one of the King of Sicily's many gifts, including control of Malta, for helping the King claim the Sicilian throne. The old pirate turned noble had recognized Harold's galley from his fortress on the hill. It was easy for an experienced seaman like Brindisi to do because it was a bit longer and had four more oars on each side than most galleys.

I was still standing on the roof of the galley's rear castle watching as we approached the quay when Brindisi dismounted from his horse and waved. I waved back and was still walking across the deck to go ashore when Harold vaulted on to the quay even before we finished mooring and approached him with much arm waving.

"Oh, my friend, I am so sorry," Brindisi said a minute later as I walked up to him and he swept me into his arms and kissed me on both cheeks. "But, welcome to Malta and peace. Now it is time for us to go to the tavern for some wine and you can tell me all about what happened if you can bear to do so. If not, we will talk of other things."

Brindisi was a man that would have risen in any land; unfortunately, he had been born here on this very small island and would be, accordingly, an outsider and doomed by the place of his birth not to rise anywhere else.

******

Somehow it helped to talk about Anne and what happened and so I did after we reached his favourite tavern and the wine began to flow. Brindisi listened sympathetically and did not interrupt.

"So that is why it happened," Brindisi finally said with a sigh and a shake of his head. "I had somewhat the same problem here with the church until I explained to the local bishop that I would be the only one collecting money from the merchants and landowners in the future.

"I did not go so far as to say I would gut him and throw in the harbour, mind you; I was much more gentle and appealed to his reason. I merely told him that God had decided the next coin he collected outside one of his churches would be his last before he died. Fortunately for him, he believed in God and we have gotten along famously ever since.

"Now, tell me, what is the news from Europe? Will it be Otto or Frederick who would be the next Holy Roman Emperor and are either of them claiming Italy?

"I hope both claim it, for there will be fighting for sure if the new Emperor claims the Italian crown. The Pope wants all of Italy for himself, as I am sure you know. Sicily will surely be next if he gets it.

"If it happens, a war, I mean," he said with his great roaring laugh, "and I get called to serve by my dear lord to whom I owe so much, the King of Sicily, I will probably become deathly ill or the sweating pox would break out on the island so that my men and I are not welcome in his army. Perhaps both if it looks like it might be a long war."

I said I did not know that of the two German princes would get the Pope's blessing—and I certainly did not say or even hint that it would be whoever prince paid the most for the silver-coated head of Saint Paul. All I told the old pirate was that I intended to look for some of the priceless holy relics missing from Constantinople because we had heard in Rome that the Pope was offering big rewards from them.

Then I lowered my voice and confided that we had a leg up on the other searchers because we knew where the priests that took the relics went ashore with them— because the priests who took them had fled Constantinople in our galleys.

"So searching for the relics is what I intend to do whilst I am out here this year."

That, of course, is the story we wanted to get around; what we did not want is for anyone to know we got away with the relics when Constantinople was falling and already have them in Cornwall.

We stayed three days and I tried to forget about Lisbon by drinking too much and living on the galley instead of ashore in a tavern room. Brindisi and Harold accompanied me every night to make sure I got safely back to the galley.

It did not work. I could not get Anne out of my mind. I kept thinking of all the things I could have done to protect her.

******

The rowing drum began its beat on the morning of our fourth day in Malta and we headed east into the open sea bound for Crete. Two days later, we got lucky; we came across a big Moorish three-masted ship escorted by a couple of war galleys.

We could tell the ship was a Moor from the cut of her sails. Three-sided they were, very queer-looking, indeed. She was beating towards us into the wind and sat so low in the water that we knew she was heavily loaded.

"She is heavily loaded and heavily guarded," said Harold enthusiastically after he climbed down from the mast after taking a good look. "Either her cargo or passengers, or both, are valuable or else she would not be so heavily guarded."

Our men cheered lustily as the order was given to break out the weapons and reset our sails. They ran to their rowing and sailing stations with a will. Talk of prize money and how it might be spent was on every man's tongue.

Harold and I had talked constantly during our voyage about what Thomas and George had told us about how the deck of the big Moor they took had been swept by a single archer high on a galley mast. We had spent much of the trip trying out different ways to make such a nest and lengthening our boarding ladders. It was no surprise when one of the first things Harold had the sailing sergeant do when we saw the big Moor was send the makings of an archer's nest up to the very top of the mast above the lookouts.

"Bigger Moorish cogs and ships with more masts and higher decks seem to be the coming thing," Harold had said several times after we heard George and Thomas tell the story of their prize. "We have got to have a way to take them. Some kind of archer's nest at the very top of the mast may be the way to go. Perhaps even taller masts."

We had already agreed that when we got to Cyprus we are going to see if we could extend the masts of all our galleys so each galley would be able to put its best archer, or even two or three of its very best archers, way up into the sky above the archers in its lookout's nest.

Harold had thought it possible, but he was cautious.

"We have got to be careful, do not we? If we put the weight of too much wood and too many men way up there it might overbalance even the biggest galley and tip it on its side in a heavy sea."

In any event, the seas were not extremely heavy, and we would be going after the big Moor with Harold's best archer at the very top of the mast. The nest our sailors quickly built was not much to look at, just a couple of short boards lashed to the mast on that the archer could place his feet and a line he could tie to the leather belt around his waist. It worked because the archer could lean out from the mast with both hands free to pluck arrows out of his quiver and push them down into men below them on the deck of the intended prize.

Pushing out arrows from up there at the very top of a swaying and jerking mast was not the easiest thing to do, but it was possible and several of the galley's best archers practiced doing it every day whilst the village dancing and archery practice was happening on the deck.

The competition among the archers on each galley to be chosen for the position at the top of the mast had been intense. One of the reasons every archer wanted to be selected was probably because I had decreed that the archer serving at the top of the mast when a high-decked cog or ship was taken was to get a double portion of the prize money to that his rank entitled him. Harold had thought it might be a good idea, and he was right—there had been numerous volunteers.

"Harold, I understand the appeal of double prize money but I wonder if they realize that whoever is up there is going to be a big target if there are archers on the enemy ship?"

"Do you think we should buy them chain mail shirts?" was his response.

Chapter Twenty-one

We take a prize and are surprised.

The big Moorish three-master and her escorts did not wait to see if we were hostile. They immediately turned to run before the wind. We were not nearly close enough, so the archer assigned to the top of the forward mast and the two who would be in the lookout's nest were still sitting on the deck to rest their arms for the fight to come. We did not know how big a fight it would become.

"Harold," I said, "the big Moorish three-master Thomas and George took as a prize was also convoyed by two galleys, was not it? Do you think it was a coincidence that this one also has two escorts?"

"Yes, that is strange. But what is even stranger is that these three all turned and ran from just one galley? I would have thought they would at least have come for a look."

"Perhaps they heard of our reputation," I suggested.

"But how would they know it is us?" was Harold's reply. "They could not be sure at this distance. All they would know is that we are a war galley and they outnumber us."

"Maybe they think there are more of us out here?"

******

We passed through a little rain squall and when we came out of it, to our surprise, there they were straight ahead of us, all three of them. What was even more surprising was that they had turned around and were coming back towards us with their sails down and rowing hard. Little wonder. The sea beyond them was dotted with war galleys, dozens of them, and they were all rowing straight at our three would-be prizes and us.

"The three-master and her escorts must have known that armada of galleys was out here somewhere and thought they had come upon it when they saw us. That is probably why they turned back so quickly and tried to run."

Harold said it to me with a little chuckle after he swung our galley around, ordered the sail brought down, and sent every man to the oars. Then he added an observation.

"We should be safe, but they would take the sailing ship we have been chasing for sure and maybe the two galleys convoying her as well, unless they have enough strong rowers on their oars to out-row the best of that lot."

"I think we should stay well ahead of them and do a 'wounded bird,' I suggested to Harold. "Maybe we can pick off a thruster or two. Do you agree?"

"Aye, Captain, that be what I be thinking myself. Maybe we take one of the galleys from yon armada and find out who the hell they are and what they were about. It is strange to see so many heathen galleys all together in one place. They must have been on a raid."

"Or going on one," I suggested ominously, "perhaps to hit Cyprus or the Christian ports along coast of the Holy Land. I wish to God we knew that way they were headed, and why, before we chased the big ship and its two escorts right into their hands."

My God, I hope our post on Cyprus has not been surprised and overrun.

******

I went up on the mast with Harold for a look of my own. It always worried me to climb a galley mast what with all swaying back and forth, but I did it. What I saw when I had gotten as far as I could go was not a heartening sight. It was as if a huge pack of wolves was rushing down upon a missing sheep and the two dogs guarding it.

The three-masted ship with the triangle sails did not have a chance. The first galleys of the armada caught up to her and had her surrounded almost immediately. We did not stick around to see what happened next. Harold ordered the sail lowered and every man to the oars. We spun around and went back the way we had come as fast as you could say "Bob's your uncle."

The captured ship's two guard-dog galleys were not caught so easily by the armada we chanced upon, if they were caught at all. At least one of them had not been taken by the time the sun finished passing overhead on its endless trip around the world. The two galleys had immediately separated and the last thing we could see from the lookout's nest before the sun finished passing overhead was a chase. The men of the guard-dog galley we could still see from the mast were rowing for their very lives with a number of thrusters from the armada of galleys in hot pursuit.

It was initially hard to tell if they were closing the gap. And then it was getting dark and they were gone over the horizon.

We knew the rowers of the fleeing galley were pulling for their lives because we had to exert ourselves a bit with two strong archers at every oar to stay well ahead of the runner and its pursuers. Without a doubt, the men of the fleeing galley had joined the slaves on her rowing benches. We had not a clue as to the fate of the three-master's other escort.

"We have no choice but to keep rowing hard on our current course until either the sun comes up or the clouds clear enough and we can see the horizon in the moonlight," said Harold disgustedly after he gasped in a deep breath.

We were sitting together and rowing an oar on one of the upper rowing benches so that two of our archers could take a break. They were both already stretched out and sound asleep on the deck. It seemed like we had just sat down and I was already winded and gasping without even trying to talk.

After a few more strokes, Harold took a particularly deep breath and spoke rather loudly.

"If we slow down and they keep coming, we could wake up in the morning and find ourselves in the middle of that whole goddamn armada. Two or three would be fine and we could take them, but not scores of the bastards all at the same time. They would wear us down until they got us."

I smiled to myself. *Of course, Harold wants the men to know what we are doing and why.*

"Aye, you are right," I agreed with a gasp and a grunt as I leaned forward after what seemed like a particularly heavy pull.

After my next pull I managed to gasp, "If we keep this up, we will be well ahead of them in the morning." And then after my next pull, I somehow added, "Then we can rest and start looking for stragglers."

My God. I cannot quit so soon. What would the men think?

******

Morning brought an empty sea except for a dot on the distant horizon that could be seen from the top of the mast. We waited and rested our arms as it got closer and closer.

"It is a Moorish galley, by God," said Harold as he joined me after climbing the mast to see for himself. "No telling whose it is, but most likely from the armada because there were so many of them."

Then he got to what had been worrying me as well.

"Do you think our Cyprus post will be able to hold out if that is where the Moors are going?"

Harold's really asking if his wife and children and those of his men are safe.

"Of course, it would. They have got their own water well and enough siege supplies to last for a year, and probably more. Besides, there are not enough Moorish sailors and pirates in the whole world to get over a wall defended by our archers, let the alone the three walls we have got on Cyprus. They were fine. *I hope.*

"At the very most, the Moors may have gotten into Limassol city and sacked it or taken some of our galleys and cogs that were in the harbour. It was our galleys and cogs I am worried about, not our people for they would almost certainly be inside our fortress and safe."

I mentioned the safety of our people loudly enough for the men standing nearby to hear. Word would get around quickly as it always does on a galley. Harold's galley was home-based on Cyprus; some of the men probably have women there and were likely to have been worried.

Hmm. I wonder how many galleys and cogs we usually have in the harbour or coming and going in their normal sailings. It used to be five or six with a new arrival or departure almost every day. I will ask Harold later when no one is around. There is no hurry; there is nothing we can do about it if the Moors have already been there or are headed there. But what do we do if they are?

******

Taking Moorish galleys was something Harold was quite good at doing. He had the grappling lines coiled and set out and the arrow bales opened. Then he sent most of our men to the rowing benches. He wanted to clear the deck long before the lookouts on the on-coming galley could get close enough to mark them.

"We do not want the lookouts on their mast to see fighting men on our deck, do we?" he said to me with a determined smile as we pretended to flee. "Not until we have grappled them so they cannot get away."

Harold and I and our apprentices and his loud-talker and sailing sergeant were standing on the roof of the rear deck castle. We appeared to be alone on the roof with three or four unarmed sailors rushing about on the deck and looking anxiously at the approaching galley as we tried to escape with only some of our oars rowing.

In fact, the arrow bales had been laid out on the deck and both castles were jammed full of archers and pike men who would come rushing out when the fighting started. We had six of the galley's big land-fighting shields lying on the roof with us and ready to be picked up on a moment's notice if our pursuer had archers.

Our galley looked exhausted and feeble. Our sail was low and drooping all the way to the deck on one side and only the oars of the lower deck were rowing. And they were rowing as slowly as they would if we had only one exhausted slave at each oar. Harold also had half the oars on each side of the upper bank of oars rowing, as would be the case if most the galley's sailors and fighting men had been sent to the oars in a desperate effort to escape.

The Moor, or whatever it might turn out to be, took the bait. There might have been archers on the Moor, so we had only one dependable sailor man in the lookout's nest. He had been selected because he had particularly good eyes. He had one of our big fighting-on-land shields up there with him in case he needed protection from enemy arrows.

We would know soon enough if there were archers on the approaching galley. If not, the sailor with the long distance eyes would be quickly replaced by two of our best archers.

"Hoy, the deck. They's deck be crowded with fighting men. They means to board us."

A few minutes later a small initial flight of arrows came up from our pursuer and flew towards our lookout. *Damn, they have archers; but not very many, from the looks of it, and they are not very good.*

"Hoy, the deck. Archers. They be having archers with short bows," our lookout cried down to us as he crouched behind his shield.

His warning was not needed. We were standing on the roof of the stern castle and all of us had seen the arrows as they began fly flying towards him.

The roof of the stern castle, as everyone knows, is the best place from which to command a galley in a fight—even if the galley you are fighting has archers. This one

certainly did, so we all crouched down behind the big
shields that had been laid out just in case; the big shields
our first three lines of pike-carrying archers use when we
fight on land.

****

The enemy galley approached us with much cheering
from its deck full of armed men waving their swords.
There was no doubt about it—they were Moorish
pirates. What was unique was that some of them were
carrying the shields of men who fight on land.

They were part of a force that is been organized to
fight on land. Is this some kind of an invasion fleet?

Our men maintained good order and were silent.

"In oars," shouted Harold as the Moorish galley
came up alongside. There were the usual sounds of a
few oars being broken off, and a few seconds later our
hulls crashed together with enough of an initial bump to
send several men on the enemy galley to their knees. At
the same instant, grapples began to be thrown on to our
deck from the Moor and an arrow thudded into the
shield of Andrew Priest, my sergeant apprentice.

The two galleys were still ten or fifteen paces apart with the Moors hauling on their grapple lines to bring them together side by side when Harold and his loud-talker screamed the words our men had been waiting to hear.

"Now. Throw your grapples. Attack; now. Attack."

It was as if a weir had burst. Our fighting men and grapple-throwing sailors came charging out of the deck castles and the upper rowing benches, where they had been hidden out of sight and waiting. They did so with great shouts. It was something our archers and sailors practiced at least once every day when the weather was not too foul. I was looking carefully around the corner of my shield and saw everything including the astonished looks on the faces of the Moors standing only a few feet away on the deck of their galley.

Seriously stunned and surprised was the only way to describe the looks on the faces of the men on the Moorish galley as our men suddenly charged out of where they had been hiding.

Our own grapples were quickly thrown as our archers ran to their assigned places and began to pour arrow after arrow into the mass of men a few feet away on the Moorish galley's deck. The Moors were close, and our archers rarely missed. It was pandemonium as the decks of both galleys were covered by shouting and screaming men. Now it was our grapple throwers who were pulling the two galleys together.

Everyone on the castle roof had come out from hiding behind our shields as soon as the fighting started. We immediately realized there were only a few archers on the enemy galley, and they could not loose their arrows because they were jammed into the disorganized crowd of Moorish boarders who were waving their swords and shouting on our enemy's deck.

We pushed arrow after arrow into the would-be boarders from our positions up on the castle roof. Other archers on the deck below us did the same from their various, carefully assigned shooting positions, and so did the handful of archers on the roof of the forward castle and up on the mast.   We took the enemy archers and thrusters first. Four of Harold's best archers came out of the castle below and joined us on the roof.

A handful of the Moors who had been waiting to board us managed to climb on to our deck when the galleys were pulled together. Bad luck for them. They were instantly chopped down by the pike men who had led our archers out on to the deck for just such a situation.

A virtual storm of arrows poured into the Moors and the handful of Moorish bowmen we could initially see were gone almost instantly. I used my longbow to push an arrow at a Moor attempting to get to the safety of his galley's forward castle. My arrow and at least one other took him just as he reached the entrance. He staggered and fell through it.

I never did find out what happened to him.

It seemed like the fighting lasted a long time. But it did not. Many of the Moors were wounded but still alive as our archers poured on to our deck and castle roofs to take their shooting positions—and then on to the Moorish galley, that was now tightly lashed to ours by a number of grapple lines.

Wounded Moors who tried to run or fight back were quickly hacked down or stabbed by our pike men and had more arrows pushed into them by our archers. Some of them attempted to escape by jumping down into the upper rowing benches and then ran further down to get in amongst their slaves on the lower rowing benches.

It was mostly over in a few short minutes. Andrew, my apprentice, and I stood on the castle roof and watched as our archers began to shoot down into the bowels of the Moorish galley at the Moors who had attempted to temporarily escape their fate by jumping down to the rowing benches.

What would happen to those we take alive was Harold's decision to make as the sergeant captain of our galley. They would almost certainly go into the water if they are pirates; we will hold them to be exchanged for Christians and Jews if they are soldiers and sailors. Since our prize looks to be a pirate galley with land soldiers on board, it was likely some of them would be going for a swim after we question them.

"Hoy, the mast," I shouted as Harold moved over to our new prize to direct the mopping up and engage in the nasty business of deciding who should get mercies and who could be saved.

"Are there any sails in sight?"

Chapter Twenty-two

Our response to the alarming news.

The hold of the Moorish galley we took was packed full of recently captured Christian slaves including, to our shocked surprise, three of our own men and some of their passengers. They had been caught by the Moorish fleet when their cog was surprised as it entered Beirut's harbour. They were all, as you might imagine, ecstatic at being freed. *Our hearing that the Moors had already been to Beirut was the first confirmation we had that the Moorish armada we had encountered was moving westward after raiding the Holy Land's Christian ports.*

We plied our newly freed men and Moorish prisoners with questions about what happened and what they had seen and heard.

It was with great relief that we learnt that the Moors had raided Limassol on their way west after raiding Beirut and the coastal ports along the Holy Land coast, but that raid had been largely unsuccessful, limited to the taking of an ill-fated cog, that had been approaching the harbour with a load of refugees and cargo from Constantinople. The Moors also sailed away with a barely seaworthy unmanned galley we had been using for training purposes.

No effort had been made by the Moors to land and try to take our fortified post or the city. According to the captives we released, our people had been in our citadel and ready to fight because one of our galleys had escaped from the Moors' raid on Acre and come in a day earlier with a warning that the Moors were out in force.

Yoram and Randolph had taken the warning to heart and immediately moved all of our men and their families inside our walled fortress. They had also sent our galleys and cogs in the Limassol harbour to safety with skeleton crews by sending them north into a rarely visited part of the Mediterranean in the middle of nowhere. The gates of the city and our fortress had been shut and the walls manned by the time the Moors arrived. The Moors had taken one look at the deserted harbour and quay and had made no effort to come ashore.

According to Harold's interpreter, the Moorish armada was returning to Tunis, Algiers, and some of the smaller Moorish ports after raiding the Christian ports along the Holy Land coast to take slaves for the Moorish King to sell. They were on their way back to Tunis and had hit Cyprus on their way home. According to one of the merchants we rescued who could jabber in Moorish, there had been talk among the Moors of also raiding some of the Greek ports, and, possibly, Malta or Crete on their way back home. *Malta?*

It quickly became apparent that we had somehow run into the galleys of the Moslem King ruling Tunis and Algiers, the one who was fighting for control of Spain and the entire Islamic world.

There had been rumours that the King had begun using his galleys to take Christian slaves to sell in order to help pay for his wars and this would seem to prove it—his galleys had come from Algiers and Tunis and hit Christian ports all along the Holy Land coast before they started back and reached Cyprus four days ago. They had almost certainly raided elsewhere along the Cyprus coast in addition to Limassol.

The worst news of all was that the Moors may have captured some of our other galleys and cogs when they launched their surprise raids on the Holy Land ports up and down the Christian coast. Among the prize's rowers was one of our Company's sailors, a man from Hartlepool who had been taken only a few days before from another one of our cargo cogs. It had been anchored in the harbour at Acre whilst waiting its turn to move to the quay and load cargo and passengers bound for Alexandria.

******

Limassol's safety was good news, and there was nothing we could do about our lost galleys and cogs except revenge them and try to free any of our men and passengers who had been taken captive. But Harold and I still had a big problem—the galleys and prizes of the damn Moorish armada could be anywhere in the sea around us. Accordingly, we were not sure in that direction we should sail because we did not know where the war galleys of the Moorish armada might be located. All we knew is that we had rowed hard all night so that the armada of Moorish galleys was likely to still be between us and Cyprus.

"Should we sail on to Cyprus or back to Malta or head elsewhere? And where should we send our prize— Malta? Or should we all stay here and rest until they pass us by?" Those were the questions Harold and I asked each other.

Finally, I made a decision. Both our new prize and Harold's galley would stay right here and bob around in the sea for a few hours whilst we feed our men and rest and reorganize.

"When the men are thoroughly rested we will sail straight for Cyprus and row right past any Moors we encounter along the way unless they look like an easy prize.

"We will put the Moors we have taken and their newly freed captives and slaves on the oars of both galleys and move enough archers on to the prize to make it hard to take if it comes to a fight at sea. Our archers would rest so they would have fresh arms if and when we need them."

Archers inevitably had strong arms and shoulders. No galley rowed by slaves and Moorish pirates had any hope of catching one of ours when there were two of our archers on every oar.

That is why, normally, I would not have been at all concerned about having our galleys row right through the Moorish fleet. The problem, of course, was that we had put some of the archers from Harold's galley into our prize as a prize crew and replaced them with Moorish slaves and captives with weaker arms.

******

We raised the sails on our two galleys several hours later and began slowly moving eastward towards Cyprus without rowing. Sure enough, that afternoon we began to see sails in the distance. The Moorish galleys were clawing their way into the wind towards us as they moved westward towards Tunis and Algiers.

Everything changed when we saw the distant sails. Our decks were cleared and we began slowly rowing towards them using only the lower bank of oars—just as we would if we were a slave-rowed Moor heading east.

Our best deception, suggested to us by a newly freed merchant from Acre, was to put a line of seven or eight men in Moorish robes on the roof of the stern castle praying towards the east. Harold and I were among them so we could jump up and take command if our ruse failed. The others were archers.

It worked even though it was hard on my knees. Everyone we passed heading in the other direction looked us over with great curiosity but without alarm. The only responses from the Moorish galleys were arms lifted in greeting as we went past them. We raised ours in return.

******

We kept the sail up and rowed easterly all that night in an effort to get well clear of the scattered Moorish fleet. It worked. No sails were in sight the next morning, and we reached Cyprus the day after that.

Limassol Harbour was a welcome sight, although, our arrival caused much initial running about as the few people out and about ran for our fortress and the city gate. They slowly returned as we rowed up to the quay and moored. The quay was empty. Not a cog or galley in sight and not a person standing on the quay. The gates to the city and our adjacent fortress were closed.

"Hoy," Harold shouted to one of the men tentatively approaching us from our fortress next to the city walls. "I will give you copper if you will run to the English post and tell them that Captain William has arrived with a prize."

Chapter Twenty-three

We wait anxiously and make plans.

Within minutes, people began pouring out of our fortified post and then from the city gate. They rushed to the quay in ever-increasing numbers and it was soon packed with celebrating people. It was as if our arrival with a prize had signalled the end of the Moorish threat. And, at that moment, it seemed that it did. *Little did we know that it did not.*

Yoram and Randolph were appalled and Lena began crying when I haltingly told them about Anne's death as we walked along the cart path from the quay to the entrance of our post. It was so absolutely senseless. That evening there was a great sadness in Randolph's voice as he summed up the situation quite well as we sat outside in the moonlight. Harold and I had just finished going over the details once again.

"What is done is done. Lisbon is an important port for us because it has so many merchants, I will grant you that; but if it becomes too dangerous to stay we could always move our hospital and post to a smaller port along the coast and stop there for water and supplies."

Yoram agreed.

"We would lose some custom if we move our shipping post out of Lisbon, but we could appoint a local agent from among the merchants so we would not lose it all."

I just nodded. I was not ready to make a decision because I was still quite down about Anne and Lisbon. In the weeks that followed, my lieutenants and I would spend long hours discussing how we should react to the various things that might happen as a result of my message to the bishop.

I did not tell them I intended to kill Bishop Resende; but I knew it would not surprise them when I did.

****

During the uncertain days and weeks that followed, we spent a lot of time talking about both the Lisbon attack and the Moorish raids. We were anxious to know how many men and bottoms we had lost and if any of the ports we served had fallen to the Moors. We endlessly speculated as to our future in Lisbon and what the Moorish raids meant for the future of the Holy Land and for our Company—were they one-off events or did they portend great change?

Mostly, however, we discussed the need to conduct an "intensive search" for the missing relics and how we should do it so word would get out that we were searching and might have them to sell. It was our great and closely held secret that we already had the relics in Cornwall.

What we never did get was any kind of response from the King of Cyprus about the raid or even from his local governor. The French knight serving as the King's local governor abandoned his castle on the hill behind the city and ran for the safety of Nicosia with his men within an hour of our arrival in the harbour—as soon as he thought it was safe to venture outside his castle's walls.

We never saw the governor again, and he certainly did not find safety with the King and his guards when he reached Nicosia. The new King was still a mere boy and his guardian and courtiers, and thus the King's guards and the rabble in his army, were living far across the Mediterranean in the bigger and more exciting city of Beirut.

At least, the King and his men were living in Beirut the last time we heard. On the other hand, the shipping in Beirut's harbour was attacked by the Moors so perhaps they moved inland. *Oh well, we told each other, it did not matter all that much; we will find out sooner or later.*

There had been a time when we would have seen the departure of the governor as an opportunity to buy or seize the governorship and move into the governor's castle. Not now. Our fortified post was now much stronger than the governor's castle. We now had three complete curtain walls and their battlements and bastions, and a fourth and similar curtain wall well on its way to completion.

We did, however, make one decision whilst we waited for word to arrive about our losses. We decided to hold the Moors we had captured in the abandoned governor's castle whilst we try to trade them for our men and other Christians.

The castle was mostly deserted except for a few servants with nowhere to go. We walked right in and by the end of the day had moved our prisoners into its dungeon. They were fearful of their fates but they need not have been—we would feed and water them to keep them alive so they could be exchanged or ransomed.

******

It was not until almost a week after I returned to Cyprus that one of our galleys came in from Acre and another a few hours later from Beirut. They could have sailed earlier but had their sergeant captains had, quite properly, waited until the coast was clear. We hurried to the quay to get the news.

The news we received was both bad and strangely encouraging. Both Acre and Beirut had been raided by the Moorish fleet and so had some of the ports and villages along the coast. The Moors had been after slaves and prizes to sell, not a fight to the finish or a city to conquer.

The good news was that the Moors had swarmed aboard and taken several of our lightly defended cogs, but had quickly pulled away from attacking our galleys as soon as they realized they would be vigorously defended.

"They were not trained fighting men," sniffed the sergeant captain of the galley that came in from Beirut. "They were untrained heathen sailors and fishermen looking for unarmed sailors who would not fight back. They surprised us by sailing into the harbour where we were anchored, I will give them that, but they retreated in dismay as soon as our arrows began taking them."

******

Our losses to the Moorish fleet turned out to be substantial and growing as more and more of our galleys and a number of our cogs did not arrive at their intended destinations—already we knew that we had lost four of our cogs, three refugee-carrying galleys, and almost two hundred men of whom more than one hundred were archers. On top of that, our credibility was damaged because at least two of the missing cogs and three of the galleys had been loaded with passengers, cargo, and merchant order parchments.

On the other hand, there had been some relatively minor offsets. Harold's galley had taken a prize and the Moors had suffered heavy losses, including the loss of a galley, when they mistook one of our pirate-taking cogs for a two-masted cargo transport. A number of Moorish galleys had surrounded our pirate-taker and grappled it and tried to board it. There were so many galleys involved that they all got away except for the first—but to hear the cog's captain tell it, and I believed him, the Moors suffered hundreds of dead and wounded from his archers before they were able to cut their grapple lines and withdraw.

Our successes were a small comfort.

"Prizes and cargos be damned; we have got to do something to get our men and passengers back," said Harold for the third or fourth time, "at least those who are still living."

"Aye. We must; we surely must. But how?" asked Randolph.

"It was either an exchange of prisoners or a ransom or both," suggested Yoram once again. "It was the only way."

"You are right," I said. "We want our men and passengers back so we will go with both."

******

In the weeks that followed, we put out the word in every port we served that we would trade for British and French prisoners and the passengers taken from our galleys and cogs. Our offer had a strange and unexpected effect—one after another, to our great surprise, our port sergeants reported that their custom increased. It also, according to Randolph and Harold, greatly heartened our men whose greatest fear was being abandoned after being captured or injured.

What we did not tell anyone was that we had begun planning a great raid for the spring when I returned to Cornwall to sell the relics. We had decided to make an all-out effort to reduce the number of Moorish pirates in the Eastern Mediterranean and take prisoners to trade for our captured men and passengers.

Chapter Twenty-four

Searching for the relics and preparing a raid.

We stepped up our training and recruited some additional apprentice archers from among the former slaves and others of our workmen whilst we waited for word to trickle in about our losses to the Moorish fleet. Good food and lots of it had strengthened some of them to the point of having enough strength to push arrows out of a longbow over and over again. And, of course, our arrow works and smiths remained constantly in operation turning out ever more long, bladed pikes, arrows, and longbows. They also began producing grappling irons and longer boarding ladders.

Whilst we waited for word of our losses from the Moorish raids, we inspected our fortress and paid particular attention to the work now being done to surround it with a fourth curtain wall and further strengthen the three inner walls and their crenelated battlements.

We also agreed on the next thing we could do to strengthen it and provide work for the steady stream of arriving refugees and released slaves—we would build a great, long, unfortified wall of stones and timber to enclose the hovels, gardens, and grazing lands of the sizable village of construction workers and artisans that had sprung up next to our fortress. We would either dig a new well for their use or, perhaps, partially reroute the little river serving as the city's water supply.

Our big question, at least as it related to our fortress on Cyprus, was whether or not it should somehow be connected to the existing city wall of Limassol so that people could safely pass back and forth between our fortress and the city during a siege, perhaps with a tunnel? Or should we just put in an escape tunnel running from the lower room of the main citadel as we were doing in London?

My answer, after much discussion, was yes, to both. We decided to start by connecting our fortress to the city with a long, narrow, walled path running all the way from our second or third curtain wall to the city wall. It would have strong gate towers at each wall it passed though and there would be additional battlements overlooking it from the city and from each of our curtain walls.

Moreover, we decided to build a small square tower over the middle of the new walled path in the open area between the city wall and the new village wall. The tower would be very much like the gate towers in our curtain walls—it would have two doors and "murder holes" in the room above the path and on all sides of it. All the gates would, of course, be shut and barred on both sides at night and during times of war.

Cyprus was by far our most important post outside of Cornwall and we wanted it to be able to hold out for a very long time if it came under siege, years if necessary. We even considered digging a walled canal to the sea so we could launch our galleys from inside our village wall during a siege. *It turned out not to be a very useful idea; we rejected it.*

Yoram was pleased to overflowing when he was told that he could proceed to dig a well inside our fourth curtain wall and build a narrow walled path to the city; and he was absolutely ecstatic when I told him that, when they were complete, he could begin building a very long unfortified wall to enclose both the fortress and our workers' village and the lands around it.

"Thank you. Thank you. That is wonderful—it would keep our people in work and food for many years to come." He was very pleased.

Yoram was very honest and very family oriented. He was always in favour of anything and everything that might make his family and our coin chests safer. I liked him very much.

******

Harold and I finally set off for the Greek coast with five galleys to "search for the relics" three weeks after we arrived in Cyprus. The Moors were long gone and we had a fairly good idea of the losses they had inflicted on us.

Yoram, Randolph, and quite a crowd of well-wishers were on the quay to see us off. They waved and cheered as we cast off our mooring lines, the rowing drums began to beat, and our galleys began to be rowed out of the Limassol harbour bound for the Greek coast.

This was the first step in our intense efforts to find the "missing" relics. We would use the excuse of delivering passengers and money orders at several ports along the way to make sure everyone knew we were searching for them. Randolph did not go with us. He remained behind on Cyprus to help Yoram prepare our men and equipment for the great raid we intended to carry out when we returned to Cornwall in the spring to sell the relics. It was a secret known in Cyprus only to Yoram and Randolph.

We sailed with five well-supplied galleys packed with enough archers to put two men on every oar. Spirits were high. In our minds, and in those of our well-wishers and men, we were obviously capable of fighting off anyone who tried to stop us from finding the missing relics.

Our archers and sailors were excited. They had known for over a week that they would be sailing to search along the Greek coast for the missing Orthodox Church relics. More importantly, we had deliberately misled them; they had been told that there would be significant prize money if they found them. They also knew that many of our other galleys would also be searching for them.

My lieutenants and I, of course, had told our men it was a secret they might soon have more prize money and had cautioned them not to tell the women in the taverns exactly where we would be searching along the Greek coast to recover the relics. And, above all, we warned our men not to borrow against their prize money from the local moneylenders as they might not find them.

As you might imagine, and as we had intended, the news spread rapidly that we would be sailing to the Greek coast with galleys packed with fighting men; that we would be searching for the missing Orthodox relics; and that they were worth huge prize monies to whomever of our crews found them.

Our search was, of course, soon known to every merchant and priest and sailor on Cyprus and the news was quickly carried to all the ports in the Mediterranean.

What the men in our five galleys did not know was that they would not be successful when they went ashore to search—another galley based in another port would "find" them.

The relics were, of course, already safely in Cornwall.

Our crews would have to be content with the extra time they would be given to visit the taverns in each port so they could, quite unknowingly, spread the word of our search and the huge prize monies on offer. Sooner or later the news of our search was bound to reach the princes, and give our offer to sell them great credibility.

******

We reached Athens's port of Piraeus after stopping at Crete and Rhodes to deliver money orders and passengers, and take on water and supplies. At each stop we had cautioned the men not to tell anyone in the taverns where on the Greek coast we would be stopping to search for the missing relics. They could not, of course, because the relics were not there and never have been. But that did not stop our men from endlessly speculating and arguing in the taverns and wine bars about where we would search, what we would find, and the size of the prize money.

By the time we reached Piraeus after two days in each port, every merchant and spy in Crete and Rhodes, and every sailor in their harbours, knew the English archers were actively searching for the missing relics— and expected to find them because they knew the various places where the priests had landed to hide them, and how long they had been gone. It was the galleys of the English archers, after all, that the fleeing priests had chartered.

******

Piraeus was more of the same, in the sense that our archers and sailors were given liberty so they would talk about our search and, in so doing, convince everyone it was real. But spreading the word that we were actively searching was not the only reason we called in here before proceeding up the coast towards Constantinople. We had another purpose for being in Piraeus that only my lieutenants and I knew about—contacting the Patriarch of the Orthodox Church to see if he would like to secretly buy any of the relics "if we find them."

I could not go to see him myself, of course, because Rome had spies everywhere. Instead, Harold sent his apprentice sergeant on a wandering walk to the Patriarch's residence to deliver a secret parchment my priestly brother Thomas had scribed. It purported to be from an unnamed English sergeant who would be able to obtain the relics from the archers and sell them to the Orthodox Patriarch "if we find them and you would pay enough."

The unknown sergeant proposed that, if the relics were found, he would provide a description of each relic and the amount of coins required to ransom it. The payment coins would be exchanged for the relics in the Beirut harbour. The Patriarch's men would be allowed to inspect the relics before they paid.

Harold and I took no chances. We stayed on the galley and did not go into the city except during daylight, and then only with a large number of heavily armed guards. We primarily went into the city's great market to buy tools for our men to use in our search for the relics—shovels with long and short handles, hoes, picks, and mattocks.

After negotiations that lasted almost an entire day we ended up buying just about every tool in the market that could be used for digging.

"We need them to take back to Cyprus for use in farming," Harold assured each merchant as I counted out the coins from my pouch. They inevitably nodded in agreement with a knowing look on their face and offered to have more available within a few days.

******

Our five galleys left the harbour in the middle of the night, two days later, without the rowing drum beating. Of course, we did; we wanted everyone to know we had a big important secret we were trying to hide. Our efforts seemed to have worked; several merchants providing us with supplies and tools had warned Harold that we would be followed by treasure hunters when we left the harbour to begin our search. More of our galleys were scheduled to arrive in three or four days. Their sergeant captains had been carefully instructed to repeat the tool-buying process and sail for other sites along the coast.

From Piraeus, we rowed our way north along the coast until the next afternoon. That is when Harold and I began holding up a parchment map as if we were studying it.

"Ah, you are right, this may be it. This could be where they landed," I said to Harold loudly enough for some of the men to hear.

"This could be the little creek they put their bow in and drew water whilst they were waiting for the priests to return."

It was all ox shite, of course. But it was for a good cause. How else could we convince the princes and the Orthodox Church to part with so many of their coins without being blamed for stealing the relics?

"This could be the place, Richard," Harold shouted over to the sergeant captain of the galley that had come up next to us.

"They landed here and spent one and a half days before they returned," I shouted over to Richard. "And do not forget that it was priests, many of them elderly, who were carrying the crates of relics and digging in the ground to hide them. Most were not strong men; they may not have gone very far inland."

Richard and his men were to go ashore here and search. From where we were standing on the deck of Harold's galley, we could hear the orders being given to the rowers on Richard's galley.

Harold's men watched with keen interest and jealous looks as Richard's galley nosed into the beach. Richard's men were enthusiastic and had already picked up their tools and weapons. They were jumping down into the surf and wading ashore as we began rowing north along the coast to the next search site. The hunt for the missing relics had begun.

******

We completed our rendezvous in Piraeus thirteen days later when the last of the galleys finished its search and returned to Piraeus to resupply. Similar to those that had come in earlier, it too had arrived empty handed. By the time it returned, however, a rumour had spread among our men, and thus to everyone in the city and in the harbour, that Harold and I had received a parchment telling us the relics had been found. It seems one of our galleys searching out of Antioch might have found them; or perhaps it was a galley from Latika or Beirut.

Our men were not sure that galley had been successful or where it had been based, but they had discussed the various possibilities and the amount of prize money its crew would be sharing every evening in the local wine shops and taverns while we waited for the return of the final galley.

"They would be chuffed," they told each other gleefully about the crew of the galley that was still out there searching, "when they find out they was a searchin' an a diggin' and them crates of old bones is already been found."

All anyone actually knew, of course, was that a galley had come in with a parchment that had caused Harold and I to begin whooping and jumping around like young boys. That evening numerous men moped over their bowls of wine in the local taverns and swore to each other and the tavern girls that they knew someone on Harold's galley who had heard me very distinctly say, "They found them, by God, they found them." *That is more or less exactly what I said.*

"Well, at least now we can go home to where the wine is better and the girls do not smell so bad," said one of the archers as he sipped at his bowl of wine. It seemed to be the prevailing sentiment among our men.

Whilst we waited for the last of the searching galleys to return and the men consoled themselves over their lost prize coins, Harold and I continued to work on our plans for the great raid we intended to lead in the spring. Our intentions were simple—we were going to fall upon the Moors and we were going to do it when we were on our way back to Cornwall to begin meeting with the princes to sell them the relics.

"One thing's for sure," Harold assured me as we once again discussed what had gone right and what had gone wrong in our previous raids, "this time we will be hitting them with more galleys and men, and this time we will be bringing more prize crews and a better way to put fire to the Moorish cogs and galleys we cannot carry away."

Our basic plan was simple and very ambitious. We intended to hit all the major Moorish ports between Cyprus and England. This time, however, we were going to try to stay long enough to greatly reduce their pirate fleets and their ability to carry cargos.

"And that means taking or destroying everything that floats, including their fishing boats. And that is not all; if possible, we are going to burn their shipyards; and, if we can get through the gates and take them by surprise without having to lay a siege, sack their cities and take prisoners we can hold for ransom or exchange."

"Why would we go to the trouble of doing all that?" Harold and Yoram had asked when I first outlined the kind of raid I wanted to lead. Harold had just asked me again.

"Why, for the coins from the prizes we take, of course; but also because we want the coins to keep coming in the years ahead when George and his sons and grandsons command the Company.

"The Moorish pirates in these waters are getting so strong they are starting to discourage the Christian pilgrims and reinforcements necessary to continue the fighting between the Saracens and Christians for control of Jerusalem and the rest of the Holy Land.

"We need to reduce the Christians' fear of the pirates so the crusaders and pilgrims keep coming. That way we can continue to carry them and the refugees without the Moslems ever winning and ending our trade. We will be back in Cornwall with no way to earn our bread if one side ever gets strong enough to win."

Yoram, of course, had understood immediately when we first talked about a raid to reduce the Moorish pirates, but not destroy them.

"It is just like our limited support for King John, is it not? We do not want to totally defeat the Moors or the merchants will not need to pay us a premium to guard their shipments. Similarly, we do not want the rebel barons to defeat John, or John to defeat them, because then John will not need to leave us alone. It is better for our Company if everyone stays at each other's throats."

"Exactly so," I had said as the others looked on with various degrees of understanding.

"Our Company needs wars and conflict to continue without a winner if we are to continue to enrich ourselves and our families. It is how we earn our bread."

Chapter Twenty-five

The great raid.

Fifty-seven of the Company's galleys and over three thousand archers and almost two thousand sailors prepared to sail "for England." It was by far the biggest force we had ever assembled. Who would have thought it possible? But it was. What was a secret was the size of the Company fleet that would be sailing and that we intended to stop along the way to "visit" a number of Moorish ports.

We assembled our fleet very quietly; we merely ordered the four-stripe sergeant captain of each galley to sail for Cornwall on a certain date, "at the request of the Pope," to help guard important religious relics as they passed through the pirate waters between Malta and London.

Each of the captains was told he would be expected to arrive in Malta with a specified number of additional sailors and pilots to replace those in our Lisbon and London fleets who had been lost last year to the pox.

Sailors and pilots were easy to recruit. They all wanted to serve on our galleys because we had a reputation for treating our sailors and pilots properly and paying them on time.

It was Harold's idea to have the orders mention our need to replace the men who fallen to the pox instead of admitting that we were recruiting prize crews. We did so because our galleys would be calling in at Cyprus, Crete, and Malta for water and supplies, and probably other ports as well. Mentioning prize crews, or even saying nothing while recruiting additional sailors, might have alerted the Moors.

We took no chances about the Moors discovering our plans. We waited to tell our men about the raids and form them up into a fighting fleet until after they reached Malta.

The sergeant captains of the galleys did not know it, but the 'secret' sailing dates we gave each of them would put them all into Malta on the same date if the weather cooperated—which, of course, was not likely.

Separately and quietly, two of our cargo cogs were sent from Cyprus to Malta with the additional food, longer boarding ladders, and fire-throwing pots the archers would need for an attack on the Moors' city walls.

We capped off our efforts to gull the Moors by sending twelve large wooden chests to Malta. We sent four of them in each of three galleys packed with additional sergeants and archers "in case of pirates." Their sergeant captains were ordered to deposit the chests in our Malta post and use all of their archers to guard the post even if it meant leaving their galleys unguarded in the harbour so that they were lost.

"The chests are everything," Harold told them most solemnly as I nodded my head in agreement. "Put them in your stern castles under heavy guard and did not let them get wet or be lost to pirates. Parade your men and stress the importance of the chests you are carrying. Take no chances. It is better to lose your galley than the chests."

I reinforced what Harold said about the importance of the chests.

"Your galleys are nothing compared to the importance of guarding those chests. Lose your galleys if you must but guard those chests. Make sure your men understand that in case you fall in battle defending them. We will be sending additional galleys as reinforcements to help you convey the chests safely from Malta to London."

We did not tell the galley captains and their men that the chests they were guarding contained the missing Orthodox relics for which we had been searching. That, after all, was a secret. And, of course, with so many men involved, every tavern keeper and spy in the Mediterranean soon knew exactly what we were doing.

******

It was a brisk spring day in the middle of April when Randolph and I sailed from Cyprus on Harold's galley. Yoram waved us as we rowed out of the harbour, and then went back to close the gates into our fortress with its greatly reduced guard force and three crenelated defensive walls with battlements and a fourth under construction.

Until we returned, Yoram would have to defend it primarily with a thousand or so able-bodied workmen and women. We did, however, leave him with thirty good archers and several very good sergeants—every man of them with a family inside its walls who needed defending.

Yoram and our men's families would be safe in a highly fortified citadel with its own water well and a huge amount of siege supplies. By our reckoning, taking our Cyprus fortress would require a large army willing to conduct a long siege and take many thousands of casualties.

As you might imagine, a serious attack was not expected although one can never be sure with Moors and crusaders. The city of Limassol, on the other hand, would be easier to take and provide more plunder.

Sailing out of the harbour with us were a number of galleys carrying almost all the archers we could mobilize including a number of newly promoted apprentices and the veteran archers taken from our pirate-taking cogs. Other archers would be sailing or had already sailed from other ports as needed to reach Malta on or about April 28th. Nine more were coming all the way to Malta from England and Lisbon "to help guard an important shipment."

Our pirate-taking cogs and several others had already sailed for Malta with enough supplies on board to make it all the way without stopping as we would usually do at Crete for supplies. They were loaded with the additional food supplies, ladders, fire pots, and arrows our raiders would need.

The sailors and archers in the crews of the supply cogs did not know it yet, but they would not be allowed to go ashore when they reached Malta or made any unscheduled stops. Why? Because we did not want anyone to find about the cargos they were carrying; word might reach the Moors and alert them to the possibility of a raid.

******

Our main fleet of galleys left Cyprus ten days later and reached Malta despite a rather severe storm that scattered us all about. The harbour was soon crowded as more and more of our galleys and cogs arrived. We were more than ready to stop for a rest. It had been a difficult trip because of the storm, with a stop at Crete for water and supplies.

"So you found them, eh?" the old pirate and long-time friend, Brindisi, said as he lifted his bowl in his favourite tavern and looked at me intently. "Or did you?"

"My men are not allowed to say anything so I cannot tell you either," was my reply with a big beaming smile on my face as I took a sip of wine. "This is very good wine, by the way."

I was trying to change the subject, but it did not work. Brindisi would not let it go.

"I am aware that you have three almost-empty galleys in the harbour whose men are all ashore guarding your trading post, and that you have heavily loaded cogs anchored in the harbour whose men are not allowed ashore. And now you are here with all those galleys and men. Everyone is talking?"

He said it as a question and looked at me carefully to see my response.

I lowered my voice and responded.

"It is not the pirates I fear," I admitted. Then I leaned forward and confided the truth to Brindisi, at least some of it.

"It was King John and all the princes. They all want the relics because the Pope has promised great things to any prince who donates them to the Church, even the crown of the Holy Roman Empire and no time in purgatory. They were worth a fortune.

"The problem is that everyone wants them, but not everyone is able to pay the high price needed to buy them. I fear there would be an attempt to steal the relics from us in England or Germany unless they are well-guarded. So I have called in all my archers to guard them until I can sell them."

My answer delighted the old pirate.

"I knew you were smart, William, but you have outdone us all with this one. Where would you sell the prizes you take?"

I took my elbows off the wooden table, rocked back on my stool, and looked at him in astonishment.

"*Do* not worry, my friend. I am too old and out of touch to try to take your place and do what you are doing. I thought about doing it years ago but never had enough men. Besides, it would be good for Malta and Sicily if you succeed in reducing the number of pirates. I would not say a word."

"Lisbon and London, I should think," I finally said with a shrug and a resigned and disbelieving shake of my head. "At least, at first; just as we did with the French fleet."

Chapter Twenty-six

Our men are surprised.

It took almost a week for the last of our storm-blown stragglers to come in. The final arrivals were the galleys of a couple of sheepish sergeant captains who had been travelling together. They had gone past the island in the night and continued on for three days until they realized they needed to turn around. The harbour was already packed with anchored galleys and cogs, and our galleys moored to the quay three and four deep by the time they arrived.

******

We began our final preparations "to leave for London via Ibiza and Lisbon" as soon as our last two arrivals finished taking on water and supplies and the weather and wind improved.

Everyone, including the locals who thronged the street to cheer and cross themselves, were quite impressed when we ceremoniously carried the crates from our post and loaded them on Harold's galley. It was a solemn procession led by a gaggle of chanting priests from the city. Of course, the priests were leading the way; we had asked them to accompany the crates to the quay with prayers, and suggested that a donation would be forthcoming if they did.

The sea was calm with favourable light winds when Harold assembled our galleys and cogs out to the middle of the big harbour for a meeting to talk about "how we are going to convoy an important cargo to Lisbon and London." It was a chilly spring day on the Mediterranean coast and spirits were high.

Harold moved away from the quay, dropped his anchor in the middle of the harbour, and ordered one of his sailors to wave the "all captains" flag. We were soon bobbing in the waves surrounded by galleys and cogs. Everywhere there were dinghies rowing towards us and every one of them had a somewhat excited sergeant captain on board.

The "captains call" had been expected. One does not, after all, sail all the way to England without someone telling him what to do and where to go. And it had to be done so that no one would go ashore afterwards and reveal our plans.

I greeted each captain by name as he climbed aboard until they were finally all assembled. *Harold had to help me with some of the names*. There were so many of them that they packed the deck. I climbed on to the roof of the forward castle to talk to them. Harold and Randolph joined me.

"Now I can finally share some things with you," I told them. "And they are secret things you must not share with your sergeants and men until you have cleared the harbour and can no longer see Malta.

"You all believe, I think, that we are here to escort some important religious relics to England. Well, it is true we are on our way to England with some important crates. But it was not true that we are out here *only* to guard some religious relics.

"That is all ox shite we put out to gull the Moors. What we are really doing out here is getting ready to raid Tunis for prisoners we can exchange for the archers and sailors the Moors recently captured, and to take Moorish galleys and cogs as prizes." *And after that we are going to raid other Moorish ports as well, but I will tell you about those later.*

There was a moment of stunned silence at my announcement. Then the sergeant captains began cheering and laughing and throwing their caps in the air. Then the chanting started and got louder and louder as it rolled out over the water to the galleys and cogs surrounding us and they punched their fists into the air with each word— "Archers. .. Archers. .. Archers. .. Archers."

After a while I held both my hands up for silence so I could continue. *The men on the galleys and cogs must be beside themselves wondering what the hell is going on. Well, they would know soon enough, would not they?*

"This raid would be different from all our previous raids. There are important relics and we have them. That means we are sailing under God's special protection. So, whilst we are protected by God, we are going to raid Tunis for prizes and prisoners, we are also going to try to get into the city and completely destroy its boat works and shipping, even its fishing boats.

"When it was all over, we will send our prizes to Lisbon and London to sell, and use our cogs as prisons to carry our captives to the abandoned governor's castle at Limassol. That is where we will hold them until we can exchange them for our captured men and their passengers."

The cheering and chanting started again.

******

My lieutenants and I spent the entire rest of the day talking to small groups of the galley sergeants about the role each would have in the raid. We were highly organized with specific written orders for each and every galley and cog—where to go in the harbour to take prizes; where to land its archers and who they were to follow; when to withdraw; what to do with prisoners; where to send their prizes; where to rally afterwards if we were forced to leave the harbour.

There was a long list of instructions for each and every galley and cog. *Little wonder in that; we had spent months working on the list for each of them.*

The sergeant captains could not read, of course, so each had his orders loudly read to him and his questions answered whilst his fellow sergeant captains stood by and listened intently. Every one of them had already been on at least two or three major raids in one capacity or another, and so already had a good idea of what he and his men were expected to do. Even so, there were a number of good questions and some foolish ones that suggested a couple of our galleys might have the wrong man in command.

Too late to change captains now, I thought to myself; it was always that way, is it not?

******

Messengers rowed dinghies out to the galleys whilst we were talking to the captains. They ordered them, in Harold's name, to bring their galleys to the cogs to begin taking on special supplies such as the longer boarding ladders and the fire-starting bundles of twigs and the fire pots.

We stayed together in the harbour all that night, and, as you might well imagine at a port that was likely to be full of Moorish spies, no one was allowed to go ashore for fear he might reveal our intentions.

Of course that is what we did; our men had not yet been told that we would be raiding on the way to England to deliver the relics as they had come to believe, but they knew about the boarding ladders and such being loaded and it would not take too sharp of a spy to know a big raid was coming.

******

As soon as the sun came up the next morning, I once again had one of Harold's sailors wave the "all captains" flag from the mast. It was brisk and chilly as the sergeant captains once again assembled. They stamped their feet to stay warm and ate chunks of cheese and hot flat-bread while they waited for our meeting to begin. Harold's cook had stayed up all night getting it ready.

Once again I stood on the roof of the forward castle with my lieutenants and summarized what we were going to do and how we were going to do it. Then we again called on each captain to briefly tell us what his galley and its archers were to do and ask if he had any questions or suggestions. As you might expect, the answers and suggestions got better and better, and the questions fewer and fewer, as the sergeants listened to each other. There were many questions. They were asked and answered loudly so everyone could hear.

Finally, many hours later, there was silence when I again asked "Any more questions and suggestions?"

The sergeant captains were sent back to their galleys and cogs and about thirty minutes after that Harold hoisted the "follow me" flag and we led a long line of galleys and cogs out of the harbour.

The cogs had to be towed out of the harbour because the wind coming off the island was not right. They had waited offshore for a couple of days to insure our secret did not get out. Then they had returned to wait for the prisoners we hoped to bring them and for some orders they would not expect.

Chapter Twenty-seven

We visit Tunis.

We sailed all that day and all the next two with Harold's galley leading the way and the others close around it. The cogs left us at the end of the first day to sail back to Malta to await our return.

No effort was made to hurry. To the contrary, the men were provided with all the food they could eat and rowing was kept to a minimum. This was done so every man's arms and strength would be at their best when we hit Tunis. Each night our galleys showed candle lanterns on their masts and we stayed so close together that there were a number of very minor bumps and collisions. They were inevitable.

Twice our lookouts saw sails in the distance and twice we ignored them. They were cogs whose captains wanted no part of a fleet of war galleys. We never did see a Moorish galley, let alone one that might have been able to get to Tunis to sound the alarm.

Had we seen a galley we would have chased it down and taken it for sure. Harold kept two of our fastest galleys close to his for just such an eventuality. They would have quickly caught a slave-rowed Moor and put a permanent end to its crew of sailors and the untrained thieves and cutthroats of its boarding party.

******

Harold's galley led fifty-five of our fifty-six war galleys into Tunis's great harbour as if we owned the place. Harold and I and many of our men had been here before and it had not changed. We knew exactly where to send our galleys and what each should do. Harold's was not the first of our galleys to enter the harbour however. One of our galleys was already here. It had rowed slowly into the harbour last night right after the sun finished passing overhead and quietly anchored just off the quay opposite the big gate through the city walls. Its deck was empty and it was dark. No one saw the more than two hundred archers jammed into its castles and rowing decks.

The only men on the galley's deck had been two Christian Arabs from Beirut, long-time members of our Company and former galley slaves with an intense hatred for anything Islamic. They stayed on the galleys deck all night. Had anyone inquired of them, and no one did, they would have replied in fluent Moorish and attempted to gull them. In the darkness, no one even saw the steady stream of men who, one at a time, came out of the deck castles and off the rowing benches to piss and shite in the harbour.

When the sun arrived the next day, the two Moorish-speaking men were joined in their early morning prayers by six men who went below when they finished praying. A few minutes later the galley slowly rowed towards the quay. No one paid a bit of attention to the galley, though, had they thought about it, they might have found it strange that someone was in the lookout's nest when the galley was in the harbour. Perhaps he was fixing something.

What was not strange at all was that the two Arabic-speaking men climbed on to the quay, moored the galley, and began leisurely walking up the path towards the city gate. A moment or so later, two other men came out of the forward castle dressed as Moorish sailors and followed after them. No one said a word and no one hurried. Before they reached the gate, the four men turned off and went to the city wall forty or fifty paces from the gate. There they squatted down to wait. They were obviously waiting for someone.

******

A quiet word and gesture came from the lookout as soon as he saw Harold's galley enter the harbour and head straight for them. It was moving at top speed with its oars beating the sea around it to a froth.

The handful of early morning Islamic workers and sailors still praying on the quay and on the decks of the nearby transports suddenly began to sit up and stare at the recently moored galley. They were dumbfounded as the quiet and virtually deserted-appearing galley suddenly erupted into frenzied activity.

Several hundred men carrying long, bladed pikes and longbows suddenly began pouring off the newly moored galley and running as fast as they could down the quay and up the cart path towards the recently opened city gate. The running men never said a word, not one word, as they passed through the open gate and into the city. The only sound was their heavy breathing and the slap of their sandals on the cart path running from the quay to the gate.

It was a big and heavy gate. The handful of city guards who had opened it an hour or so earlier when the sun arrived had not seen the sudden activity on the galley moored to the quay. Even if they had seen it, they would not have had time to close the gate before the four men who had been lounging nearby cut them down. The four men checked the dead guards as they stripped off their Moorish sailor clothes—that had been covering the distinctive hooded Egyptian gowns of English archers with the stripes of their ranks sewed on to their fronts and backs.

The huffing and puffing archers running up from the quay were alert and excited as Randolph and his three men greeted them and put them into their assigned positions. It was something they had practiced together over and over again using one of the gates to our Cyprus fortress.

This time it was for real and the four men's initial assignment was simple—they were to do whatever was necessary to hold the city gate open until reinforcements could arrive from the galley to relieve them.

******

Harold had his rowers rowing hard as we came charging through the entrance to the big harbour and headed straight for the quay in front of the city gate. More than forty galleys similarly packed with archers were right behind us. Others coming in behind us headed for the Moorish galleys pulled up on the beach off to the left of the quay, and five moved into position to block the harbour entrance so none of the Moorish shipping could escape. We had surprised the Moors just as they had surprised our galleys and cogs at Beirut and the other Holy Land ports.

"Follow me," I shouted as Andrew Priest and I vaulted over the galley railing and led more than a hundred archers from Harold's galley on a run towards the city. All around us galleys were unloading archers and their sergeants were hurrying them to the city gate as fast as they could run.

Almost every archer was also carrying a land-fighting shield and either extra quivers of arrows or a bladed pike. Many were sweating from their exertions as they reached the gate even though there was still a chill in the morning air. It was very exciting.

Randolph and his reinforced Company of archers were not waiting at the gate for me and the archers following me. He had already rushed off with his apprentice sergeant and men to the city's huge central market. It was his task to lead his men to the city's market and capture it as soon as the city gate was secured.

******

Our raid had taken the Moors of Tunis by surprise just as the Moors had surprised us at Beirut and elsewhere when they made their great raid a few months ago. Within minutes, we had over two thousand heavily armed archers inside the walls of Tunis.

Our casualties and the Tunisians were minimal as there had been no fighting of any significance. The only casualties were the three gate guards Randolph and his men cut down. They were off to the side of the gate and already covered by swarms of flies attracted to the pools of rapidly drying blood around them.

Tunis was mostly silent except for barking dogs, and its winding and narrow shite-strewn streets were empty as I double-timed the archer Company from Harold's galley to join Randolph's Company in the market. The few people we saw in the streets took one look at us and either darted inside their shops and homes or hurried away down the narrow side lanes.

We passed through the open gate and turned right to go to the city's main market next to its great mosque. The sound of our running feet and heavy breathing was all that could be heard as we pounded down the narrow lane. No one said a word to us as we passed, but we could see and feel people watching us from the rooftops and the window openings in the sleeping rooms above the windowless rooms and courtyard walls at the street level.

A few minutes after we passed through the city gate we reached the city's central market. It was a huge area of merchant stalls and workshops next to the city's main mosque. Randolph and the bulk of the men from his galley were in the open area between the stalls and the mosque arrayed in battle formation. A smaller force of his men was at the holding pens at the far end of the market where the slaves and live animals were sold.

"Hoy, Lieutenant. What is the word?" I asked with a gasp as I came to a stop and bent over to ease the pain in my side and catch my breath. *I am getting too old for this shite.*

"So far so good, Captain. The heathens' morning prayers were over by the time we got here and we have seen no one carrying weapons, at least not yet. That is going to change, of course, and this is where the fighting is likely to start. The merchants have disappeared from the market as you might expect.

"The good news is that we found four of our men from one of the cogs we lost. Over there in the cages of the slave market they were; some of their passengers were with them.

"Two of the archers we released," Randolph said with a shrug, "promptly gutted one of the slavers we caught who had been guarding them. They said he had killed one of our men and they had sworn to kill him if ever they ever had a chance."

"Good work. Keep to the plan, Lieutenant—do not let any of the heathens get into the mosque for the priests to organize and do not let your men start burning the city until we see what happens. Maybe, just maybe, the merchants will return to the market and we can work out something to get our captured men back peacefully whilst we finish destroying the city's shipping—but I doubt it so do not wait a heartbeat if you see people carrying weapons. Go for them instantly and kill them.

"Alright then," I concluded. "Lieutenant, I am going to go on to the king's palace to see how Edward the shepherd and his men are faring, and then back to the quay to see how Harold and his men are doing in the harbour."

Randolph and I spoke loudly and formally so the archers around us could hear. It was important for the men to know we were organized and following a plan; gives them confidence, does it not?

More and more archers continued to pour into the market as we spoke. Randolph was already assigning them to positions in his battle formation as I waved my arm in a circle above my head and then pointed in the next direction I intended to lead my galley Company of archers. It was time to visit Edward Shepherd and his men at the castle inside the city's walls where the King lives.

Edward's a steady old archer who had run away as a lad from his father's life as a shepherd serf. He was not one of our original Company but both Henry and Peter thought highly of him and had recommended him for a fifth stripe and a leadership role in our raids. Edward had, I hoped, led six galley companies of archers, about five hundred men, through the city gate and all the way to the royal castle on the little hill beyond the great mosque. At least, that is where he was supposed to lead them.

******

Edward saluted by knuckling his head and calling his men to attention when I puffed my way up to him with my bad leg beginning to hurt the way it does in England when the weather is cold and wet. I knuckled mine back and gave him a great friendly clap on his shoulders. His

Our new senior sergeant's men were in battle formation. I could see from the bodies on the ground that there had been fighting between Edward's men and the Moorish king's guards whose barracks were in a big square building next to the King's castle.

From where I was standing with Edward and his men, I could see what looked to be a galley's Company of archers in a smaller battle formation further on along the castle wall. I could also see a number of dead Moors on the ground in front of us between the King's castle and the nearby barracks. A dozen or more archers were moving among them to pick up reusable arrows and strip the dead Moors of their weapons. We would be taking them with us when we left, the weapons that is.

Edward quickly filled me in as to what had taken place.

"Them Moors out there on the ground are likely to have been castle guards who were away from their posts when we arrived. They came a charging out of that building over there in an effort to get into the castle and we cut them down with our arrows. Unfortunately, the castle gate was closed when we got here; yes it was."

Many things soon became clear—that the surviving guards had retreated back into their rooms with their wounded, that Edward had both the castle and the rooms of its guards surrounded, that he was keeping his men back far enough from the castle's walls and the guards' rooms to be out of crossbow range, and that he did not have nearly enough men.

Edward's men were in positions that we wanted to hold, so I quickly sent Edward with a guard of several dozen archers double-timing back to take command of our reserves at the main gate—with orders to send six more galley companies here to the King's castle immediately. I would take over the command of the men who were already here.

******

I waited until the six heavily armed galley companies of archers arrived, all breathless and puffing, and were distributed in the open area around the walled palace and the barracks. Then I pulled back the men in front of the palace gate and sent one of our interpreters forward unarmed, shouting, and waving a piece of linen over his head. *He knew to jabber Moorish because he was a long-time slave who had made his mark and joined us after we freed him; he volunteered to go forward alone and would put on a stripe for it.*

After a fairly long wait, a man wearing a very large turban came out of a small low door built into the gate. It was almost funny because he had trouble ducking his head down low enough to get out through the door.

The two men talked for a while with many hand gestures. The turbaned man then went back through his little door and our interpreter returned to me.

"He is gone to get a higher ranking official. I did as you said and told him that we had taken the city and that one of our captains was here and wanted to talk— and that, if the talks were not successful, we would begin burning down the city in addition to destroying all the shipping in the harbour."

We waited.

Suddenly, we all jumped and a shiver ran through our ranks as the big gate swung open for a few seconds and an ornately dressed man wearing an absolutely huge turban stepped out. A man with a much smaller turban accompanied him, obviously some kind of attendant or interpreter. The gate immediately closed behind them.

It was a good thing Big Turban did not try to use the little door in the gate; he would not have gotten through it. I had to repress a smile at the thought.

I put down my sword and shield and walked forward with my interpreter. Whilst we were walking towards the two men, I noticed Big Turban looking aghast at the bodies of the Moorish guards on the ground where they had fallen. I did not say a word when I stopped about ten paces from the two Moors; I just waited.

Big Turban finally spoke for quite some time. My interpreter listened carefully and then repeated it to me in English. "He says his master wants to know who you are and what you want." *He sure as hell said more than that.*

"Tell him we are from England. … Tell him we are here because Tunisian galleys attacked shipping and ports east of Malta. … Tell him we would stay here until we finish destroying Tunis's shipping and Tunis frees every one of its Christian and Jewish slaves. … Tell him that if the Christian and Jewish slaves, every single one them, are not at the city gate by sundown we would sack the city and burn it to the ground.

"Also, tell him if we ever again find one of Tunis's galleys east of Malta, or hear of Christian or Jewish slaves being in Tunis or on its galleys, we would return and kill you and your king and destroy Tunis."

Finally, I told him exactly why we had come.

"I am here with my men because your galleys and those of your Moorish friends captured over one hundred English archers and sailors, and several hundred of their passengers, during your big raid on Beirut and elsewhere a few months ago.

"All of them in Tunis must be returned today; and all those being held elsewhere must be immediately freed and sent to Ibiza. If you already sold them, you best hurry to get them back and free them. My men have been ordered to return and burn Tunis to the ground if we ever hear of so much as one Englishman or one of our passengers being held or sold as a slave."

Then I leaned forward, poked the poor sod in the chest with my finger, and made him a promise.

"We want those people immediately freed. Failure to do so would result in me returning and personally cutting your king's stomach open and pulling his guts out while he is still alive and pissing on them—while my men do the same to every one of his courtiers, including you."

Big Turban's eyes got bigger and bigger as my interpreter told him what I was saying. His mouth was hanging open with a look of disbelief and his hands were shaking by the time I finished.

He was clearly aghast at what he had been told. "I would convey your request to my master."

"That was not a request," I snarled. "It was a promise and your master best believe it and act quickly if he wants to avoid a very painful death."

I said it emphatically and loudly and gave him a hard look whilst I waited for my interpreter to finish. The archers standing at the front of the men behind me heard what I said and nodded their agreement most grimly.

Later, Peter and Harold both told me that I looked quite fearsome what with my face all chopped and such. It seemed to work; Big Turban began shaking.

I continued after my interpreter finished.

"We are English archers and we always keep our promises and are willing to fight to keep our passengers and cargos safe; that is why the merchants in every port prefer to use our galleys and cogs. I have made your master a promise of taking his head and guts, and yours, and I have made it in front of my men. It was best for your master that he believes what I have said to you. He will die most foul if he does not, and so would you."

After I gave him another hard look I told him what needed to be done to save the city.

"Now it was time for your master to do what is needed to save Tunis and his castle from being burned to the ground—and he must do it immediately.

"First, he must send unarmed men out from his palace to announce throughout the city that all those prisoners and all the Christian and Jewish slaves in the city are to be immediately sent to the city gate in front of the harbour. Every single prisoner from the recent raid and every single Christian and Jew in the city must be there by sundown or we will sack the city and find them for ourselves.

"Second, before prayers can begin again in this church your King must deliver twenty thousand gold bezants or its equivalent in silver and gold to me for my men's trouble. If he does not bring us the coins and free the prisoners, we would supply ourselves by sea and stay here until his castle falls—and we will tear down that big church over there and burn the city to the ground whilst we are waiting.

"But mark you this," I said with a snarl as I again poked his chest with my finger.

"Even if the coins are paid and the slaves freed, if we ever find even one Christian or Jewish slave on a Tunisian galley or transport, or even one Tunisian galley east of Malta, we will return and I would personally take your King's head and guts and those of all his courtiers and sack the city. That is my promise to your master in front of my men." *My men nodded; they approved.*

"I would tell my master what you said," the man agreed.

He started to turn away to return to the palace. But then he turned back and asked, "Is your master the man they call Richard?"

"No," I replied. "Richard is dead. God took him because he did not keep his promises when his enemies surrendered to him. Now the captain of the English with longbows and galleys in these waters is William and he always keeps his promises. Then I exaggerated.

"William and his men are ten times more powerful than Richard."

I exaggerated our strength and I lied about Richard. He was not dead because he did not keep his word when prisoners surrendered; he was dead because he was foolish enough to get too close to the wall of a castle he had no need to attack and a boy got him with a crossbow. But Richard's dead, so it really does not matter if we use him to get what we want, does it?

Chapter Twenty-eight

Tunis surrenders and I regret my decision.

As the day wore on and rapidly got warmer and warmer, a well-guarded runner brought me a message from Edward who was now in command at the city gate. More than forty of our missing men and passengers had already arrived at the gate along with over a thousand newly freed slaves, many more than we had expected.

All of the released archers and their passengers were ecstatic at being freed, he said, and so were the Jews. Some were in terrible condition and ill-clothed, but many were not.

But there was an unexpected problem, Edward reported. Some of the newly freed slaves who showed up at the city gate wanted to stay in Tunis and remain as slaves. They said they were too old or too settled to start a new life in someplace new and begged to be allowed to remain in Tunis. Not even assurances from the former slaves in our ranks about the availability of work and a good life on Cyprus could change their minds.

"What should I do?" Edward asked.

An hour or so later, servants came out of the door in the castle gate with chests holding the coins needed to ransom the city. Actually, not all of the ransom payment was in coins; there was an extensive amount of women's gold and silver rings and necklaces in the chests. It looked about right, however, and I accepted it.

I sent the servants who delivered the ransom back with a message to the city's ruler. I told him that he could keep the Christian slaves who wanted to remain in Tunis without losing his head or guts, and then I sent a message to Edward saying he could send them home.

******

All of the Tunisian cogs and galleys were either anchored in the harbour with prize captains and crews on board or burned by the time the sun finished circling the earth and darkness fell. So were eight cargo transports from distant lands and three unlucky Tunisian transports that had sailed into the harbour after we arrived. We took them all.

The Tunisians never did make an effort to retake our prizes. They could not have tried even if they wanted, according to a message I received from Harold, because we had taken or destroyed everything that floated.

"No one can get to our prizes anchored in the harbour unless he knows how to swim" was how Harold put it.

It was an important message because it meant our galleys and prizes could safely stay in the harbour overnight as we had hoped and planned. I promptly sent a message to Randolph telling him to hold his position until my men and I fell back on him in the morning, and another to Edward and Harold telling them Randolph and I would lead our men in to the city gate tomorrow late the next morning.

We stayed overnight because I had a great fear of leaving men behind in the confusion if we tried to leave in the dark with our newly freed men and the slaves. We had long ago decided that it would be better to leave the next day when we were better organized and each sergeant could count his men.

******

That night our forces remained concentrated in the open area between the market and the mosque, at the city gate, and around the King's palace. We made no attempt to patrol the city. The market and mosque remained closed and empty; the city's narrow lanes remained deserted. The people of Tunis were fearful and rightly so.

There had been a few scattered incidents during the day, so we expected the worst and remained alert and ready in battle formation all that night. We were not disappointed. Scattered groups of Tunisians came at us in the dark. The darkness made them braver and it was hard to see them until they were almost on top of us. All in all, we lost two men killed during the night and a number of our men were injured, many from stones that were thrown in the darkness. Most of the injuries were not serious.

******

On the morning after our raid, we burned the city's two shipyards to the ground and carried off all of the shipwrights' tools we could find. The newly freed slaves, many of whom had spent a nervous and chilly night in the darkness waiting outside the harbour-side gate, were loaded the next morning on some of the newly taken cogs for carrying to Malta. Smoke from the burning shipyard drifted over the harbour as the slaves filed aboard our galleys.

"We will sort them out when we get back to Malta," Harold told everyone who inquired about our plans for the slaves. *Yes, we were going back to Malta instead of westward towards Lisbon and London; there were still too many Moorish pirates afloat and we did not know where they might be. We did not want to risk losing our lightly crewed prizes to chance encounters.*

Harold had come ashore at dawn to help supervise the loading of our men and the newly freed slaves from the city and from the galleys we had taken. Under his direction, some of our archers were returned to their galleys but many, perhaps even most, were assigned to our prizes as guards. For the safety of their prize crews, the galley slaves, except for a few who were British and French, were well fed and watered but remained in chains. They would be freed as soon as they reached Malta.

The British and French who had been released, including nine of our men who had been taken at Beirut, were immediately armed and sent to the galleys and cogs carrying the released slaves who wanted to leave Tunis.

It was late in the afternoon when I nodded to Harold and he had one of his sailors climb the mast and wave the "follow me" flag. A few moments later the sound of rowing drums began to reach us from across the water. It was time to go; we needed to clear the harbour whilst it was still light enough to see.

Tunisians crowded the shoreline, the rooftops, and the quay to watch us go.

I had second thoughts as I passed through the harbour entrance into the sea beyond and I have held them ever since. I still regret how we behaved in Tunis. We should have sacked the city while we had the opportunity, driven the Arabs into the desert, and tore it down as the Romans did to Carthage.

Chapter Twenty-nine

The archers are surprised at what happens next"

"That was a bad mistake, William, one you will come to regret even though you took so many prizes and broke their backs for years to come."

Enrico Brindisi, the former pirate and long-time ruler of Malta on behalf of the King of Sicily, looked at me sadly as he said it.

"You are right, my dear friend Enrico, you are right," I admitted somewhat drunkenly. "There is no question about it; we should have stayed and destroyed Tunis before we came back to Malta."

After a pause and a disgusted shake of my head, I tried to explain.

"What is worse, I knew it as soon as we started rowing out of the harbour and I looked back at the city. I guess I was too anxious to get to England with the relics."

That was my excuse because I did not want the old pirate to know what I was going to do when we leave

Malta. But it was not a very good excuse since the relics were already in England. I wondered if he had figured out what we were going to do next?

"Ah well. Who am I to speak, eh? I probably could have taken Tunis when I got back from my horrible year as a prisoner in Germany. But I dithered and let my galleys decline and my captains leave and go elsewhere until it was too late. Now all I can do is sit in the sun and drink wine."

"Tell me about Germany, Enrico. What are the German princes like? Can I trust them if they say they would buy the relics? The only ones I ever met were crusaders"

******

It was an exciting time to be in Malta with my men. Our return from Tunis with so many prizes had initially resulted in a great celebration with drunken men and women crowding the quay and the city streets and frequent fights over women and wine skins.

Order was finally restored when I ordered the men confined to their galleys and cogs and for them to be anchored in the middle of the harbour so none of our men could get ashore. A sergeant carrying a sword and shield and two similarly armed chosen men from each galley had been sent ashore to help keep order; that had helped reduce the turmoil even more.

I also dried up the sale of wine on credit by announcing that the prize coins due each man would not be paid until the prizes were sold, and that no coins could be withdrawn from those on deposit until the men withdrawing them were away from Malta.

As you might expect, the restrictions caused the men to grumble as good fighting men always do; but they were not angry because the orders were so obviously necessary and reasonable. Thereafter, our archers and sailors were only allowed to go ashore in groups of three and only for a short time to have a bowl of wine and a quick dip of their dingles in the local tavern girls—with each man standing surety for the other two. Then they had to return to their galleys and cogs so another group of three could take their places.

Once we regained control of our men and newly released slaves, my lieutenants and I spent the next couple of days inspecting our prizes and trying to decide that of them to send to Lisbon and London to sell, and that to send to Cyprus to have Yoram enter into our service. Those going east to Cyprus to enter our service would carry released slaves who wanted to head in that direction and skeleton crews of volunteers, primarily sailors. We sent them with only a few fighting men on board because, as everyone knew, we would need our archers elsewhere to help guard the relics.

It was somewhat of a risky decision to send our prizes and freed slaves east with only sailors and a handful of archers to maintain order. However, after much discussion, we had decided it was a risk worth taking, both because we had knocked out the most easterly part of the huge Moorish fleet, the Tunisians, and because any pirates who met our galleys and cogs would be fearful of approaching them because they might be loaded with hidden archers and boarding parties as was our custom.

Besides all that, and most important of all, we wanted to take as many fighting men as possible to England to help guard the relics.

In any event, not all the released slaves and prisoners would be sailing to Crete and on to Cyprus and the Holy Land ports. Some of them signed on to join the Company as apprentice archers and sailors and would go wherever we ordered them to go; others wanted to travel west with us to the Spanish coast and even all the way on to England and France.

If those who chose to sail west with us had known what we are going to do on our way to England, many of them probably would have opted for Cyprus. The only thing certain was that they had to go in one direction or the other—Brindisi did not want any of the freed prisoners and slaves staying in Malta "because their idle hands would undoubtedly cause unrest and thievery to rise."

Brindisi was a wise man who would have made a fine king of a great state.

******

The prizes we decided to take into our service were long gone on their way to Cyprus and it was a windy and lightly raining day when we once again began sailing west from Malta. It began in the morning when Harold had the "all captains" flag waved from his mast. The quay was empty except for Brindisi's city guards; all of our galleys and cogs were anchored in the harbour

The sergeant captains of our remaining cogs and galleys had been told to expect the "all captains" signal. They promptly got in their dinghies and had themselves rowed to where Harold's galley was anchored in the middle of the harbour.

It took a while for all of them to assemble; the addition of some of the prizes we took in Tunis made our westbound fleet much larger than it had been before our raid. It was the first "all captains" for the newly appointed sergeant captains of the prizes we were taking to Lisbon and London to sell.

We talked and bantered as we waited for the late arrivals, and Harold and I made it a point to greet the newly promoted prize captains and get to know them better.

All in all, it was quite a happy and optimistic band of men who climbed over the railing and on to Harold's deck. There was no surprise in that—we had won big in Tunis, our losses had been minimal, and every man on Harold's deck was looking forward to a goodly amount of prize money. On top of that, the prize captains had been told that they would keep their new ranks and their commands if they got their prizes to London.

Some of the men on Harold's deck had never been to London before and were asking those who had already been there about the tides, making one has way up the crowded Thames, and such-like—the kind of questions that inevitably come up whenever the sergeant captains of our cogs and galleys get together to discuss ports and operations.

They all looked up expectantly as Harold and Randolph and I climbed on to the roof of the forward castle to tell them how their cogs and galleys were going to fit into the convoy guarding our precious cargo during its voyage to London via Ibiza and Lisbon. *They all knew about the chests of relics scattered through the fleet, the ones we were secretly taking to London; it was a secret that had somehow gotten out and once out, could not be contained.*

I began by addressing what had been a major topic in the taverns and around the water barrels during the past few days—who would be in the crews of each of the galleys and cogs going to Ibiza and when would some of the archers and sailors still crowded into the galleys start moving to their new berths in the under-crewed prize cogs?

"I am sure you are all wondering why each of our galleys has taken on so much more in the way of supplies than would normally be shipped for a full crew going to Ibiza and Lisbon and on to London. You are probably also wondering why some our galleys are still stuffed with archers and prize crews whilst our cogs and the prize cogs we are taking to Lisbon and London to sell have taken on similarly large amounts of supplies and did not have archers on board to protect them.

"The answer could be," I said with a big smile as I threw my arms wide, "that Lieutenant Randolph and I enjoy buying supplies in the market and that in all the excitement Lieutenant Harold has forgotten how to assign archers and sailors to crews."

That got a big round of happy laughter and friendly shouts and calls.

"And you are right, we should redistribute our archers and sailors more evenly so that every one of our galleys and cogs is better able to protect itself and our valuable cargos as it sails from here to Ibiza and then on to Lisbon and London."

Then I dropped a rock on them when I added, "Except not everyone is going directly to Ibiza—some of you would be going on your galleys with Senior Sergeant Edward Shepherd to look for Moorish prizes in all the little ports along the coast west between Tunis and Algiers including Bizerte." *I emphasised the word "some."*

I smiled at the resulting "ohs" and "ahs" and exclamations that came from the assembled men; and after a long pause while things settled down, I raised my hands for silence and added, "And neither are the rest of our galleys going directly to Ibiza—we are going to sail to

Algiers first and take more prizes." *And try to destroy the place.*

There was a moment of stunned silence before the cheering erupted.

******

Edward Shepherd and his eight captains were the first to be given their orders. Edward was given the overall command of nine fully crewed galleys. Their orders were simple—they were to stay together and move along the Moorish coastline and look in at all small ports along the way.

Why did I want them to look in at the small ports? Because we had been told, and it sounded reasonable, that many of the Moorish coastal villages usually had a couple of locally-owned cogs and a pirate galley or two in their harbours. That, apparently, was how the people of the smaller Moorish ports earned their coins and served their King instead of paying taxes. It was very much like the way we archers and the portsmen of Hastings and the other Cinque Ports earn our coins and serve King John.

The orders for the sergeant captains and crews of the prizes being taken to be sold in Lisbon and London came next. They were to stay quarantined here in the middle of the harbour for at least three days and then sail in the next good weather straight to Ibiza. They would rendezvous with us in Ibiza's harbour—some or all of our galleys were expected to be there when our cogs and prizes arrived.

In the event our galleys had not yet arrived, our cogs and prizes were to stay anchored in the middle of the harbour on high alert, and not tie up at the quay or allow their men to go ashore until enough of our archer-crewed galleys entered the harbour to be able to protect them. *Our precautions were warranted; Ibiza was, at the time, caught up in the religious conflict between the Pope who wanted it to become a Papal State and the followers of the Orthodox Patriarch who wanted it left alone with Orthodox priests and nobles in control.*

Amidst many congratulatory cheers and much manly hugs and back-slapping, a sergeant captain recommended by Harold was told to put up another stripe and take command of the cogs and prizes going directly to Ibiza to await the arrival of our galleys. And, as you might imagine, the cogs and prizes going to Ibiza were quarantined and told to wait here in the harbour for a couple of days before they sailed for Ibiza; we did not want to take a chance that they would be taken by a

Moorish pirate and word of our raid would reach Algiers before our galleys arrived.

The orders for the galleys going to Algiers came next and took the most time even though they were very similar to the orders we gave to the sergeant captains for the raid on Tunis.

"Basically, it would be the same as Tunis except that afterwards we will sail to Ibiza instead of Malta."

That is what I told the captains before we started talking about what each of them was to do when we reached Algiers. Then, just as we did before we raided Tunis, every sergeant captain was called forward and, as the other sergeant captains listened carefully, loudly told what he was to do and what would be expected of him. It took all day because the layout of the harbour at Algiers was very different from which of Tunis.

There were many questions and quite a few good suggestions.

Chapter Thirty

We visit Algiers.

We did not sail for Algiers immediately. We stayed in the harbour overnight and had another "captains call" in the morning just as we did before our raid on Tunis. *It was always surprising how many questions and concerns arose when a galley captain had an entire night to talk to his sergeants and think about a new assignment wherein he might lose his life. The next morning some of them climbed out of their dinghies all chipper and alert and confident; others had obviously stayed up all night worrying and thinking. They all had questions and concerns that needed to be addressed.*

Four hours later, the sergeant captains returned to their galleys in their dinghies, the "follow me" flag was waved from Harold's mast, and the rowing drums began their rhythmic beat. The crews on our temporarily quarantined cogs lined their deck railings and cheered lustily as we left the harbour bound for Algiers.

****** Lieutenant Randolph

My assignment and that of my galley was to repeat what we had done at Tunis—sail quietly into the harbour at Algiers late in the day as if we owned the place and then, the next morning, go ashore and be ready to capture one of the city gates as soon as our fleet of galleys begins to enter the harbour. Since I had to be in the Algiers harbour a day earlier than everyone else, mine was the only galley that sailed as soon as the first "all captains" meeting was finished.

It was late in the afternoon three days later when our lookout first reported seeing the entrance to the Algiers harbour and the great city stretching out behind it. It was a large harbour, and, as we got closer, our lookout reported he could see were numerous masts. That was good news. It meant the harbour was full and bustling as we had hoped and expected.

The sun was just finishing going down as we slowly made our way towards the barely visible harbour entrance using some of our oars on the lower rowing benches, just as we would if we were a slave-rowed Moorish galley returning from a long voyage. Only a few of my men and I were on the deck as we approached the harbour entrance. We were all wearing Moorish clothes.

Things started to go badly from the very beginning. We were still some distance from the entrance to the harbour in the fading light when one of the archers on our mast shouted a warning.

"Hoy, the deck. There be galleys in the harbour and many cogs."

"How many galleys? Are they pulled up to the beach or at the quay?"

A few seconds later there was a worrisome report.

"Hoy, the deck. They be galleys near the harbour entrance. Forty at least, maybe more. A few are pulled up on beach but most are in the harbour."

In the harbour? They should be nosed into the beach or at the quay, particularly at the end of the day. Something is wrong. I better climb up and look for myself.

There was a new report before I could jump down from the roof of the forward castle and make my way back to the mast.

"Hoy, the deck. A couple of them buggers is coming out. We count sixty plus sails anchored in the harbour and at the quay. Many cogs and ships."

I jumped down from the roof and walked rapidly to the mast. Everything was quiet except the slow swish of the oars we were using. Gulls were swooping and crying overhead and there was not a cloud in the sky. The sunset was glorious.

Climbing a galley mast was something I was something I never got used to doing. Ours was not swaying much at the moment because the sea was calm, but a rope ladder was always a problem for me. It had been a dry day, so, at least, the rope ladder would not be wet and slippery. I kicked off my sandals and climbed with my feet bare; I moved slowly, one step at a time, with each foot down solidly before I raised the other.

It did not take long to get high enough to see into the harbour. What I saw when I got high enough gave me a great shock. There were two galleys coming straight at us and rowing hard with their sails up.

The two galleys did not shock me. They could have been coming out most normal-like, trying to get out to sea before darkness fell. What shocked me was that there were so many galleys behind them in what appeared to be some kind of defensive formation—and I could see the periodic glints and flashes on the deck of the two galleys coming towards us that would only occur if the sun bounced off bared swords.

My God. They know we are coming. What should I do?

******

My initial reaction to the outbound galleys was to turn and run. On the other hand, darkness was coming so if we rowed right on past them and into the harbour we might be able to lose ourselves amidst all the shipping. Finally I decided.

"Turn us around, Tommy," I told my sailing sergeant. "Right smartly if you please. All hands to the oars. Drummer beat to maximum speed. Raise the sail. Sharply, lads, sharply."

I did not know what else to do. I could not just ignore the galleys coming towards us and sail into the harbour. It was still light enough for them to follow us and find us where we moored. Besides, it would not be surprising for an innocent captain to turn and run if he saw two armed galleys coming for him with their decks crowded with fighting men.

We spun around and they did indeed come charging out of the harbour to follow us. We went straight out to sea and lost them soon thereafter when darkness fell—I ordered the sail lowered in case they could see it outlined against the moon and made a hard turn to starboard. We did not see our fleet even though we knew it was out here somewhere preparing for tomorrow's raid.

Now, what? Should I stay out here and try to warn William or should I go back and try to enter the harbour despite the darkness? My head hurt thinking about it. Finally, I decided. It was the moon that decided me. There was only a quarter moon; so we are going to go back and try to enter the harbour in the darkness.

******

It took quite a while to find the harbour entrance. We used the moon to mark our position and tried to retrace our path. It did not work very well even though we rowed longer to make up for the extra distance the sail would have given us. Unfortunately, all we could see when we got to where we thought the harbour should be was the dim outline of the coast. The wind must have blown us off course when we were backtracking.

I was just about to give up in despair and head back out into the blackness of the sea when there was a call from one of the men in the lookout's nest.

"Hoy, the deck. We saw a light flicker off to our port. Distant it was. It might have been from Algiers City."

Climbing the mast in the dark was not pleasant. I am not a sailor man and I had never done it before. But I did it, even more slowly and cautiously than before. At first, I did not see anything and I was not even sure I was looking in the right direction. It turned out I was not.

Finally, one of the lookouts climbed down to where I was clinging to the rope ladder and tried to show me where to look. Nothing. And then there it was; I could see a couple of faint lights flickering in the distance. Perhaps smiths or bakers were working at night when it was cooler or women were cooking their families' suppers.

"Stay up here and pilot us towards the lights," I told the unknown lookout. "Sing out if you need food or water or to piss or shite but did not take your eyes off those lights until someone comes up to relieve you."

We rowed hard until we reached the harbour entrance. And even then we almost missed it because of the dark.

"Everyone quiet," I said in a whisper as I walked along the rowing benches. "No talking, and muffle your oars." .. "No talking, and muffle your oars." ..

I must have whispered it twenty times as I padded along the aisle between the rowing benches. I had already sent Tommy Small, the sailing sergeant, up the mast to the lookouts with the same message. There were now three lookouts up on the mast. They were told to climb down if they had anything to report, not shout.

We slowly rowed into harbour. Nothing stirred. All we could hear was the periodic creak of our galley's wood and rigging and the swish of our muffled oars. The harbour was dead silent. We had three lookouts in the bow with long pikes to push us off any galley or cog we might come upon in the darkness.

Our progress was slow because we were only using six lower-deck oars on each side as a slave-rowed galley might do as it entered a harbour at night when visibility was limited. I deliberately took us in along the edge of the harbour so the loom of our ship would not be seen outlined against the moon.

We all held our breaths as we passed what must have been the western end of the galleys that had been waiting for us. I needed to piss so badly I lifted my tunic and let go when I heard voices drift over the water from a cog we were slowly passing.

"Keep going deeper into the harbour," I whispered to Tommy. "We will anchor as far away as we can get from the galleys."

I had already told him that twice before but I could not help repeating it for fear he might have forgotten. I was so excited my arms were tingling and shaking as if I was in someplace cold.

A few minutes later I asked for my sailing sergeant's opinion.

"What do you think, Tommy?" I whispered. "Would this do for us?"

"Aye, Randolph. It was as good as any. I will go pass the word to the rowers. I am going to put the anchor down myself so they would be no splash."

* * * * * *

Dawn found us silent and alone near some Moorish cogs. Voices began to come across the water from the city. Their priests were in their towers calling the faithful to prayers. Almost immediately we began to smell the smoke of cooking fires and fresh bread coming from the cogs around us.

I whispered instructions for our "prayer men" to come up on deck wearing their Moorish clothes. They were ready and there were soon six of us on our knees in a line on the roof of the stern castle. The sailor who led us in our bowing had been a Moorish captive for many years. He would pretend to be the galley's sergeant captain and respond in Moorish if any questions were asked.

It was not until dawn broke and we could hear the calls of the city's priests coming out of the water that I realized how poorly we had anchored. I could see the harbour entrance from here alright, but one of the Moorish cogs anchored nearby was blocking me from seeing the gate in the city wall my men and I were supposed to hold.

I was not taking any chances. Even before the heathen priests began calling there were only the three of us who could be seen from the nearby Moorish cogs and ships, me and Tommy and the sailor posing as the sergeant captain who knew how to jabber in Moorish-speak. Everyone else was out of sight below deck, hungry because we could not light a cooking fire to make bread, and ready to either instantly put their oars in the water and row like hell, or grab up their weapons and come running out for a fight.

We could not feed the men because cooking a lot of bread might have alerted the Moors that we had many men on board; the same for the men coming on deck to use the shite nest to put their turds in the harbour where they belong. They would just have to go hungry for a while and use the buckets Tommy put out for them. They were used to using buckets from when the weather was too heavy to safely use the shite nest in the stern. It was not a problem.

****

The more I thought about the galleys waiting at the harbour entrance, the more I worried about our plan to take the galley to the nearby quay and for the four of us to walk up to the gate in the city wall the way we did in Tunis. If the Algerians expected an attack, moving a strange galley to the quay might have been seen for what it was, the beginning of an attack.

"Tommy," I told my sailing sergeant, "I have changed my mind. My three lads and I are going to take the dinghy to the beach and walk up to the gate real casual-like. You are stay here real quiet-like and not bring the galley to the quay until you see our galleys start to enter the harbour. We will not move against the gate until we see you get to the quay."

After I was sure Tommy understood what I wanted, I set my worries aside. My mind was made up. I climbed off the castle roof and went to fetch my three men. It was time to begin our assault on the city. It felt a strange kind of relief to finally be doing something. As I walked across the deck I wondered how soon William would come through the harbour entrance. He waited until almost noon when we raided Tunis.

Just thinking about William's arrival made me hurry. What if he arrived early and we were not ready to take the gate?

Chapter Thirty-one

Randolph and the Algerian Horsemen.

I was suddenly very anxious and it seemed like it took forever for the one sailor among the four of us to row our galley's dinghy to the strand on the north side of the quay. But we did reach it and were able to pull the dinghy ashore. The strand was surprisingly deserted except for some old fishing boats that had been pulled ashore for repairs or to be lived in. No one was about and that too was worrisome. It looked increasingly as if the Algerians knew we were coming.

After we pulled the dinghy ashore, and turned it around so we could leave quickly if it became necessary, we set out to walk up to the city gate; four nondescript and unarmed men wearing Moorish tunics and head linens. We might have been walking into the city to find work or to meet someone.

One of the men, not me, carried a bundle on his shoulder. Hopefully, it looked like something he was bringing to sell in the market or perhaps that he might be a workman carrying his tools. Actually, and not put too fine of a point on it, he was carrying the tools of our trade—galley swords. We did not, of course, carry our bows and shields; we had no way to conceal them.

Three of us knew how to use our swords, quite well as a matter of fact. The fourth hardly at all; he was a wiry and dependable two-stripe "chosen man" sailor from Portsmouth, one of the slaves who made his mark and joined us after we captured the Moorish galley on that he had been chained to a rowing bench to sit in his own shite and piss until he died. He had learnt to jabber Moorish right good during the years he sat there.

The name against that our interpreter-sailor made his mark on our Company's roll was Edward Portsmouth Sailor, known to one and all as "Eddy." Eddy walked on the strand in the front of our little group of men because he would do the jabbering if any Moorish jabbering needed to be done. As you might expect, Eddy, being a good sailor, was the man what rowed the dinghy we pulled up on the strand.

Eddy was a careful man. We adjusted the Moorish clothes covering our tunics and waited impatiently while he made sure the dinghy was turned around to face the water and its oars were hidden under it. But we did not complain; to the contrary, we wanted to be able to get away quickly if things turned to shite at the city gate.

****

My three men and I reached the city wall and began to walk on the cart path that ran along the wall towards the gate. Several times we nodded and walked on without speaking as we met people coming towards us on the path. Everything seemed normal until we came around the corner of a wall bastion and got our first look at the gate at the end of the cart path running up from the quay—it was closed.

The hairs on my arms suddenly prickled. This did not feel right at all. It should be open this time of day. This is not possible. What should we do?

I did not have time to think about it when one of the archers gave a gasp of surprise and motioned with his head toward an area of the strand about a ten or fifteen minute walk further along the city wall, the area of the strand beyond the wall where we had been told the city's galleys would be moored at the water line or pulled out of the water for repairs.

"Lieutenant Randolph, look!"

There were a small number of galleys floating in the water and lined up along the beach, just where we expected to find them—and so were a large number of men on horseback; fighting men for sure. Even at this distance it was clear that they were mounted soldiers, Moorish knights and light cavalry, the men that the Moors use when they fight on land. I had seen them myself many times when we were fighting the Saracens for Richard and Edmond.

Dear God, they must know we are coming. That is why the gate was closed and most of their galleys were waiting at the harbour entrance.

"Everyone try to look natural-like. We are going to walk as fast as we can back to the dinghy and row back out to the galley. We have got to get to sea and warn our men that the Moors know they were coming. Quickly now, there is not a moment to lose."

It was not to be. We were about half way back to the dinghy when my heart sank—our galley was slowly rowing towards the quay using some of its lower oars as if all was well and this was just another day. William and our fleet must be entering the harbour.

******

My men and I watched in horror and disbelief as the oars of our slow-moving galley bit into the water around it. There was no way we would be able to get to our dinghy and warn them. The archer chosen man standing next to me moaned a fearful "no" out loud. He understood as well as I did. We four were trapped. Now what should I do?

"Quick, lads, run for it. The dinghy's no good to us now. We have got to get to the quay and board our galley if we are to get away from here alive."

We stripped off our Moorish clothes so our archer tunics could be seen and began running for the quay as if our lives depended on it, that they surely did. We knew that the galley would not stay long if the city gate was not open. Tommy might wait a minute or two to see if any of us were still alive, but probably no longer, not with that mob of Algerian horses and soldiers on the strand next to where the Algerians moored their galleys. If Tommy's lookouts saw the closed gate and did not see us running down the path to meet them at the quay, they had think we were lost. Then they would push off from the quay to join the rest of the galleys in the taking of Moorish prizes.

It was going to take us at least ten minutes to get to the galley and it would surely leave if they did not see us.

My men and I had barely gotten started and we were running hard and waving our arms to attract their attention when Tommy brought the galley up against the quay and heavily laden archers began pouring off and running up the cart path to the city gate.

I was so surprised when the archers began coming off the galley and running up the cart path that I stopped and stared in disbelief. That is when I realized the city gate was now open. Our archers were heading into a trap.

******

The sight of the galley's archers running towards the now-open city gate stopped me in my tracks, but not for long. Even so, my three men were well ahead of me when I lowered my head and resumed running. My running did not last all that long. I was still quite a ways from the galley and I could hardly breathe when I slowed to a walk. My heart was pounding and I had to stop and lean over with my hands on my knees to breathe and rest before I could once again begin staggering towards the quay.

My three men did not share my weakness. First one and then the two others reached the galley before I even got close to the quay. That is when things got a bit blurry.

Suddenly, I realized that sailors from the galley were pounding down the quay and up the strand towards me. I did not have the strength to thank them when they grabbed me by my elbows and half-carried me the rest of the way in a limping and gasping sort of run. When we got there, I was so tired I could not even lift my leg to get over the galley rail; one of the sailors had to lift my leg over the deck railing and push me over into the arms of the sailors on the deck.

There was shouting and cries of alarm all about me. If the sailors who had caught me had not held me up, I would have fallen for sure. I almost wish they had not caught me for then I would not have seen what happened next.

******

I watched in horror as the men on horseback on the strand in front of the beached Moorish galleys gathered themselves together and began spurring their horses towards the archers running up the cart path to the now-open city gate. Someone among the archers must have seen the horsemen and sounded the alarm. After a moment's hesitation, about half of the heavily laden archers turned around and began running back to the galley. Only those closest to the gate continued running towards it and passed into the city.

Most of the archers who remained on the cart path did not have a chance. A fleet-of-foot few who had been at the back of the gate-bound group dropped their heavy burdens and dashed all the way back to our galley and safety. They literally dove onto the deck of the galley as the horsemen thundered down the quay towards them.

Many of the horsemen were carrying short bows and, being Moorish horsemen, knew how to use them. They pulled their prancing and rearing horses to a halt in front of the galley and immediately began loosing arrows down at our sailors and the breathless archers who only a few minutes before had thought they had reached safety.

Our deck was littered with dead and wounded men before we drifted far enough away from the quay to be out of range of the Algerian riders. Only the fact that I fell to the deck and played dead saved me from the Algerian archers that were loosing their arrows down on to our galley from their horses on the quay. It would have been a different story if we had had more archers on board. We would have decimated them. But we did not; except for my two companions and the few who had made it back to the galley, all of our archers were either in the city or trapped in the open on the cart path.

We on the drifting galley at least had a chance. The archers on the cart path had none. Several small groups of our men came together either instinctively or at the orders of a sergeant and tried to make a stand. They were ridden down even though a number of the Moorish horses and riders went down to the archers carrying long-handled, bladed pikes and those who were able to respond with their longbows.

The only resistance from the galley came from the two archers who had been with me and the handful of men who had made it back to the galley with their bows.

My two companions had rushed to get their bows and joined the returnees in loosing arrows at the Algerians who galloped up to the galley; I was somehow so weak that I was unable to get to my bow and help them. Even so, those few dozen of our archers were able to loose enough arrows to drive away the Algerians who had galloped up the quay to where we were moored. They left the quay littered with dead and wounded men and rider-less horses. I watched as one of the Algerian horses bolted forward into the water when it was hit and almost landed on our deck as we were drifting away from the quay.

I was not hit, at least I did not think so, but I was aware of being on the deck with a great pain in my chest. Then the pain stopped and everything faded away.

Chapter Thirty-one

William and the battle for Algiers.

We waited together off the Algerian coast all night and began rowing for Algiers when the sun came up. Our lookouts had only reported one worrisome sail yesterday, a double-masted cog wearing all her sails that might have been heading south on its way to Algiers. It had a good wind behind it and went past us well to the north just as the sun went down on a night in that there was but the smallest sliver of a moon.

The unknown cog's lookouts might or might not have seen the candle lanterns we had already hung on our masts in order to stay together for tomorrow morning's raid. If our lookouts had seen it earlier, we could have chased it down; but there was no way we could have found it in the darkness and we did not even try.

******

I was on Harold's boat and we had three pilots on board. When the sun arrived to start the day, they had all agreed that if the wind held and we did not row it would take us about three hours to sight the entrance to

Algiers' harbour and another hour to enter it. I had listened to them with a piece of warm flat bread in one hand and a slice of cheese in the other; then I gave the order everyone expected.

"Lieutenant," I called out to Harold, have the "follow me" flag waved from the top of the mast and set your sail for Algiers. No rowing until we near the harbour entrance; we will want the men's arms rested when we meet the Moors."

Activity on the galley was both excited and subdued in the hours that followed. The archers continued to nap and eat. Many worked quietly on their weapons. Only the sailors were active on the rudder and sail and up in the lookout's nest. The rest of our galleys followed close behind us.

******

I was on Harold's Moorish-built galley, the big one with four extra oars on each side. Forty-eight of our galleys, our entire strength in the Mediterranean, were following close behind Harold's as we led them through the harbour entrance.

Harold's galley was to lead some of our galleys to the long quay in front of the city gate where they would disembark their men. Others would either go for prizes in the harbour or peel off and head for the strand where the Algerians nosed in their useful galleys and beached those that needed repairs. Six would block the entrance so the shipping in the harbour could not escape. Each sergeant captain knew where he was supposed to go and what he was supposed to do.

Our galley was as ready for a fight as Harold could make it and so were the galleys coming into the harbour on either side of us and behind us.

The roof of our galley's stern castle was packed with men as were the castle roofs of every galley in our fleet. With Harold and I on the castle roof were our apprentice sergeants, Harold's loud-talker, and his sailing sergeant.

Six of the galley's best archers were also on the roof with us. Five more were on the much smaller roof of the forward castle, three were up the mast in the lookout's nest, and one man, Harold's very best archer, a chosen man from a village south of London called Haywards Heath, was lashed to the very top of the forward mast.

About sixty archers stood at the ready along the deck railings on both sides of the galley; another sixty were pulling oars on the upper rowing bank and ready on a moment's notice to rush to the deck with their weapons and join in the fighting. Bales of arrows were open and stacked up everywhere. A handful of sailors manned a few of the lower rowing benches, primarily to help the rudder men steer.

Our longbows were in our hands and our swords and pikes and shields nearby as we swept through the harbour entrance—and came face to face with the waiting Algerian fleet formed up in two lines of galleys one behind the other.

"The cog must have alerted them," Harold said quietly as he stood next to me on the roof of the stern castle.

"Keep to the plan, Lieutenant." I said it loudly so the men standing about us could hear. "Go for the quay."

After a second or two, I began adding more instructions. "Sweep their decks as we pass them." And then, "Try to take out their oars as we go past so they cannot get away."

******

"Loose your arrows as soon as you can reach a man;" ... "loose with a target, I say; loose with a target." ... "Stand ready to ship oars." Harold gave the orders as we closed on the two lines of Algerian galleys and his loud-talker and sergeants repeated them.

We bore down on the waiting Algerians as fast as our sail and the archers rowing on our upper benches could manage. The Algerians' decks were full of shouting men waving swords.

The Algerian galleys were roughly arrayed inside the harbour in two lines facing the harbour entrance. The storm of arrows we loosed began to fall on them as soon as we got within range. Every archer was loosing arrows with fresh arms and determination as Harold headed us towards an opening between two Algerian galleys in the first line of the two lines of galleys.

The rowing drum beat loudly and all about me was the sound of constant grunting as all of our archers, including me, pushed out arrow after arrow into the mass of men on the decks of the two Algerian galleys in front of us. *Every man on our galleys has a battle position and fights. We have no slaves and servants as is the Moorish custom.*

Both of the galleys we were attempting to pass between in the first line of Algerian galleys had lookouts on their masts. They were among the first to go. As I pushed an arrow at a heavily bearded man wearing a turban who was standing on the forward castle of the portside Moorish galley with a sword in his hand, I caught a glimpse out of the corner of my eye as the lookout on the other Algerian galley fell end over end to his deck.

From where I was standing, I could clearly see the man in the lookout's nest above the turbaned man on the galley to the south as my arrow hit him squarely in the stomach; the lookout was slumped down with both of his arms dangling over the edge of nest. Someone had already gotten him.

I had initially aimed at the lookout but he had collapsed before I loosed so I had dropped my aim and pushed my arrow into the belly of the turbaned sword waver. At this distance, he had been impossible to miss.

A moment later Harold shouted, "Ship oars," and we began passing between the two Algerians, snapping some of the oars of the one on our port side. The other Moor was fifty or sixty paces away to starboard so we did not come close to snapping any of its oars. All the while I was pushing out arrows as fast as possible I could hear the loud shouts and screams coming from the men around me and on our deck as the archers lining our deck railings pushed their arrows into the Algerians. At this distance, we could hardly miss.

Most of the arrows we pushed went towards the men waving their swords on the decks of the two galleys we were passing between. One moment they were waving their swords and shouting their battle cries; the next, they were falling and scattering in great disarray. Even so, the Algerians on the portside galley, the one with the snapped oars, somehow threw at least two successful grapples that I could see.

Their grapples held and our galleys crashed together and stayed together for a moment. But not for long. Our sailors assigned to be grapple men during a battle did not throw their grapples. Instead, in response to Harold's bellowed orders, they picked up their nearby grapple axes and within moments had cut the Algerians' grapple lines.

Those few moments while we were lashed together were both good and bad for us. They were good because we were close alongside the Algerian long enough for our portside archers to finish clearing the Algerian's deck; they were bad because our forward movement towards the second line of Algerian galleys was totally stopped.

******

We came to a complete stop as a result of the Algerian grapples and stayed that way until we floated far enough away from the Algerian galley so that Harold could get our oars back in the water. The men about me and I took advantage of the lull and scrambled to rearrange our supply of arrows. While we were doing that, Harold was bellowing out the rowing and rudder commands necessary to move us through the gap between a couple of enemy galleys in the Algerian second line.

I looked around as Harold gave his orders. Our galleys had mostly broken through or gone around the Algerian first line and were closing on the second. But not all of them; some of our sergeant captains had seen Harold's galley stop in the Algerians' first line instead of continuing to move towards the quay. They had then stopped to fight, thinking, quite reasonably, that following Harold's lead was what they were now supposed to do.

Finally, our rowing drum began booming once again and we began moving toward an opening between two Algerian galleys in the second line. Once again Harold ordered our oars pulled in and we scraped up against an Algerian galley—and this time we were not going fast enough to snap its oars.

Worse, much worse, this one had archers on board; fortunately, it did not have many and we cleared its deck as we slowly drifted past it with our oars shipped—but not until we took a number of casualties, including a man on the roof near me being hit in the middle of back as he pushed arrows at the other galley we were passing between. Fortunately, the impact of the strike only knocked him off the roof and onto the deck instead of into the water; unfortunately, he was most likely dead or soon would be.

No grapples were thrown by the Algerian galleys in the second line as we passed between them. As soon as we were clear of the Algerian second line, Harold gave the order for everyone to resume rowing and we headed for the quay in front of the city gate with our rowing drum beating rapidly.

We could not see the quay for all the cogs and ships in the harbour, but we could see the open gate in the city wall on the hillside above the quay—and the heavy fighting that was obviously going on around it.

****

At first I did not realize what I was seeing. Then I understood—the gate was being held by our men against a large attacking force of several thousand men that included horsemen—and for some reason the men holding the gate were moving out of the city to fight the Moorish horsemen. It was quite a foolish thing to do and Randolph was not a foolish man.

Finally, I understood—our men at the gate were being forced out through the gate by the Algerian fighters inside the city. They would be slaughtered if we did not hurry.

"Hurry, Harold," I said as I pointed towards the distant gate. "It looks like our men are being forced out of the city into the arms of that lot outside the gate. They would be slaughtered."

Harold sent more men to the oars and ordered the sail to be temporarily raised. Our galley tore through the harbour towards the quay. Only about twenty of the thirty-one galleys that were supposed to be with us, were with us as we approached the quay. The others were almost certainly engaged elsewhere with the two lines of enemy galleys or heading for the strand where the Algerians were moored their galleys along the shoreline—that they would probably find empty since many, if not all, of the Algerian galleys had been manned to confront us.

There was no doubt about it, our careful plan that we had worked on for so many months, was falling apart in front our eyes.

"Lower the sail." ... "Landing party to the deck." ... "Standby to back oars." ... "Back oars."

All over the deck of Harold's galley our men were busy gathering up their weapons and getting ready to carry them ashore. They would be heavily burdened. In addition to their longbows and quivers, they were carrying either extra quivers of arrows or bladed pikes and land-fighting shields. Many of the archers also carried galley shields on their backs and sheathed short swords on their belts.

It was a hot and sunny day for a fight. A few men were smart enough or thirsty enough to run to the water barrel for a quick drink before we got to the quay. *I should have thought of water; I should have told some of our men to carry water skins.*

"Harold," I said loudly. "Stand by to have some of your sailor lads start carrying water skins up there."

******

Harold brought his galley up to the quay with our deck packed with heavily laden archers. I was at the deck railing ready to lead them ashore. The noise from the fighting in front of the gate was quite loud and there was a great cloud of dust hanging over the battlefield. A few of the Algerians in the Algerian rear had seen us arrive at the quay. I had already passed the word that the men were to quickly form up on the quay and advance in the tight fighting formation we used when enemy horsemen were present.

I leaped on to the quay wearing my mail shirt under my tunic and was already quite warm as I held my hands wide apart to indicate how and where I wanted the men to form up on me. It did not take long before we were in our tight horse-fighting formation with the first three men in each file being pike-holding archers with land-fighting shields. We were in a line about fifteen men wide and seven men deep as we double-timed up the slope towards the dust-covered battle in front of the gate. It was slow going because of the slope, the heat, and the weight of the weapons we were carrying.

Some of the men standing in the rear of the Algerians attacking the gate had turned and stared at Harold's galley as we reached the quay. But they paid us no particular attention even after we began pouring out of the galley and began climbing up the path towards them. They likely thought we were reinforcements coming from their fleet of galleys.

Everything began to change when we formed our battle formation and they saw our other galleys begin to reach the quay and discharge their archers. That is when the men in the rear of the mob in front of us first began to realize we were coming to fight them, not to reinforce them.

They learned too late to do themselves any good. A few seconds later I dropped my raised fist and we began pushing a stream of arrows into the mob of men who were mostly facing away from us. We took them down as a scythe cuts the rows of wheat in front of it.

In less than a minute, six or seven similarly formed galley companies had run up from the quay and begun adding their arrows to ours. The men in front of us quickly turned into a panic-stricken, leaderless mob with those on horseback trampling their own men in a desperate effort to get away.

It was all over rather quickly—and the gate into the city remained closed. Men from Randolph's galley were lying all over the ground in front of the gate amidst a much greater number of dead and wounded Algerians. Only a small handful of Randolph's men were alive and many of them had been wounded more than once. They were huddled into a corner of the wall where they had gone to make their last stand—where a bastion protruded out from the wall so they had a corner that would shelter them on two sides.

We also found some wounded men from Randolph's galley in front of the gate who were still alive, but no Randolph. Dead and wounded Algerians were everywhere. We were too busy attending to our own men to deal with the Algerian wounded, some of whom were attempting to drag themselves away, others were crying out and pleading for help. It was the usual battlefield chaos that exists when the fighting stops.

******

Our dead and wounded men were being gathered up and carried to the quay when one of the archers who had gone with Randolph to the gate came up from the quay and sought me out. That is when I first began to understand what had happened—about Randolph finding the gate closed and hurrying back too late to warn the galley; and how the galley's Company of archers had started up the path with some of the men continuing and some turning back when the Algerian horsemen charged.

It was a heart-breaking story and I only heard part of it as we hurried back to the quay with our dead and wounded men; some slung over the shoulders of our strongest men, others being led and helped to walk. The day had become very warm and the men suffered greatly.

"He just fell to the deck and died when we got him back to the galley. There was not a wound on him," the anxious archer told me as we trotted back towards the galleys along the quay.

I did not have time to lament Randolph and our lost and wounded men. We were hurrying to the quay because I had no idea as to how the fighting was going in the harbour between the Algerian galleys and ours; all I could think about was that we needed to get our galleys and men back into the fighting in the harbour before the Algerian galleys won the day.

The Algerian army, if that is what it was, had been at least temporarily routed; our standing around in the sun in front of the city walls waiting in case the Algerians reformed and returned would accomplish nothing. It was time to rescue our wounded and move on to what we do best—take prizes. The city would have to wait.

******

My blood was overly heated by the sun by the time I reached the quay and began shouting orders and motioning for the men to re-board their galleys. The heat was so bad while Jeffrey and I waited impatiently for our archers to return that I wobbled and had to stop for a moment to rest while Jeffrey had one of his sailors throw water on my face and tunic to cool my blood.

Peter reached the quay with his rear guard and ran down the quay to Jeffery's galley temporarily to report. I agreed when he suggested he should lead his three galleys into the harbour to take prizes. I did not have time to tell him about Randolph.

My impatience finally got the better of me after my blood cooled sufficiently for me to think again—we left a senior sergeant on the dock to direct our late-arrivals and casualties to a couple of galleys whose sergeant captains were ordered to remain at the quay until every man was boarded. We had no choice but to concentrate all our efforts on defeating the Algerian galleys and securing the cogs and ships in the harbour as prizes; we would have to wait and deal with the city later.

Randolph's galley with the body of my dear friend remained anchored just off the quay. A battle was raging in the harbour and I did not have time to stop and pay my respects.

Chapter Thirty-Two

The harbour at Algiers

As we rowed away from the quay with the drum booming, Harold and I could see galleys in every part of the harbour and what appeared to be several pursuits involving one of our galleys chasing an Algerian galley through the crowded harbour.

It was hard to tell exactly what was happening or who was winning. One reason for the difficulty was because just about every transport in the harbour had raised its anchors and was either attempting to escape or had been taken by one of our prize crews who was trying to get it out of the harbour

Some of the transports were being towed towards the harbour entrance by small boats powered by desperately rowing Moorish sailors; others were prizes being towed by one of our galleys. Others, either prizes or Moors trying to escape, had raised their sails and were trying to claw their way out of the crowded harbour despite the wind coming in from the sea.

Everything was absolute chaos, and there were numerous collisions and near-collisions. Compounding the confusion, dozens and dozens of dinghies and small boats crammed full of Moorish sailors were attempting to row ashore to escape being captured.

It was hard to tell what was happening or who was winning. Were the galleys I could see in the harbour some of the Algerian galleys that had been waiting for us at the harbour entrance, or were they prizes we had taken that were trying to find transports to tow away as prizes? The other, and perhaps more important question, at the moment, was who controlled the entrance to the harbour?

There was only one way to find out, so I decided to temporarily forego attempting to join the fighting or the taking of prizes and ordered Harold to row straight to the entrance of the harbour so we could see what was happening there.

"We need to make sure the entrance is blocked so the Moorish transports and galleys cannot get out unless they are prizes," I said to Harold by way of explanation as he loudly gave the necessary rowing orders and his loud-talker and sergeants repeated them even more loudly.

I did not say a word as he gave his orders, merely nodded and poured another bowl of water on my head. It felt wonderful and I suddenly realized I so desperately needed to piss I could not wait. So I lifted my wet tunic and aimed downwind even though pissing on the deck of his galley was as close to a mortal sin as an archer could get. My brother would have had a fit.

******

Rowing through the shipping in the crowded harbour was an exciting experience with Harold's sailor sergeant constantly shouting rudder and rowing commands to turn us this way and that. Shipping and galleys were everywhere moving about in an effort to get clear of the fighting going on about them.

We saw two collisions and nearly had one of our own when a small boat of Moorish rowers attempting to tow a single-masted cog to safety crossed right in front of us. We passed over its tow line and listened to the screams of its rowers as the stern of their dinghy was dragged down under the water.

Less than two minutes later, we came around a three-masted ship just as it finished raising its anchor—and found ourselves head to head with a fleeing Algerian galley with one of our own galleys coming right behind it in an effort to capture it as a prize. We quickly shipped our oars and began snapping off the Algerian's oars as it came past. It already had dead men on its deck and our archers added to them as it slid past us—and promptly put its bow straight into the side of the cog whose dinghy we had sunk.

Our archers and sailors cheered mightily and pumped their arms as our sister galley pursuing the hapless Algerian shipped her oars and came slowly sliding past us at distance of no more than ten paces. Its men cheered and shouted to us with equal enthusiasm and many waves and arm pumps of their own.

From my position on the roof of the forward castle, I could see sailors in our sister galley's bow swinging grapples in circles around their heads. They were preparing to throw them on the hapless Algerian as we passed going in the opposite direction. After the grapple throwers came a deck packed with enthusiastic archers and finally a beardless young one-stripe lad in the shite nest in the stern of the passing galley dropping a turd into the harbour.

The young archer in the shite nest waved at us with a big smile as we slid past. I smiled broadly and lifted my hand to acknowledge him. So, I am sure, did all of our men who saw him—it was one of the most amusing things I had ever seen in the midst of a battle. The sergeant captain of the pursuing galley had obviously thrown his bales of live chickens in the shite nest to clear his decks and they were bouncing up and down all around the lad whilst fluttering their wings all about and complaining loudly as he dropped his shite.

Even the ever-serious Harold smiled when he turned to me and asked,

"Have you ever wondered what it would be like to have flapping chicken wings wipe your arse?"

******

My worries fell away as we approached the harbour entrance. The two lines of Algerian galleys were gone. We had either scattered them or taken them. Some had obviously been taken—there was already a line of galleys and cogs lashed together with their anchors in the water to the north, prizes for sure.

More importantly and just about the only thing that had appeared to have worked as planned, eight of our galleys were either arrayed in their assigned blocking positions across the entrance or boarding and seizing cogs and ships attempting to leave the harbour. *At first, I had been confused by the cogs in the line of prizes, but then I realized that they must have been taken by our entrance guards when they tried to leave the harbour.*

"Where to now, Captain?" asked Harold with a smile as he nodded towards our blocking force and the line of prizes.

"Let's make a run through the harbour to see if we can find an Algerian galley that needs to be taken or a galley of ours needing help to capture a prize."

******

Smoke was billowing up from a cog on fire in the harbour and people were pouring out of the city to watch the battle. Both of our "rescue galleys" were still waiting at the quay with their cargos of wounded archers from the fighting in front of the city gate. The quay itself was empty of people; the longbows of the tow galleys' archers were keeping the onlookers far away. There was no sign of the horsemen and their attendants.

We spent over an hour rowing through a harbour that was in a state of total chaos. Unanchored cogs and ships were drifting aimlessly about everywhere; others were being towed by their dinghies and ship's boats in the hope that they could somehow reach the harbour entrance and escape into the sea beyond it. Some of the dinghies and small boats were rowing fleeing Moorish sailors ashore from the cogs and ships they were abandoning.

More importantly, and to my great satisfaction, every Algerian galley we came across either had one or more of our boarding parties aboard or was awaiting their imminent arrival with its deck covered with dead and wounded men. All in all, the fighting was subsiding. Many of the transport cogs and ships in the crowded harbour, however, had not yet even been boarded. Even so, not one of our galleys needed our assistance. I had been reduced to an onlooker and it was very frustrating.

Everywhere our longbows and archer-heavy galleys had reaped a grim harvest of the slave-rowed Algerians with their untrained and ill-equipped sailors and fighting men. Bodies floated in the water everywhere in the harbour. Some had been killed during the fighting and fallen in the water; most, however, had been tossed overboard by our prize crews as they cleared the Moorish decks.

For the most part, at least so far as I could tell, our men were following orders—the surrendered Moors on the Algerian galleys were not being treated as pirates and immediately killed. I had forbidden it because we had taken them in their home waters. Besides, as I had explained to the sergeant captains before we sailed, we needed hostages to exchange.

******

The results of our raid were fairly clear to me and my lieutenants by the time we finished patrolling the harbour. There was no question about it, we had control of the harbour and all the shipping in it—and the Algerians had control of the city and all the land around it. In other words, my plan to take and destroy Algiers had failed. Instead of the whole city, we held only the quay.

I used Harold's loud-talker to shout orders across the water to three of our galleys that had finished sending off their captured cogs and ships. They were to row to the quay and relieve the galleys that had loaded our survivors from the battle at the city gate so they could row to the relative safety of harbour entrance and thence to Sardinia.

The sergeant captains of the three galleys and their crews were pleased and cheerful when they received their new orders; they had taken all the prizes for that they had prize crews, and they were pleased to know that getting our wounded to safety and barbering them was a priority.

We led the three galleys to the quay and Harold brought us alongside one of the two galleys carrying the survivors from the battle at the gate, John Plymouth's. Harold's sailors used their long-handled pikes to hold their galley against John's whilst Harold and I climbed aboard. We wanted to see for ourselves the state of his galley's supplies and the condition of the men he had on board.

"Hoy, John, what do you have aboard? How many survivors and how many prize crews?"

"Hoy, Captain, and you too, Harold. Welcome aboard. We followed you straight here to the quay and stayed as you ordered—so I have got every man I sailed with plus sixteen of Randolph's men; and all five of my prize crews, of course. I had seventeen of Randolph's men but one went dead on me, that he did, and there is another who might be needing a mercy."

"Try to keep him alive in one of your castles and happy with the flower paste if you can," I replied. Then I gave him his sailing orders.

"Now here is what you are to do, John. We have got our prizes all lined up nice and tidy-like out there by the harbour entrance with Henry White in command. I want you to row out there and see Henry. Tell him you have brought him five prize crews and that I said he was to give your galley fifty Christian or Jewish rowers from among the galley slaves, Englishmen, Frenchies, and Island men if he is got them. You keep your archer sergeant and three files of archers.

"Turn all the rest of your archers and their share of your arrow bales over to Henry White for him to use on our prizes—then you sail for Sardinia. Wait at least two days for me or Harold or Lieutenant Peter. If we do not show up, you are to go on to Cyprus via Malta and Crete, but only after you take on supplies and get the wounded barbered up most nice."

I thought for a minute while he nodded his agreement to my orders and asked a couple of minor questions. Then I expanded on my order to him.

"Oh, and one more thing, John. Do not forget to feed up the slaves real good with double rations and let them do whatever they want after you get them to Sardinia. They can go with you to Cyprus, or stay on Sardinia, or head westward rowing on one of our galleys bound for England. It was their choice as is our custom. Give them the choice and make sure they have safe places before you leave Sardinia."

Harold listened and nodded his approval. So did John and the men standing nearby. It was little wonder that they did. Taking care of our wounded men was important to everyone and we have gotten some of our best archers and sailors from the galley slaves we have freed. Two of my lieutenants, Harold and Henry Lewes, for example, were among the first of the many slaves we freed. On our very first galley was where Thomas and I found them.

******

It was with heavy hearts that we rowed the short distance to visit Randolph's galley where it was anchored nearby. Tommy, Randolph's sailing sergeant, had Randolph laid out on the deck with his eyes closed. It was all I could do not to weep in front of the men who stood in a circle around us watching. *We had been in the*

Company and sailed together with King Richard all those many years ago, had not we?

"He was a good man, a very good man," I finally said as I crossed myself and mumbled a little prayer under my breath. "And a damn fine archer."

Then I took a deep breath to clear away my black thoughts, and turned away to give Tommy, Randolph's sailing sergeant, command of the galley and basically the same orders I had just given to the sergeant captains at the quay with the wounded from the battle at the gate. He was told to stop at the harbour entrance and get fifty of the slaves we had taken as rowers from Henry White, and sail for Sardinia, and then on to Cyprus, using the newly freed slaves and his archers as rowers.

Unlike the galleys at the quay with our dead and wounded men, however, Tommy's galley was desperately short of archers as a result of so many of its archers being been lost or wounded in the fighting at the gate. I promoted one of Harold's archers, a chosen man both Henry and Harold had already recommended for promotion, to sergeant, and assigned twenty of Harold's archers to move to Tommy's galley under his command—all were volunteers who raised their hands to indicate that they were willing to return to Cyprus instead of continuing on to England to help "guard and deliver the relics."

Finally, with a great sigh, I turned back to Raymond.

"Wrap him tight so he does not smell too much and move him to a galley going to Cyprus when you get to Ibiza. That way we can keep him with archers permanent-like by burying him in our cemetery with the proper words. Tell the galley's captain I said Yoram was to have a priest say the words all proper-like when they bury.

"Do you have enough supplies and water?" I asked Raymond. "If not, be sure to get them from Henry White."

Chapter Thirty-three

A sour victory.

There was much cheering each time we rowed past one of our own galleys or a prize being towed to the ever-growing line of prizes Henry White had anchored near the harbour entrance. The men were happy, but I was not—my plan to take the city had fallen apart and Randolph was dead along with many of our archers. I had failed.

Our men's happiness about all the prizes was all well and good; and my unhappiness with our failing to take Algiers, and with losing so many men in the effort, was understandable, but neither did anything to solve my basic problem— that I was not certain as to what should we now do.

I called my lieutenants together to talk about it. We decided to hold the harbour indefinitely in order to take arriving galleys and cogs and exact a ransom for returning the harbour. We had already taken our first additional prize, a Moorish cog with strange sails came in right past our row of prizes and entered the harbour. Its crew had not known of the battle and had been surprised to find themselves captured.

It was a little two-master with only one castle and filled with amphorae of coloured dyes, bales of Egyptian linen, and a little chest full of pearls. Henry White promptly anchored it at the end of the row of prizes and went aboard to check its cargo.

"How long do you think we can stay here and control the harbour?" I asked my lieutenants as they gathered on Harold's deck.

"As long as you want, Captain; as long as you want," said Harold. "We have more than enough galleys to keep control of the harbour and fetch supplies even if we send all the prize cogs to England to be sold and all the prize galleys to Yoram in Cyprus to be added to our fleet."

"Well then, how many galleys should we keep here as a garrison?" I asked Harold.

"A dozen galleys would be enough if they were fully crewed with archers. Then we would be strong enough to hold the harbour even if three or four of them were away fetching supplies."

"Make it so," I replied, as Henry and Peter nodded their approval.

******

My lieutenants and I were fairly sure we could stay in control of the Algiers harbour for as long as we wanted because we could, if necessary, bring in enough food to maintain our men. We knew, even if our men did not, that there was no need to hurry to get to England with the crates stored in the holds of three of our galleys; we alone knew they did not contain the missing relics. They were already in Cornwall.

Finalized our plans for Algiers after the four of us spent two days inspecting our prizes and moving men and supplies about. We decided to send our prize galleys and Raymond's body to Cagliari as the first stop on their voyages outbound to Cyprus. Similarly, we decided to send most of the prize cogs and ships to Ibiza as their first port of call on their way to London. A few of the best, however, were sent to Cyprus to add to our fleet of cargo transports and pirate-takers.

It was also a profitable two days—we took two more trading cogs and a big three-masted ship with a crew from somewhere in the east. They were not expecting us so they just sailed into the harbour and fell into our welcoming arms.

The three-master was interesting because its masts were higher than any of us had ever seen, and its sails were made of some kind of heavy linen instead of leather like ours. Harold and almost all of the sailor sergeants went aboard to marvel at it.

"That one next to it has a new hull design. It also should go to Cyprus for our shipwrights to see," said Harold. "The three-mast ship's crew, as well, so our sailing sergeants can be learnt how to sail it."

******

Only nine fully crewed galleys, and two Moorish cogs that had sailed into the harbour yesterday and become prizes, were all that were left in the harbour as the sun finished passing overhead on the fifth night after the raid. So far, we had made no effort to contact the Algerians and they had made no effort to contact us.

"They probably thought we had come to raid them and would soon go away," suggested Peter as we sat on the deck of Harold's galley drinking bowls of wine from some skins that Harold had bought in Malta before we sailed.

"They ought to be getting uneasy about now; I know I would," Henry volunteered.

It was a dark night and quite comfortable now that the sun had gone down. We could see a few lights flickering in the distant city from cooking fires and lanterns. Our galleys were showing no lights, but we instinctively knew they were anchored nearby and could periodically hear snatches of voices and the familiar and somehow reassuring creaking of nearby hulls.

After a while, I rolled up some of my bedding for a pillow and fell asleep on the deck. As I drifted off, I could hear the sound of snoring and the quiet conversations and sensed the movement as sleeping men rolled over or got up to piss from the shite nest in the stern. It was altogether quiet and peaceful. I slept soundly.

"Alarm. Alarm. Everyone awake. Here they come." The cry pierced my ears and I jerked awake with a snort and sat up. For the briefest moment, I did not know where I was. Then I tripped over someone as I scrambled to the railing of the galley to look.

Coming straight at our cluster of anchored galleys were two fire boats. And, within seconds, three more bloomed into flames, and then at least a dozen.

Cries and shouts of alarm began on the galley next to us and instantly spread to every one of the galleys anchored around us. Within moments, shouting and the sound of running feet were everywhere and we could see as many as twenty boats on fire and coming straight at us.

The light from the more distant fires backlit boats in front; we could see their shapes outlined against the more distant flames—fishing boats with their sails up and piled high with dry twigs and branches—and there were men on board sailing them straight at us.

******

"Sailors, man your pikes to push them off; archers to the oars," Harold roared. And then, "Raise the anchor, George; raise it. ... Hurry, lads, hurry."

I was so confused I instantly started to run to the forward castle to get my longbow, mail shirt, and wrist knives. I had actually taken two or three steps when I realized how stupid that would be because I might have to swim. Instead, I ran to the anchor rope in the bow to help pull it up. Several sailors were already there and I was not needed.

All I ended up initially doing was standing with both hands on the deck railing and watching in disbelief as the fire boats came across the harbour towards us. I did not even know Peter had joined me until he spoke at my side.

"My God, the Moors on those boats are committing suicide. They would never escape," Peter exclaimed. "Why would they do it?"

Then a thought struck me.

"Quick, let's get pikes and help hold them off," I shouted.

We started running for the nearest pike rack at almost the same moment the first of our rowers began rowing and Harold's galley lurched forward.

A flaming fishing boat reached us before we got to the rack. Just before it hit, we could see it was piled high with flaming twigs and brush. Our galley was just starting to move forward and two sailors, including Harold himself, had pikes and were trying to push its bow away as it collided with us.

Our being slightly underway combined with the pikes pushing on its bow caused the fire boat to bang the side of its hull up against ours instead hitting us straight on with its bow. The sharp sound of our oars breaking off could be heard over the screams and shouts of our men as burning twigs and branches from the top of the pile on the boat spilled over on to our deck and forced Harold and his men to drop their pikes and jump back away from the flames.

The flaming boat stayed next to us for only a few seconds until the momentum from our rowing carried us away from it—with burning debris on our deck. I watched in dismay as our men tried to pick up the twigs and brush where they were not yet burning and throw them over the side, and several burned themselves quite severely when they grabbed hot embers.

A smart young sailor with a pike saved the day. He began using his pike like a hay fork and began pitching the burning twigs and brush over the side. Within seconds, every man with a pike was desperately copying him, including me and Peter.

"Bring up the water skins, lads. Bring up the skins," I could hear Harold shouting as he used his bladed pike to pick up some kind of burning shrub and toss it over the railing.

******

Darkness began to return as the fires flickered and died down on the dozen or so fishing boats that were still burning as the wind pushed them past our galleys.

All we knew initially was that several of our galleys had fires on their decks that were soon extinguished and one of them was seriously on fire and burning out of control. We did not know whose galley it was that was burning, and Harold and our sergeant captains did not wait to find out. Every one of our galleys rowed towards it to take off our men.

Some of our other galleys reached it before we did; all we could do was stand off and watch in the dim and flickering light of our burning galley as one of our galleys came alongside and its crew used their pikes to pull the hulls together. We did not know whose galley that was either.

"Phillip's, I think," said Harold as we stood on the roof of the stern castle and watched the rescue begin. "He was anchored over that way."

As soon as the two hulls banged together, shouting and desperate men from the burning galley poured over its deck railing and on to the deck of their rescuer. Many of them were desperately clutching their bows and other personal items they had managed to scoop up before they fled to safety.

******

Dawn's early light revealed a chilling sight: the galley torched by the fire boats had burned down to the waterline and was still smoking. It was Richard Farmer's and anyone on it who had not escaped to the deck of Phillip's galley was surely dead.

Phillip's galley had initially been absolutely packed with men. By the time dawn arrived, however, most of the rescued men had been taken aboard several of its sister galleys. They had come alongside in the darkness and off-loaded them. My lieutenants and I had talked about what we should do while we waited in the darkness for the arrival of dawn's early light. Finally, I decided.

"Nothing," I told my lieutenants. "We do nothing except stay here and take every sail that enters the harbour as a prize—and keep a better watch at night in case they try again."

"And with two men sleeping by each anchor rope, a man in the lookout's nest, and every galley's bailing buckets and empty skins on deck and filled with water," added Harold emphatically. We all nodded in agreement.

"What do you think they would try next?" asked Henry to no one in particular.

******

The small boat rowing toward us had a man in the front waving a shirt above his head and blowing of some kind of horn. Two men were rowing and there were only four men in the boat. The man sitting in the stern was obviously coming to talk. Harold had his sailing sergeant row us slightly towards them so they would know where to head if they wanted to talk.

I moved to the side of Harold's galley and raised my hand in greeting to the approaching small boat. It was not a friendly greeting, just an acknowledgement that I recognized them and that I was the man they should address. My lieutenants stood with me.

The man in the boat did not try to stand up as it came alongside. He was clutching the side of the boat for dear life. *He was obviously a landsman who did not know how to swim.*

"Hoy," he said in passable French. "Who are you and why are you here and what do you want?"

"I am an Englishman," I replied. "Algerian galleys and others recently attacked our trading post in Cyprus and took several of our cogs in Beirut harbour. What did you expect would happen after you attacked Englishmen and their transports, eh?"

"I was not involved in that; I am a grain merchant. My name is Muhammed Beller. I was sent to you only because I speak French. What would you do? How long would you stay?" he asked.

"Oh, food supplies are easy to bring in, are they not? So I would think we will be staying here in the harbour at least until next year or, perhaps, the year after that. Certainly, we will be staying until trading cogs and ships stop coming to Algiers for us to take as prizes; and after you release our men and your Christian slaves, of course."

He looked thunderstruck and amazed, so I ploughed on with encouragement in my voice.

"We are hoping, of course, that some of your king's friends would come here and attempt to relieve Algiers. My men can never take enough prizes, can they? So, I would be pleased to carry a messenger from your king asking his friends to come to his aid: perhaps, he could look westward to Tangiers or Oran for assistance. Their kings might send their galleys in an attempt to relieve you."

Then I continued and really rubbed it in.

"Looking eastward to Tunis for assistance would not work for your king, of course. In case you have not heard, the Tunisians were foolish enough to join with you Algerians in your recent raids against Beirut and Cyprus; so a couple of weeks ago we visited Tunis and took all the Tunisian galleys and all the cogs and ships in Tunis's harbour. They freed their Christian and Jewish slaves and paid us gold bezants to leave. Algiers would have to do the same."

The Algerian, Muhammed something or other, listened to me with a look of absolute astonishment and dismay on his face. Ten minutes later, his two rowers began rowing him back to the city with a list of demands for his king to consider.

******

Muhammed and I talked back and forth for three days before we were able to hammer out an acceptable agreement. In the end, we agreed to leave the harbour and the Emir of Algiers, *apparently, that is what the Algerians call their king*, agreed to pay a ransom for the harbour of nine thousand gold bezants and free all the Christian and Jewish slaves in the city and in lands around it, including their spouses and children.

The next day my lieutenants and I were on Harold's galley as it cautiously made its way to the quay. The coins were waiting so we immediately began counting and loading them—and then watched somewhat remorsefully when a big three-masted ship innocently entered the harbour and promptly began unloading its cargo at a berth further down the quay.

"Perhaps we should have waited a few days," Harold suggested with a teasing smile in his voice and a nod towards the new arrival.

Peter looked up from where he was counting coins and laughed. We were well satisfied. The Emir's coins were more than enough to pay our men's prize money; we would be able to keep over a thousand gold bezants and everything our prizes fetched.

On the following day our cogs and galleys came to the quay at dawn and began loading the newly freed slaves. There were thousands of them and they formed three great, orderly lines, and little wonder they were orderly—our galleys lined the quay with our archers instructed to kill anyone they saw carrying weapons or starting trouble. Some of the slaves were carrying children and large amounts of personal items such as bedding and bowls; others had only the rags on their backs and nothing more.

One of the lines was for the slaves who wanted to be taken to Ibiza and ports to its west; one for those who wanted to be carried to Sardinia and ports to its east; and one for those who wished to stay in Algiers as slaves.

It took all day to sort out and board the slaves. Many of whom were ecstatic and dancing about, and even more who were pensive and worried even though we had men who had been former slaves themselves walking up and down the lines assuring them that they really would be free and that we would, if they so desired, let them work in exchange for their food and clothing.

As was our practice, we allowed those slaves who said they want to remain in Algiers, to return to their homes. And once again, a surprising number asked to be allowed to remain in Algiers as slaves. Each inevitably said it was too hard to start over someplace else; they preferred to be subservient and secure with the Moslems than free and destitute with their fellow Christians and Jews.

I was surprised to find myself understanding their thoughts. Change and uncertainty was difficult once one has life settled into place.

******

Harold's galley was the last of our galleys to leave the quay and the last to move through the harbour entrance and out into the Mediterranean. I was listening to the swishing of the oars and thinking about what to do next. It did not take long for me to decide. We had given the princes long enough to think about buying the relics. It was time to sell them.

"Where now?" Harold asked me as we cleared the harbour entrance.

"Row for Cornwall."

*** END OF THE BOOK ***

There are more books in *The Company of Archers Saga*.

All of the books in this exciting and action-packed medieval saga are available on Amazon as individual eBooks. Some of them are also available in print and as audio books. Many of them are available in multi-book collections. You can find them by searching for *Martin Archer Stories*.

This book is book ten of the saga and can also be found in a bargain-priced collection containing books 7, 8, 9, and 10 entitled *The Archers' Story: Part II*. The three books after that are collected as *The Archers' Story Part III;* and the four after that are collected in *The Archers' Story: Part IV*. There is also a *Part V* with the next three and a collection entitled Part VI after that.

A chronological list of all the books in the saga, and other books by Martin Archer, can be found below.

Finally, a word from Martin:

"I sincerely hope you enjoyed reading the stories about the hard men of Britain's first great merchant and military company as much as I have enjoyed writing it. If so, I hope you will consider reading the other stories in the saga and leaving a favourable review on Amazon or Google with as many stars as possible in order to encourage other readers.

"And, if you could please spare a moment, I would also very much appreciate your thoughts and suggestions about this saga and its stories from the dawn of Britain's rise as a great economic and military power. Should the stories continue? What do you think? I can be reached at martinarcherV@gmail.com."

Cheers and thank you once again. /S/ Martin Archer

Books in the exciting and action-packed *The Company of Archers* saga:

The Archers

The Archers' Castle

The Gold Coins

The Emperor has no Gold

Protecting the Gold: The Fatal Mistakes

The Alchemist's Revenge

The Venetian Gambit

Today's Friends

The English Gambits

The Englishman (coming late 2020 or early 2021)

eBooks in Martin Archer's epic *Soldiers and Marines* saga:

Soldiers and Marines

Peace and Conflict

War Breaks Out

War in the East (A fictional tale of America's role in the next great war)

Israel's Next War (A prescient book much hated by Islamic reviewers)

Collections of Martin Archer's books on Amazon

The Archers Stories I - complete books I, II, III, IV, V, and VI

The Archers Stories II - complete books VII, VIII, IX, and X

The Archers Stories III - complete books XI, XII, and XIII

The Archers Stories IV – complete books XIV, XV, XVI, and XVII

The Archers Stories V – complete books XVIII, XIX, and XX

The Archers Stories VI - complete books XXI, XXII, XXIII

The Soldiers and Marines Saga - complete books I, II, and III

Other eBooks you might enjoy:

Cage's Crew by Martin Archer writing as Raymond Casey

America's Next War by Michael Cameron – an adaption of Martin Archer's *War Breaks Out* to set it in the immediate future when Eastern and Western Europe go to war over another wave of Islamic refugees.

Sample pages from the first book in the saga.

I decided to leave George with the archers whilst my brother Thomas and I went into the city to try to find the Bishop and collect our pay–four bezant gold coins from Constantinople for each man. And we would get more for every man in the company who had lost his life or balls whilst with Edmund. It was quite a bit for only two years of service, but we had paid dearly for it by so many of us losing our lives.

At least we tried to get in see the Bishop. The guards at the city gate would not let us through the gate even though Thomas was a priest.

One of the guards looked a little bit smarter and greedier than the other two. Thomas motioned him aside and blessed him. I watched as they huddled together for a moment talking in low voices.

Then Thomas waved me over.

"William, this good man cannot leave his post to tell the Bishop we are here. And that is a pity for we only need to see His Eminence for a few minutes to deliver the important message we are bringing him.

"It is a problem we need to solve because it would not be a Christian thing to make someone as important as the good Bishop upset. He is sure to be unhappy if he has to walk all this way just to have a word with us."

"Ah. I understand. The guard wants a bribe to let us in.

"Let us in and you and the others can come with us when we sail away from here," I said.

"Forget it, English. I have a wife and family here. I am not going anywhere."

It was time to take another tack. I reached into my almost empty purse and pulled out two small copper coins—enough for a night of drinking if the wine was bad enough. I pressed them into his grimy hand.

"We only need a few minutes to deliver a message. We will be out and gone before anyone knows."

The guard looked at the coins and then again at us, sizing us up was what he was doing. And he did not like what he saw. We looked like what we were, poor and bedraggled.

"One more copper. There are three of us on duty and no one is supposed to enter. But we will take a chance, since it is for the Bishop and our sergeant is not here."

I agreed with a sigh and dug out another copper.

"We will not be long and the Bishop will appreciate it." *No, he will not.*

Thomas waved the wooden cross he wore around his neck to bless the guard as he put our coppers in his purse, and then he waved it at the other two for good measure.

******

Thomas and I had to shoulder our way through the crowded streets and push people away as we walked towards the church. Beggars and desperate women and young boys began pulling on our clothes and crying out to us. In the distance black smoke was rising from somewhere in the city, probably from looters torching somebody's house or shop.

The doors to the front of the church were barred. Through the cracks in the wooden doors we could see the big wooden bar holding them shut.

"Come on. There must be a side door for the priests to use. There always is."

We walked around to the side of the church and there it was. I began banging on the door. After a while, a muffled voice on the other side told us to go away.

"Go away. The church is not open."

"We have come from Lord Edmund to bring a message to the Bishop of Damascus. Let us in."

We could hear something being moved and then an eye appeared at the peep hole in the door. A few seconds later, the door swung open and we hurried in.

The light inside the room was dim because the windows were shuttered.

Our greeter was a slender fellow with alert eyes who could not have been much more than an inch or two over five feet tall. He studied us intently as he bowed us in and then quickly shut and barred the door behind us. He seemed quite anxious.

"We have come from the Bekka Valley to see the Bishop," I said in the bastardised French dialect some call crusader French and others are now calling English. And then Thomas repeated my words in Latin. *Which, of course, is what I should have done in the first place?*

"I shall tell His Eminence that you are here and ask if he will receive you," the man replied in Latin. "I am Yoram, the Bishop's scrivener; may I tell him who you are and why you are here?"

"I am William, the captain of what is left of a company of English archers, and this is Father Thomas, our priest. We are here to collect our pay for helping to defend Lord Edmund's fief these past two years."

"I shall inform His Eminence of your arrival. Please wait here." *The Bishop' scrivener had a strange accent; I wondered where he came from?*

Some minutes passed before the anxious little man returned. Whilst he was gone we looked around the room inside the door. It was quite luxurious with a floor of stones instead of the mud floors one usually finds in churches.

It was also quite dark. The windows were covered with heavy wooden shutters and sealed shut with heavy wooden bars; the light in the room, such as it was, came from cracks in the shutters and smaller windows high on the walls above the shuttered windows. There was a somewhat tattered tribal carpet on the floor.

The anxious little man returned and gave us a most courteous nod and bow.

"His Grace will see you now. Please follow me."

The Bishop's clerk led us into a narrow, dimly lit passage with stone walls and a low ceiling. He went first and then Thomas and then me. We had taken but a few steps when he turned back toward us and in an intense low voice issued a terse warning.

"Protect yourselves. The Bishop does not want to pay you. You are in mortal danger."

The little man nodded in silent agreement when I held up my hand. Thomas and I needed to take a moment to get ourselves ready.

His eyes widened, and he watched closely as we prepared. Then, when I gave a nod to let him know we were ready, he rewarded us with a tight smile and another nod of agreement—and began walking again with a particularly determined look on his face.

A few seconds later we turned another corner and came to an open wooden door. It opened into a large room with beamed ceilings more than six feet high and stone walls begrimed by centuries of smoke. I knew the height because I could stand upright after I bent my head to get through the entrance door.

A portly, middle-aged man in a bishop's robes was sitting behind a table covered with parchments. There was a bearded and rather formidable-looking guard with a sword in a wooden scabbard standing in front of the table on our side of it. There was also a closed chest on the table, a pile of parchments, and a jumble of tools and chests in the corner covered by another old tribal rug. A broken chair was pushed up against the wall.

The Bishop smiled to show us his bad teeth, and beckoned us in. We could see him clearly despite the dim light coming in from five or six small window openings near the ceiling of the room.

After a moment, the bishop stood up and extended his hand over the table so we could kiss his ring. First Thomas and then I approached and half kneeled to kiss it. Then I stepped back and towards the guard to make room for Thomas so he could re-approach the table and stand next to me as the Bishop re-seated himself.

"What is it you want to see me about?" the Bishop asked in Latin.

He said it with a sincere smile and leaned forward expectantly.

"I am William, captain of the late Lord Edmund's company of English archers, and this is Father Thomas, our priest and confessor." *And my older brother, though I did not think it wise to mention it at that moment.*

"How can that be? Another man was commanding the archers when I visited Lord Edmund earlier this year, and we made our arrangements."

"He is dead. He took an arrow in the arm and it turned purple and rotted until he died. Another took his place and now he is dead also. Now I am the captain of the company."

The Bishop crossed himself and mumbled a brief prayer under his breath. Then he looked at me expectantly and listened intently.

"We have come to get the coins Lord Edmund gave to you to hold for us so we would be paid if he fell. We looked for you before we left the valley, but Beaufort Castle was about to fall and you had already gone. So we have come here to collect our pay."

"Of course. Of course. I have it right here in the chest.

"Aran," he said, nodding to the burly soldier standing next to me, "tells me there are eighteen of you. Is that correct?" *And how would he be knowing that?*

"Yes, Eminence, that is correct."

"Well then, four gold Constantinople coins for each man totals seventy-two; and you shall have them here and now."

"No, Eminence, that is not correct."

I reached inside my jerkin and pulled out the company's copy of the contract with Lord Edmund, laid the parchment on the desk in front of him, and turned it around so he could read the words in Latin that had been scribed on it and see Edmund's mark.

As I placed the contract on the table, I tapped it with my finger and casually stepped further to the side, and even closer to his swordsman. I did it so Thomas could once again step into my place in front of the Bishop and nod his agreement, confirming it was indeed in our contract.

"Our contract calls for four gold bezant coins from Constantinople for each of seventy-nine men, and six more coins to the company for each man who was killed or lost both of his eyes or his bollocks. It sums to one thousand and twenty-six bezants in all—and I know you have our money because I was present when Lord Edmund gave you many more coins and you agreed to pay them to us. We are here to collect our coins."

"Oh yes. So you are. So you are. Of course. Well, you shall certainly get what is due you. God wills it."

I sensed the swordsman stiffen as the Bishop said the words and opened the lid of the chest. The Bishop reached in with both hands and took a big handful of bezants in his left hand and placed them on the table.

He spread the gold coins out on the table and motioned Thomas forward to help him count as he reached back in to fetch another handful. I stepped further to the left and even closer to the guard so Thomas would have plenty of room to step forward to help the Bishop count.

Everything happened at once when Thomas leaned forward to start counting the coins. The Bishop reached again into his money chest as if to get another handful. This time he came out with a dagger—and lunged across the coins on the table to drive it into Thomas's chest with a grunt of satisfaction.

The swordsman next to me simultaneously began pulling his sword from its wooden scabbard. It had all been prearranged. .....

Made in the USA
Monee, IL
19 January 2021

58080774R00239